# A Conspiracy of Ravens

DAME MARGARET JAMES

# DEDICATION

For mum, dad, and my beloved Harry.

# CONTENTS

# 1 | AN ESSENTIAL CHANGE OF SCENERY

As a writer of murder mysteries, I never expected to be at the heart of such a crime, and yet here we are.

My apologies for assuming you know who I am. Please allow me to introduce myself: I am Dame Margaret James, the daughter of Andrew Sterling and Joan Willoughby, and the widow of the late Harold "Harry" James. I was born and raised in the resort town of Southend-on-Sea due directly east of London where I spent my childhood years fishing with my father and walking the beach with my mother. Southend-on-Sea is perhaps best known outside of England for its pier, which, at over two kilometres, is the longest pleasure pier in the world. To say that a child would not enjoy growing up in such an idyllic place would be a disservice to truth. It was heavenly.

I assumed my life would always take place in or around Southend-on-Sea, but that all changed the day a strapping young fellow with a severe jawline, wavy blond hair, and piercing blue eyes sauntered into my parents' gift and novelty store. That fellow was my Harry. I was sweeping the floor when he walked in, and he would never miss the opportunity to tell friends and strangers how *he* was the one who swept me off my feet that fateful day. Harry always did have such a clever sense of humour.

He was right, of course, as our casual meeting turned into a romantic dinner which turned into a months-long love affair before Harry proposed marriage one year to the day of our first meeting. Harry was 23, and I was just 19. We married in Southend-on-Sea and then moved shortly thereafter to London where Harry worked at Stillings & Sons Publishing House, one of the most prestigious publishers in all of the United Kingdom. It was through this connection to the publishing house and at Harry's constant encouragement that I began writing books.

I had always loved writing, of course. My mother and I would often sit on the beach with pen and paper, writing whatever stories came to mind that day, with the crashing of waves as our background noise. I had done some writing, short stories actually, that had been published in one of London's evening papers, but it was not until I wrote one particular story that my career as an author would really take off. The story, *The Crimes of the Vicar*, was a murder mystery set in a small, fictitious hamlet in the Midlands. Mother and father had taken me to the Midlands several times as a child, and I always found the misty, foggy setting to be such a contrast to the sunny, bright beachside town I called home. There was something darker, something more mysterious about the Midlands, and that ominous setting inspired my tale of a vicar who, having blackmailed members of his community with secrets he gleaned through his position, was found murdered. Suspicions and accusations then spread about the town as the reader of the novel attempts to figure out "whodunit."

The story stirred up quite a fervour in London, with Londoners so eager to get their hands on each subsequent issue of the paper to find out what happened next. The popularity of the tale was so remarkable that Stillings and Sons asked if I would consider turning *The Crimes of the Vicar* into a full book. "You must," I remember Harry telling me, seemingly even more delighted at this news than I had been. And so, with Harry's characteristic enthusiasm and support, I wrote my first book. Then my second. Then my third, and so on and so on until I had penned exactly 39 best-selling mystery novels. I guess you might say I was quite prolific.

As if the life of being a famous author were not splendid enough, with the fancy dinners and the lack of want for anything, you might imagine my surprise when I learned that I would have bestowed upon me the honorific title of dame by none other than King George himself! This happy news came after I had written my 25th best-selling story, *Murder by Moonlight*, which the king said was his favourite book. Never did we ever have such a delightful evening of dancing, feasting, and general merriment as we did that night!

This joy continued many more years into the future until the night that Harry took ill. I had just finished proofing my latest book, *Rhythm of the Riviera*, and sent it off to the publisher when his cough started. "It's nothing," he would reassure me, ever the optimist, yet I could see him growing weaker and more easily fatigued each passing day. Simple tasks, like bathing or raising a spoon to his mouth, became more and more complicated until they were impossible for him to do on his own. We hired an in-home caretaker, but I assumed much of the responsibility—not by necessity but by choice: my Harry had been my crutch throughout those early moments of self-doubt in my life and career, and now I would be his support in these moments where he doubted himself and his physical abilities. My world became 100% Harry for two years until one winter morning when my sweet Harry simply did not wake from his final slumber. He was just 59 years old.

You might be wondering why I felt compelled to share this brief biography with you. I assure you it was not an exercise in vanity or celebrity. No, the death of my husband has *everything* to do with the current situation in which I have found myself and was the very precursor to the events that make up the story of this book. You see, ten years have passed since the death of my late husband. The years since his passing have been full of the typical highs and lows one often experiences after the death of a loved one, like the carousel I used to ride as a girl in Southend-on-Sea. To be frank, I had not found the inspiration to write another book since his passing. In fact, I had not even attempted to write a short story in ten years' time. If I am being honest, I could have lived the rest of my life having never written another book and been satisfied, but, alas, this was not what the Fates had planned.

I was quite content with my life's story and thought it had reached its proper conclusion, but the rest of the world did not. Authors face a tricky conundrum: the more successful you are at captivating readers, the more of your books they want to read. It is a slight addiction for them, in some ways, with my words the dangerous drug they crave. After what they referred to as an "understandable period of grieving," Stillings and Sons wrote to see if I had any interest in publishing a new novel. How kind. It seemed every year of the previous decade included rumours that Dame Margaret James would be penning a new novel at long last, with fans ever so eager and increasingly disappointed each passing year.

It was not as if I had not *thought* about writing again, of course. I do fancy myself a bit of a perfectionist, you see, and it had long bothered me that I stopped at 39 books instead of a nice, even number like 35 or 40. "Certainly you have one more book in you, Maggie," I would often say to myself, but ever since Harry had gone, it seemed as though my well of inspiration had run dry, the bright fire that lit the path of my journey so many times before had burned out. I would stay at 39 books and just need to be content with that.

Non-authors often assume that creative ideas are constantly overflowing, but dreaming up new stories is challenging even for the best of writers. It is particularly challenging when the subject matter—murder, in my case—does not come naturally based on experience as it might for a top chef writing a cookbook or a refined woman writing a guide to etiquette. I *wrote* about murder; I did not *live* murder. Furthermore, although I was no stranger to writer's block, this last particular spell had been quite dizzying. My last book, *Rhythm of the Riviera*, was now ten years old, ancient by some standards. I had been producing new books at a rate of one every year or two since I started writing, even if my pace had slowed for the last few books. "Take your time," the publisher would say, which I would have believed more if their persistent nagging did not increase more and more as the weeks turned into months. I did not miss that and was not keen on signing up for it again.

Still, finishing just *one* more book would be so satisfying to the publisher, to the fans, and even to myself, as I thought that writing one last, exceptional novel would be the closure I needed on both a prolific career and a life well lived. I longed for this retirement, the opportunity to exhale, take a break, and enjoy my remaining years of life without expectations from fans and publishing houses. I just never anticipated it happening the way it did.

Here's how this most recent case began…

Harry and I had long talked about traveling to America before he fell ill. We had envisioned arriving by boat in New York, enjoying the city for a few days, and then proceeding to tour New England in the early summer months. Once Harry became sick, those plans were shelved. He made me promise that I would still make this trip should something happen to him, and I always agreed to this in order to assuage his fears, never thinking I would actually have to take the trip alone. Once he passed, I simply resigned myself to the reality that our American adventure was off the table.

One day, after sitting at the typewriter in what must have been my millionth attempt to start a new novel, I had a thought. "What if you had a change of scenery, Margaret? An escape from London that could provide some inspiration." Perhaps it was divine intervention that I happened to glance at the morning paper sitting on the desk nearby with a headline bearing New York's name in bright, bold letters. That prompted the memory of the plans Harry and I made but never pursued, and that was the moment I made the fateful decision that led to this book.

"I am going to New England, Harry!" I shouted up to the ceiling.

And, with that announcement, I began a whirlwind week of planning my American adventure. I would stay for two weeks, no, three weeks in New England: a brief stop in New York City before finding an isolated bed and breakfast that could provide some peaceful seclusion from the outside world. It was there that I intended to write my 40th novel, which I would announce as my last, so that I could return to England, publish the book, and retire. "Simple," I thought, "I don't know why it has taken me ten years to figure this out!"

Not too far into the planning process I realised that I would likely want to hire an assistant to accompany me on the journey. At 65, I did not move quite as quickly as I once had, and the idea of lugging three weeks' worth of luggage and a heavy typewriter was not so appealing. I had the means to hire someone, I thought, so why bother myself with the less enjoyable elements of this adventure when my efforts should be squarely focused on the task at hand: writing my book.

I placed an ad in the paper, which was promptly met with several responses. I opted to interview a final set of candidates, which led me to one Anna Winthrop. Ms. Winthrop was, how does one say it politely, a rather nondescript girl. She had the kind of face that one would never notice among the crowd and was neither too thin nor too round to be distinguished by her silhouette alone. She was, in the kindest sense of the word, *plain*. She was dressed in greys and blacks, which so appropriately coloured her somewhat morose and dejected personality. Anna had been born and raised in the Midlands, which caught my attention (her character certainly matched her place of origin), and came to London to work as a housemaid some years back. Although only 24, one could tell from the lines on her face that Anna had witnessed some stress in her lifetime.

Somewhat peculiarly, Anna made no mention of any family of her own, and after ignoring my attempts to get her to discuss potential dear ones who might miss her on two or three occasions, I left the issue never to return to it. I figured there were some things people just do not enjoy sharing, although I admit I was still quite curious to know more of her story.

By the end of her interview, I had made my decision: I would hire Anna to accompany me on my New England adventure. Upon returning, we could discuss extending her employment as my assistant, but for now she would be my travel companion. While some may find such a depressing travel partner to be a miserable pairing, I actually thought her silence and passive nature would be better for me: I would much rather have a quiet type than a chatty, bubbly soul unable to keep well enough alone. If Anna could carry my belongings, entertain herself, and occasionally bring me a cup of tea and biscuits, well, that would be just fine by me.

As I prepared my belongings and affairs for the trip, I tasked Anna with locating and booking a serene bed and breakfast that would serve as our home base while in America. This would be her first task. To help her along, I gave her some documents Harry had assembled when he was still healthy and excited for our American adventure. My only instructions were to make sure the location was extremely secluded, away from any large cities or towns and to book the rooms under a made-up name. You see, Dame Margaret James' work was just as popular in America as it had been in England, and because every trend took a few years to hop across the pond, one might have even said my popularity was even *higher* in the States than it was in England at the moment. The last thing I wanted was to deal with obsessive fans from the city ruining my peaceful writing retreat. Luckily, few Americans would likely recognise my visage: despite having achieved immense popularity in England, even few people outside of London would likely be able to recognise me on the street. For this

I was very thankful. It can be difficult being so famous.

Anna made arrangements for us to stay at an upstate New York bed and breakfast known as Raven's Point Manor. The estate was a fair distance from the closest city which, itself, was but a mere village. Better yet, the manor was perched atop a piece of heavily forested land that was surrounded by a rather large lake with only one access road to and from the property. The owner had warned Anna that the access road often flooded during the rainy weeks of June, but I paid little attention to what seemed like such an inconsequential detail. After all, what could be the worst outcome of a flooded access road? More private time to write?

As it turns out, there *was* a worse outcome. Much worse. Indeed, Anna and I would soon find ourselves in the most mysterious of circumstances with no way out, no exit back to safety, and no means to call for help.

One might say we had no way of knowing what dark chaos awaited us at Raven's Point Manor, so with bags packed, plans made, and the excitement that usually accompanies the start of any trip, we boarded our ship to New York and set sail for America.

The events that follow in each subsequent chapter are being typed just after they happen, often late into each evening during my stay at Raven's Point Manor. For, as you will soon see, I have been entrusted by the other guests to make a record of the strange happenings taking place around us so that, in the event we do not make it out alive, the police will have some evidence as to what occurred. In fact, as I write this, I am not even certain that *I* will see the day these pages are printed. We are all at grave risk, myself included. Please do not think it is lost on me that I, Dame Margaret James, beloved author of 39 murder mysteries, have found myself trapped within my own murder mystery. The whole charade has quite a poetic appeal to it, I suppose, but I say that I much prefer *writing* about murder than *living* it. And with that, let's begin.

# 2 | A COLOURFUL
## CAST OF CHARACTERS

After what seemed like almost a full day's drive from the city, we arrived at the one-lane road surrounded on either side by a boggy, wet marsh and proceeded up the side of a low hill just ahead in the distance. The sunny sky and vibrance of the city were now just distant memories in this rather bleak, dark enclave of nature. Fir trees created a dense, thick forest, which elicited quite a contradiction of feeling: both a breath of fresh air and the feeling of being suffocated, simultaneously. The setting just screamed of a place that should play host to some wicked event, which probably should have been our first clue.

We continued along the road, around the landscape's various curves, up and down its many hills, before one final incline led us to the estate's gates. Chiselled stones stacked ever so perfectly formed two thick columns on either side of the road. On top, a wrought-iron sign served as the bridge between the two stone columns. The sign, quite ornate and flowery in its design, spelled the name Raven's Point with the silhouette of the eponymous bird just above. The gate was open, presumably in preparation of our scheduled arrival, which was a thankful gesture, as the house was still roughly a decent kilometre or two from the gate. The estate was considerably massive. Waiting for someone to walk out to greet us would have taken a fair bit of time. This way, with the gate open, we would be able to pull right up to the house itself.

As we continued along the main driveway, I saw the most curious looking man standing off the road a bit toward the forest apparently talking to himself. His gaze was fixed straight ahead, as if he were having a conversation with a ghost, but I assure you no one was there. Just the bearded man, with a shovel in one hand and a rain smock over his clothing. As we drove past, I swore I heard him just repeating the same lines over and over again, almost as if he were singing a song, but we were too far away to make out what he was saying. Anna seemed completely indifferent to this spectacle, but as I turned to see what she was looking at I understood why: Raven's Point Manor was beginning to emerge in front of us on the horizon.

And what a house it was! A gothic manor, the likes of typically seen in the wealthy country estates of England, Raven's Point was ever the perfect picture of an architectural enigma. Cold yet inviting. Luxurious yet decrepit. Aged yet youthful. This bundle of contradictions would be our home for the next several weeks. Even if it had the air of a mausoleum from its exterior, the hope was the manor's interior would be full of warmth, character, and, hopefully, a bit of tea and some biscuits. I had grown quite hungry on the drive in from the city.

As the car pulled up, a red-haired woman, probably in her mid-50s, opened the front door of the house.

"Hello," she cried out, enthusiastically waving both of her arms in the air. Americans are a curious sort, having mastered many wonderful accomplishments in the relatively short history of the nation. Subtlety was not one of those accomplishments.

Anna and I stepped out of our respective side of the car while our driver fetched our bags from the back. No sooner did I look back toward the front door than did I see the red-haired woman just steps away from me.

"You must be Ms. Crawford," the woman announced in my direction.

"Actually, I'm...," I began to correct her before

remembering that I had instructed Anna to provide a false name to preserve my anonymity during our stay, "...I'm delighted to be here! A pleasure to make your acquaintance, Ms....?"

"Flaherty. Mrs. Kathleen Flaherty," said the woman. I knew the Irish had settled these parts after expanding beyond New York City, but I must say it was remarkable to see an Irish-owned manor. Nothing against the Irish, of course, but they were not a people history had been so kind to. I always found this so surprising considering they tended to be such a cheery, hardworking folk. History always seems to find a new group to ridicule even if it all seems so clearly silly and undeserved in hindsight.

"Delighted, Mrs. Flaherty," I responded as Anna and the driver began moving our bags from the car to the foyer of the home.

"Aye, call me Kath," the woman barked back with a jovial laugh punctuating her command. The Irish always were a bit less formal than we Brits, but America had clearly done an extra special number on this one. She was truly a blend of both cultures.

"Indeed, Kath. Such a lovely estate you have here! We are very much looking forward to our stay at Raven's Point," I said as the woman grabbed my arm and led me toward the manor.

"Not as delighted as I am to be hosting you here," she replied. "Now hurry in before it starts to rain. Swirling clouds only mean one thing in these parts. Hurry in, hurry in!"

The driver had just brought in the last of our luggage when Mrs. Flaherty ushered him out the front door almost as quickly as we had arrived.

"You had better hurry and make your way back, good sir," she said. "The water is already high, so any bit of rain at this point and the main access road is sure to be flooded. You won't make it back home for days if that's the case."

The driver scurried out the massive wooden door in just

enough time before Mrs. Flaherty slammed it closed. The winds had picked considerably in just the few minutes since our arrival, and the sky had turned a curious shade of dark greyish green, as if the moss from the ground had climbed up the walls of the manor and covered the clouds above.

The foyer of the manor was just as impressive as the exterior. Solid oak lined the walls and floors of the entryway, which itself was warmly illuminated by the most gorgeous crystal chandelier. A beautiful, ornate grandfather's clock stood ticking and tocking on the wall to my left, its pendulum swinging and reflecting the lights of the in the room. A massive staircase lay just beyond an expansive greeting area that was covered with the most ornate, plushest rug I had ever seen.

"From Persia," Ms. Flaherty whispered having clearly followed my eyes to their target.

"Most impressive," I replied. "Such exquisite craftsmanship! I would have simply assumed its origin, as one could only ever find such a fine rug in Persia!"

"I think you will find most things here at Raven's Point Manor to be only *the most* authentic and unique," Mrs. Flaherty said. "This is quite a special place, love, quite a special place."

At that moment I realised I had completely forgotten about Anna (which, admittedly, was altogether too easy to do). I turned around to see her standing near the suitcases, framed by a large window near the entry behind her. Honestly, her drab, dreary attire sort of made her blend into the darkening grey sky. Had it not been for her pale face and hands protruding from her smock, well, I would have been convinced she had left with the driver or disappeared into thin air. A few stray water spots on the window panes behind Anna confirmed Kath's prediction: it was beginning to rain.

"Let's see, I have you two in rooms six and seven, just up the stairs and to the right," Kath said. "Dinner will be taking place in the dining room at 8:00pm sharp, but you should help yourself to a drink in the library with the other guests beforehand."

It had completely slipped my mind that we would not be alone during this writing retreat. I was actually a bit worried about this when making plans: having *some* people around might be nice but too many people would get quite annoying rather quickly.

Kath seemed to read a worried expression on my face, as she quickly responded, "And do not worry your mind too much: we never have a full house this time of year, so it shan't be too noisy. Just six other guests at the moment, and there's room enough for ten!"

"Marvellous," I replied, sincerely relieved.

I walked over to Anna and the luggage to start gathering some of the bags. No sooner did I bend down to lift one of my suitcases than did the fiery Irish-American innkeeper dance a jig my direction and position herself between me and my baggage.

"Not on my watch, Ms. Crawford," she laughed, arms outstretched as if to block access to my luggage. "Me and the girl here—almost forgot she was here, this one—we will take your bags to your room. You just make yourself at home and have a look about. I'll need to be tending to the kitchen soon to prepare for dinner, so have a walkabout and enjoy your stay at Raven's Point Manor."

"Why, thank you! That's quite nice," I said.

Anna, stirred back to life by Kath's energetic spirit, began grabbing bags, dropping the same hatbox three or four times before finally getting a good grip on it. Mrs. Flaherty grabbed a few suitcases herself and started the trek up the stairs, Anna following just behind. I watched this humorous juxtaposition of a fiery, burning ember and a cool, blackened coal working together to get the bags upstairs. Laughing a bit to myself, I wandered over to a large arched doorway to begin my self-guided tour of the manor.

The parlour was every bit as exquisite as the foyer, albeit with darker woods and more comfortable furniture. The centrepiece of the room was the massively large stone fireplace on the wall farthest from the arched doorway. A fire was burning, which bathed the room in warm colours and a relaxing heat. I noticed another luxurious Persian rug in the centre of the room, along with some curiosities on the shelves lining the walls. Some sort of horned animal skull on one shelf. A mosaic vase that reminded me of some of the artisan crafts I saw with Harry during our trips to Constantinople. A dagger featuring a jade handle common to Chinese collections. Mrs. Flaherty's point about authentic and unique features was already proving true.

As I made my way around the room, exploring the interesting artefacts from every corner of the globe, I found my eyes drawn to a large painting hanging above the fireplace. My eyes must have taken some time to adjust to the fire's brightness upon entering the room because the area above the mantle had previously been shrouded in darkness. However, now that my eyes could make out details in the dim room, I saw a painting of a rather regal looking man, what appeared to be his wife, and a young child standing between them. The three people were quite stoic and expressionless, simply staring straight out into the world with no discernible expression on their faces. A lone raven sat atop the man's outstretched finger, black as night. Perhaps a bit mesmerised by the comforting warmth of the fire, I felt as though the family in the painting was actually staring right at me in the parlour…

I am not quite sure how long I had been gazing at the painting when I was startled by a voice from behind me.

"Beautiful family, isn't it?"

I recognised the voice as Kath's immediately, cutting into the peaceful silence of the room like a warm knife through smooth butter. The flames in the fireplace even seemed to dance furiously right as she began speaking, which probably added to my startled response.

"Quite," I gasped, regaining my composure.

"That lot was the family that owned this manor," Kath

went on. "The Radcliffe family. Maybe you've heard of them?"

"Radcliffe, you say? No, I'm afraid I have not," I replied.

"Ah, well, you've heard of the Carnegies and Rockefellers, of that I am certain," Kath continued. "The Radcliffes were American royalty, just like those families. Made their money in steel. Good people, they were."

"So, you knew them then?" I asked.

"Knew them? They were like family to me. Surely you didn't think this manor came to me through my lineage, did you?" Kath laughed. "Imagine that! No, dear, I was the housekeeper for the Radcliffes for many years, and my husband was the groundskeeper. Treated us just like family, they did. Good and kind souls."

"Pardon me for asking," I began, "but you speak of them as if they are…"

"Dead? That I do. Sadly, the Radcliffes passed away almost twenty years ago now."

"Oh, how tragic," I replied, and before I could temper my curiosity in a respectful manner, I found myself uttering, "What happened?"

A bit surprised I would ask, Kath gave me an odd look and then continued, "You may have noticed that Mr. Radcliffe fancied himself to be a bit of an explorer," gesturing around the room at the curiosities.

I nodded.

"That was a good and fine pastime until the day he thought he and Mrs. Radcliffe should go on safari in Africa with Mr. Radcliffe leading the expedition," Kath continued.

"Oh, dear," I said aloud. "A dangerous pursuit. Was it an animal that got them?"

"You could say that," Kath replied.

"A lion? An elephant?"

"A chicken. Mrs. Radcliffe choked on a piece of chicken bone during dinner one night at the camp," Kath said with a heavy sigh.

"But Mr. Radcliffe? How did he…"

"*That* was a lion. In a panic, Mr. Radcliffe ran from the camp to try to find help. Within minutes, a lion, having heard all the commotion from trying to clear the chicken bone from Mrs. Radcliffe's throat, was waiting in the dark, ready to pounce. According to the witnesses it all happened so quickly," Kath said looking lovingly at the painting.

"What a peculiar way to go," I thought to myself.

After a few minutes of respectful silence, I began again, "And what about this child here?"

"Ah, now that's the saddest part," Mrs. Flaherty started.

*That* is the saddest part? Surely nothing could be worse than a chicken-lion double murder?

"That's Elliott Radcliffe, Mr. and Mrs. Radcliffe's only child," said Kath.

"Was he on the safari, too, then?" I asked.

"No, the child stayed behind with me and my husband here at Raven's Point. Such a young thing at the time, just celebrated a seventh birthday, in fact. I remember because I made the biggest chocolate cake I could," Kath continued. "When the news came of Mr. and Mrs. Radcliffe's demise, the poor thing was inconsolable, weeping for days and days. We held a service hoping it would bring some closure. Nothing. The young Radcliffe inherited everything, of course, as the only one left in the family's lineage, but children are far too young to recognise the value of material belongings, too immature yet to realise that the rest of one's life would be taken care of in a way most of us could only ever dream."

"Must have been difficult," I said.

"Indeed, it was, which is why I suppose we should not have been surprised when the poor thing ran off in the middle of the night one summer evening and never returned," said Kath.

"Wait, do you mean the child just disappeared in the middle of the night?" I asked.

"Yes, that's right. My husband and I woke to the front door wide open, footprints in the mud, and an empty house save for ourselves," Kath responded. "The rain was torrential, worse than we typically see around these parts, which is saying something. The water was high, and the flooding was rampant. The local police figured the child likely got swept up in a flash flood and drowned, the poor thing, but they never found a shred of evidence to support their story."

"What a terribly tragic family tale. I am so sorry you had to suffer so many losses," I offered.

"Thanks, love," she responded. "Of course, with no living heir, Raven's Point was left next to my husband and me to maintain. I had always hoped to run an inn, ever since I was a girl growing up working in our family's inn in Dublin. My husband suggested a bed and breakfast seeing as the house wasn't really ours in the first place, and before you know it, we had established the Raven's Point Manor bed and breakfast."

Although that explained so much about my surprise of an Irish-owned manor, I couldn't help but feel a tinge of guilt about having suspicions in the first place.

"So, I guess you could say it was tragic, but in a way, it had a bit of a happy ending," Kath said, stepping away from the painting.

"It *would* seem that way, wouldn't it," I responded in a tone that came across a bit more questioning than I intended it to. "And Mr. Flaherty? Is he...?"

"He's passed, some years ago now," Mrs. Flaherty replied, grabbing the dangling heart locket around her neck. "Peter was an angel on Earth, so it's only fitting he's an angel in heaven now."

"Sorry to hear that, Mrs. Flaherty," I said. "My husband has also..." I stuttered. I found I never did like talking about Harry's passing even after all these years. "I am also a widow."

"Sorry to hear that, love," Kath replied. "I sort of figured as such with the lack of a gentleman for such a long trip and your advanced age and all."

I blushed.

"Oh, I don't mean to call you old," Kath laughed. "I just meant, I figured you're of an age when someone's husband might have…oh, you know what? Never you mind."

"No worries, Mrs. Flaherty. I admit I am impressed you have been able to manage Raven's Point Manor all alone and to keep it in such impeccable form," I said, implicitly returning the insult.

"Ah, well, yes. It is quite a bit of work, but I am not completely alone," Kath responded as the smile faded from her face. "There's Giles."

"Giles?" I asked.

"Yes, Giles. Maybe you saw him on your way in? He was supposed to be digging trenches to help redirect some of the rainwater to prevent flooding."

She gathered her thoughts for a moment before beginning again.

"After my husband passed, I realised we would need someone to tend the grounds, as I could never manage to both keep the house and manage the outdoor chores," Kath responded.

"Ah, yes, the bearded fellow in the rain smock working near the front gate?" I asked.

"That's him, alright," Kath scowled. "Why, he's probably out there right now standing in the rain like a dolt. My husband would have been so disappointed in the way he tends the grounds, leaving deep holes here and there, mounds of dirt stacked up for days on end. My Peter took such great pride in his work. Giles barely manages to trim the hedges properly."

"He seemed…distracted," I said in an attempt to learn more about Giles' odd behaviour.

"Oh, that? Yes, well, you see Giles was in the war," Kath went on. "I don't know if he was altogether there before he was sent to Europe, but I do know that the man who returned is certainly incomplete," she said as she tapped the side of her head.

I thought Kath's characterisation of Giles was a bit cold for someone who had served nobly in war, but I dared not interrupt her.

"He barely speaks and can hardly manage to do much of anything except tend the grounds," Kath said. "At least a few times a day I'll see him standing frozen in place just mumbling the same words over and over."

"Why, I believe I saw that very thing as we drove in today!" I exclaimed. "Whatever was he saying? It sounded as if he were…"

"Singing?" Kath said. "Yes, I know. He mumbles, but to me it sounds like he's saying 'Captain Liberty' over and over again."

"The war, of course," I said.

"Indeed, it's sad what happens to the boys we send to war. They leave so young and full of promise only to return a shell of their former selves," Kath said.

"If they are lucky to return at all," I added.

"So true. So very true," Kath responded.

At that moment, the grandfather's clock sprang to life from the foyer, chiming five long tones to signify that it was now 17:00.

"Ah! Do you hear that?! Wherever does the time go?!" Kath leapt into action, "I must hurry to the kitchen now. Dinner won't prepare itself, sadly. Please, Ms. Crawford, make yourself feel at home, explore the manor, and help yourself to some tea if you like. I would encourage you to stroll about the estate with your young friend, but I am afraid the rain will be keeping us in tonight."

My young friend? Oh! Anna! I almost forgot she was upstairs. So easy to forget, that Anna.

"Thanks so much for your warm welcome, Mrs. Flaherty," I replied.

"Please," she paused, "call me Kath," and with that Kath darted out of the room toward the kitchen leaving me on my own to explore Raven's Point Manor.

\* \* \*

The ground floor of the manor was surprisingly still. If there were six other guests staying in the manor, well, they must have all been corpses, as the house was as silent as a cemetery.

Now, I would rather not bore you with all the architectural details of the manor, but I do think it is worth painting a picture of our story's setting. In addition to the exquisite foyer and parlour that I have already discussed, the first floor of the manor housed a well-stocked library, a glass-paned orangerie, a wonderful dining room, a kitchen, and a game room of sorts, which housed a beautiful, hand-carved chess set and a dartboard among its many novelties, as well as a music room featuring a piano. Although I feel a bit embarrassed to write this, I feel it is necessary for completion: there was also a loo.

Just under the massive staircase in the foyer was a door that led to a cellar. I barely stepped down into the cellar after realising that it was undergoing some sort of reconstruction, with bricks and mortar strewn about, walls half exposed, and what appeared to be a wine chilling room that was fully stocked. The perfect, polished look of the main floor stood in sharp contrast to the dusty, dirty work-in-progress that was the lower level.

"I suppose you won't be spending much time down here anyway," I mused to myself. "Except maybe to borrow some of this wine?" A boozy author is a dangerous one.

As I made my way up the stairs, I swore I saw something move in the corner of my eye. A yellow robe or kimono of some sort floating in the wind before vanishing behind the slamming of one of the doors, but I was also convinced I was just imagining things. I still had not eaten anything since we left the city, and a hungry stomach can often deceive even the smartest brain. I realised at that moment that I was unsure whether I had been assigned to room six or room seven, but as I attempted to open the door to room six, its motionless handle answered my question.

"I suppose this is Anna's room," I said. "Good thing she's locked herself inside. Wouldn't want too much excitement."

I proceeded down the hall a bit to room 7, reached for the handle, and opened the door. The room was immaculately decorated, although my eye was first drawn to a framed painting of what appeared to be a raven.

"Hmm. Well, that *is* fitting, I suppose," I thought as I reached out to adjust the slightly crooked frame.

The floral print bed linens matched the window draping. Solid oak furniture adorned the room, including a large writing desk and the frame of a porcelain wash basin. The room was a whimsical mix of stark wood and soft floral, continuing the oddly balanced theme of Raven's Point Manor.

"Perfect," I thought as I set my typewriter upon the desk and imagined staring out the window into the beautiful countryside, writing what would be my final novel.

I noticed that my belongings had already been placed in the wardrobe and my suitcases neatly stacked nearby. "Thanks, Anna," I muttered to myself as I sat on the edge of the bed.

"Ooh! Soft!" I remarked as I rubbed the back of my hand over the bed linens. "I should take a quick nap and then go see about that tea and biscuits I have been thinking about."

That was all I remembered thinking before the black set in. Within seconds, I was out.

\*       \*       \*

I awoke what I thought was fifteen minutes later to the chiming of the grandfather's clock downstairs.

"One, two…" I counted in my mind, "three, four, five, six. Six o'clock? I can't believe I…seven." Seven chimes! I had been asleep for two hours, not fifteen minutes, and dinner was now just one hour away!

I remembered what Mrs. Flaherty had said about joining the other guests for pre-dinner drinks in the library. Not wanting to appear rude nor to make myself stick out in any way, I figured I should at least make a brief appearance at the library drink gathering before dinner.

I hurried to straighten my clothing and fix my hair from what was an involuntary flattened pillow styling. I checked myself in the mirror, adjusted my blue-rimmed glasses, and then stepped out of my room into the second-floor hall. I swiftly made my way toward the stairs before thinking, "Anna! I should see if she would like to join."

I double-backed and knocked on Anna's door. No response. I knocked once more but heard nothing beyond the door.

"Pity," I thought, "the poor girl is probably asleep." Rainy days do have an exhausting effect on people.

I made my way down the stairs and turned left, proceeding straight into the library. There was already much commotion and chattering coming from the direction of the library, so it appeared as though the other guests were already enjoying each other's company and spirits. I pushed the sliding doors open and surveyed the scene before me.

Standing closest to the door were two gentlemen smoking cigars. Although similar in age, the men could not have presented themselves any more differently. The taller of the two had dark, Mediterranean features. Italian, I guessed. His suit was well tailored and appeared to be fabricated using premium textiles, its deep emerald colour giving him a sort of earthy style. A man who must have paid close attention to detail, his suit was accessorised with a golden pocket square, a golden necktie, and a gold ring. He was clearly visiting from the city.

The man with whom he was speaking was almost the opposite in every way. His long-sleeve dress shirt did nothing much for his portly figure other than remind everyone that he was not wearing a dinner jacket. His badly sunned face and calloused hands implied a life of manual labour, whether a farmer or a factory worker I was not entirely sure. He spoke in lazy legato phrases, which suggested he was not someone in any hurry. Whereas his conversation partner was cosmopolitan and dapper in every way, he was as informal and oblivious as men come. He was clearly *not* visiting from the city.

Near the men, seated on a blood red sofa near a fireplace more modest in size than the one I had seen in the parlour, were two women. Whereas the men were roughly the same age, the women looked as though they could be grandmother and granddaughter but in age alone, not looks. The older of the two women was quite matronly, around my age, and extremely overdone by way of dress and maquillage. It appeared as though her wardrobe was tended to by someone with poor vision and her makeup by a circus clown. She also sat in the most peculiar way, legs crossed, back straight as a rod, and hands folded neatly in her lap, careful only to touch just enough of the sofa to be seated and no more. Her clothing was ill-fitting and drab, although it attempted to imitate haute couture, and it was clear this woman was a stranger to city life, as well.

The younger woman sitting next to her, on the other hand, was a ravishing sight, indeed. Thin, leggy, and done up like royalty, the woman wore a tightly fitted sapphire dress that glistened like a gem in the light of the fireplace. Her brown hair was styled in a way that suggested a European heritage, as the Americans were a bit behind us when it came to progressive style trends. Even from where I stood, I could detect a hint of an accent, though I could not exactly place it from so far away. Her beauty was like a beacon to everyone in the room, however, as the gentlemen smoking would often glance in her direction even as they spoke to one another. If poor Anna was consistently overlooked by everyone in the room, this young woman was the exact opposite: the centre of attention in any room she entered.

Across from this sofa were two chairs on either side of a small table. In one chair sat a 20-something year-old man and in the other chair sat a 20-something year-old woman. One might have assumed they were a couple except they could not be any more uninterested in each other. Now, it is worth noting that plenty of married couples are quite uninterested in each other and that works out well enough for them, but these two were certainly not married. If their odd personalities did not give this away then the lack of a ring on either of their hands certainly did.

The young man was an attractive lad, chiselled features but also a soft, clear visage. He wore thin-framed spectacles and had wavy brown hair through which he was currently running his fingers. In his other hand was an open book, presumably one removed from one of the library's many shelves, and he was deep in thought regarding whatever it was he was reading, seemingly oblivious and indifferent to the fact that there were other human beings in the room. His bow tie and tweed jacket suggested he might be a barrister or maybe a scholar; whatever career it was he pursued, he came across as learned.

The young woman sitting in the chair on the other side of the table was a beauty, herself, with hair styled like that of a famous actress and wearing a dress that certainly came from an expensive shop. Her youth is what stood out to me the most followed by the longing look in her eyes as if her mind was elsewhere even if she were physically here with us in this room. I noticed that she also had her attention on the first gentleman I saw upon entering the library, but I thought nothing of it at the moment, as I was more concerned with making an introduction for myself.

Oh, and Anna was there, as well, standing in the back corner of the room mingling with no one, odd girl.

"Ah, and here she is," the emerald-suited gentleman said as he approached me. "Ms. Crawford, I presume?"

Although the name still had not sunken in completely, I acknowledged his greeting with a smile and responded,

"Yes, that's me: Ms. Alice Crawford!" I nearly forgot the name Anna had given me but thankfully saw a copy of *Alice's Adventures in Wonderland* on display atop one of the tables.

The other guests all stood up at the same time and approached me. The gentlemen took a step back to let the ladies go first.

"Good evening, Ms. Crawford," said the quiet young woman who had been sitting in the chair. "Mary Jane Finley. Nice to meet you."

"Why, hello there, madam," said the older woman who has been sitting on the sofa as she did a strange curtesy. "I am Doris Powell, the wife of Mr. Albert Powell," she said as she gestured in the direction of the two men who had been smoking cigars.

"Good evening," I heard a thick French accent say. The beautiful woman who had also been sitting on the sofa kissed the air to the left of me then to the right of me and said, "I am Claudette Lavoie. Enchantée."

French, I should have known. We British aren't known for getting along particularly well with the French, which probably explained Claudette's disdainful look back in my direction as she walked away. *Quel charmant.*

Following the ladies, a line of the gentlemen had formed.

Up first was the rotund gentleman whose sweaty hand firmly grasped mine. "Pleased to meet you, Ms. Crawford. The name's Powell, Albert Powell."

"Ah, yes, I could have guessed, Mr. Powell," and it was true, I could have guessed this gentleman was Mrs. Powell's husband. They just...*went* together.

"Marvin Rossini, Rossini's fine jewellery," said the tall, tan gentlemen who followed. "Delighted to meet you," he said with such a quick, almost unnatural energy.

And, rounding out the group, was the young man who had been lost deep within a book upon my arrival to the library. "Richter, uh, Fred that is. Fred Richter," the words stumbled out of his mouth. "It's lovely to meet you, Ms.

Crawford," he said as he looked away somewhat awkwardly.

"The pleasure is all mine," I announced to the group.

At that moment, I spotted Anna in the corner of my eye.

"And I am sure by now that you have all met my assistant, Anna?" I asked.

"Oh, yes, indeed. Almost forgot the poor girl was here," Mr. Rossini responded.

Anna approached my side avoiding eye contact with everyone in the room in the same way a canine avoids eye contact as to not appear threatening. She then stuck to my side like a magnet as I wandered about the room exchanging pleasantries with our fellow guests.

Mr. Rossini, ball of energy that he was, was serving as a bartender for everyone, making sure that no glass went unfilled for too long.

"I'll have a Mary Pickford," Miss Finley said.

"I'll take a Bee's Knees," said Mrs. Powell.

"I'll have a Corpse Reviver," Mr. Powell requested.

"Yech!" replied Mr. Rossini. "I never did like the taste of Absinthe. Like black liquorice, it is. Bad enough to eat, even worse to drink, Mr. Powell."

"To each his own," Mr. Powell responded. "Besides, it just means more Absinthe for me!"

We were all a bit lost in conversation when we were startled by the front door swinging open. We could feel the chilling air of the rainstorm immediately flood into the manor, swirling around the first floor and into the library where the flames of the fire responded with a jittery flicker. The storm had intensified significantly, and there, barely visible in the doorframe, stood a man whose silhouette blackened out the silvery flashes of lightning illuminating the grounds of the estate.

The group of us in the library made our way to the arched doorway to get a glimpse of what caused this commotion. As he stepped farther into the foyer, Giles' rain smock became visible in the light from the dimmed chandelier, dripping wet and full of mud. In his left hand he carried the same shovel I saw when we had first pulled onto the grounds just a few hours before. If he noticed our group then he simply ignored us, as he walked right past the library toward the cellar door, mumbling something as he walked by.

"Captain Liberty," I heard him say. "Captain Liberty. Captain Liberty." He descended into the cellar, shutting the door behind him.

No one said anything at first, and then the silence was broken by Mrs. Powell who simply said, "Spooky."

Right at that moment, there was a bright flash of lightning followed by a roaring thunder. And then, to punctuate this coincidental symphony of nature, Mrs. Flaherty rang a small bell from the kitchen.

Dinner was ready.

# 3 | A DELICIOUSLY
## DISHY DINNER PARTY

When you live by the sea, you grow strangely accustomed to the strong smell of fish. Although the pungent odour is rather off-putting to many people, I have often found that the smell brings back fond memories of my childhood in Southend-on-Sea. Smell and memory are curiously linked, it seems, as I have often had this experience of strong smells evoking such very vivid memories.

As my fellow guests and I made our way across the foyer to the dining room, the smell of fish was unmistakable.

"Oh, my," Mrs. Powell began, "I do hope that whatever fish Mrs. Flaherty has prepared is served without its head. I simply cannot stomach seeing the face of the animal I am about to consume. Positively ghastly!"

"Do you mean to say that you will lose your head at the sight of a fish who has not lost his?" Mr. Rossini joked (or at least *attempted* to joke), sniffling heavily just after.

Everyone gave a half-hearted laugh out of politeness for Mr. Rossini's comedic effort while taking a seat around the large dining table. Mr. and Mrs. Powell sat at the end closest to the foyer, across from the kitchen. Next to them sat Miss Lavoie who, herself, was seated to the right of Anna. On the other side of the table, the side closest to the kitchen, sat Mr. Richter, Mr. Rossini, Miss Finley, and then myself, directly across from Anna. The seats at either end of the table were left open for Mrs. Flaherty and Giles, the former who sounded as if she were having a one-woman battle with the pans in the kitchen and the latter who had yet to make an appearance since descending into the cellar.

The guests around the table all sat very quietly and still for the first several minutes, going through the typical etiquette of placing napkins in laps and cleansing the palate with the water that was already on the table. I quickly busied myself with straightening the silverware, wine glass, and bread plate that formed my place setting. It appeared Mrs. Flaherty was too busy cooking food and playing housemaid, simultaneously, to do the latter job perfectly. I sincerely hoped she did not also fall short on her cooking efforts in this failed attempt to juggle so many tasks at once. My stomach was now growling with hunger, as my unexpectedly long nap earlier robbed me of the opportunity to grab some tea and biscuits.

I was lost in my daydreaming about tea and biscuits when Mrs. Flaherty broke the silence of the dining room with a boisterous, "Who's hungry?!" kicking open the swinging door from the kitchen.

"For tonight's meal, we will begin with fresh salmon mousse cups and a salmon salad followed by a main course of salmon soufflé and a delicious pineapple upside down cake," Kath announced.

Pardon me for the pun, but it was then that I should have realized something fishy was certain to occur at dinner.

"Ah, well, that *is* a relief," Mrs. Powell sighed. "My stomach could not bear the thought of seeing a real fish's head on my plate."

"But eating the animal cut into small pieces and baked within a pastry is...acceptable?" Fred, the young learned gentleman asked in a most academic way, "Interesting."

"It is not that I do not enjoy the taste of the fish, of course. I do. I just cannot bear the thought of a poor animal suffering," Mrs. Powell said. "The pain, the blood, the thought that their little fish family is now without a member of its school. And then to think of yanking the hook from the poor dear's mouth, the deboning process, the…"

Mrs. Powell continued on in graphic detail as everyone shifted somewhat uncomfortably in his or her chair. Most people simply do not think too much about how, exactly, food arrives to their plate. In fact, most people try to avoid thinking about death altogether, as this often reminds one of his own inevitable demise. This mortality salience is what makes my reader shudder as they consume my mysteries: it is not the death of the fictitious victim in a murder mystery that frightens them; it is the thought of *their own* expiration.

Perhaps sensing everyone else's level of discomfort with his wife's topic of conversation, Mr. Powell interrupted, "So, what is it that everyone does for a living? I suppose if we are all to dine together and see each other around the manor during our stay it would be nice to know what keeps us busy when we are not away on vacation."

Holiday, as we Brits would say, but Mr. and Mrs. Powell were American through and through.

"I will start," Claudette Lavoie began. "I work in fashion. My father owns a textile company in the south of France, so I had been exposed to the business since I was a girl. I started designing my own clothing as a teenager, and now I own a shop near Boulevard Haussmann in Paris."

"Smashing, I would say! I knew you must have been in fashion since the moment you arrived the other day," said Mrs. Flaherty as she circled around the table delivering everyone's salmon mousse cups. "It is not every day we have a famous French fashion designer in these parts!"

"Well, then I would guess it is not often you have a dealer of gems and luxury jewellery in these parts then either?" Mr. Rossini chimed in. "I am the third generation of a family business that began in Palermo and made its way here to Manhattan. If the lovely madame here paints your body with her beautiful clothing, then the Rossini family adds the final touches," he said, pulling on his earlobes, gesturing his neck, and showing his wrists before wiggling his ringed fingers toward the other guests.

"Oy! I have to tell you, Mr. Rossini, but your ring was indeed the first thing I noticed when you stepped out of the car here at Raven's Point Manor," Kath said as she placed Mr. Rossini's salmon mousse cup in front of him and then grabbed his hand to see the ring up close.

"Well, and I noticed your lovely locket, Mrs. Flaherty, and Mademoiselle Lavoie's beautiful earrings," Mr. Rossini replied. "When you work in my business, all you see, everywhere, is gold."

"And you, Miss Finley? What is it that you do?" Mrs. Powell asked the young woman sitting next to Mr. Rossini.

"I am a schoolteacher, Mrs. Powell. Elementary school," Mary Jane Finley answered.

"Oh, how wonderful!" Mrs. Powell shrieked. "I would love to have been a schoolteacher!"

"What prevented you from pursuing it?" Mr. Rossini asked.

"The chalk! All that pesky chalk, drying out your hands and blocking your nasal passages! Suffocating! Why, I do not know how you even manage, Miss Finley, but hurrah and three cheers for you," Mrs. Powell went on.

"Ah, yes, well, that does take some getting used to, I suppose," Miss Finley replied.

After a beat, Mrs. Powell continued, "And how is it that you two know each other?" she said while wagging a finger between Mr. Rossini and Miss Finley.

If Mr. Rossini and Miss Finley were thermostats then the air in the room must have turned sub-Arctic at that very moment, for the warmth of their cheeks drained from their faces immediately upon Mrs. Powell's simple query.

"I beg your pardon?" Miss Finley asked Mrs. Powell.

"Well, if I am not mistaken, I believe I saw you coming from Mr. Rossini's room this morning, around 7:30am, in fact. I figured you had just been chatting or something, you know, as old friends do," Mrs. Powell continued with no hint of negative intent in her voice.

"That must be a mistake, Mrs. Powell," Mr. Rossini

responded.

"No, no, I am quite sure I saw you, Mary Jane. You are staying in Room 2, and Mr. Rossini is in Room 1, and I saw you leaving Room 1 and walking to Room 2 right around…"

"Oh, you know what it is?" Mr. Rossini began again. "You *are* right, my good woman, but you have the time wrong. You see, Miss Finley stopped by my room before lunch, so perhaps you have your meals mixed up?"

Mrs. Powell had a confused expression on her face but said, "Yes, well, perhaps you are correct. Still, am I mistaken in recognizing there is some shared history between you two?"

Again, an awkward silence filled the room while the rest of us watched this tennis match play out back and forth across the dining table. Then, Mr. Rossini and Miss Finley responded at the exact same time.

"We are lovers," she said.

"We are cousins," he said.

If the silence had been thick just one moment before, it was now suffocating.

"Distant cousins," Mr. Rossini added, "as in generation upon generation removed. From the old country. Italians."

"Ah, yes, that's right," Miss Finley went on. "And we are *bird* lovers. I misspoke there for a second. In fact, that is the very reason I went to Mr. Rossini's room. I was hoping he would be able to identify the beautiful songbird I heard just outside the window."

"And did you…?" Mrs. Powell said, bobbling her head and looking toward Mr. Rossini.

"Did we *what*?!" Mr. Rossini asked, wide-eyed.

"Identify the songbird?" Mrs. Powell clarified.

"Oh, yes, of course," Mr. Rossini said, somewhat relieved. "It was a…it was a…"

"Fox sparrow," Miss Finley answered.

"Marvellous! Such a beautiful song they have," Mrs. Powell exclaimed before looking at Mr. Rossini and adding, "how very impressive!"

"And what about you, Mr. Richter?" Mr. Powell, once again witnessing his wife potentially crossing a line, turned everyone's attention to the young gentleman sitting across from him.

At that moment, Fred Richter seemed startled that he was the topic of conversation, particularly because he was caught taking some saltine crackers from the table and placing them into the pocket of his dinner jacket.

"Mr. Richter," Kath began, "if you would like seconds all you need to do is say so."

"Oh, no," Fred said, blushing a bit. "It is just that I sometimes get an upset stomach at night and thought maybe I should have some saltine crackers on hand to help settle my stomach."

"Nerves, is it?" Mrs. Powell asked.

"Gas mostly," Fred replied, somewhat oblivious to his context.

After a moment, Fred began again, "As to what I do, Mr. Powell, I am a scientist. Biochemistry, specifically. I taught, er, I teach at a university, which is also where I have my laboratory."

My suspicion that Fred Richter was a learned man was confirmed. I always was rather observant. To be fair, the fact that he was also a petty saltine cracker thief slipped by me.

"Monsieur Richter, you are in Room 4 next to mine, non? I have been meaning to ask you if you have been hearing a strange scratching noise in the middle of the night around 2 or 3:00am," Claudette Lavoie asked.

"Hmm, not that I have noticed," Fred replied. "I seem to have slept quite soundly each night since I arrived."

"Bizarre. I am certain I hear it each night. It sounds almost like a kitten clawing at a…"

"It's nothing," Fred interrupted somewhat coldly. Perhaps recognizing the terseness of his reply, Mr. Richter continued, "It is probably just a stray tree branch scraping against the house, Ms. Lavoie."

Claudette Lavoie, clearly dissatisfied by this answer, shot daggers at Mr. Richter before pursing her lips, looking away, and letting out a little puff of breath with a "pff" sound and a shrug. It was so very French of her.

By this point, Mrs. Flaherty had already delivered everyone's salmon mousse cup, but the group was so lost in conversation that no one really noticed until Mr. Richter grabbed his cup in one hand, spoon in another, and leaned in to take a bite.

Before he could bring the spoon too his mouth, Mrs. Powell shrieked, "Wait! Before we start, shouldn't we wait for the groundskeeper? Oh, what's his name again?"

"Giles," Kath said, visibly annoyed.

"Ah, yes. Giles. It is only proper etiquette if we wait for everyone to be seated at the table before starting in," Mrs. Powell continued.

At that moment, Kath pushed her chair from the table, walked over to the golden bell sitting on the shelf of a lovely china hutch, and began ringing the bell furiously.

"Giles!" Mrs. Flaherty yelled walking toward the foyer, "Dinner is served! Hurry up!" She turned back toward the dining room and mumbled, "Even dogs can respond to bells, the lazy dolt."

As she walked back toward her seat, Miss Finley began to speak, "Mrs. Flaherty, with all due respect, I gather that Mr. Giles is not operating with his full faculties and is, to my understanding, also a veteran of the war. Perhaps it would be prudent to show some compassion when speaking about him, particularly in front of a room of total strangers?"

Mrs. Flaherty, a bit caught off guard from the schoolteacher's chastisement, recognized her callousness and replied, "Aye. You are correct, Miss Finley. Please accept my apology, everyone. It usually takes a small army to run a house of this size, but it is just me and Giles here. Sometimes the stress is…overwhelming. I shall try to work on my patience. We can all do better, can't we?"

No one acknowledged her question.

Just then, the door to the cellar opened and, within seconds, Giles appeared at the doorway clearly having taken some small effort to clean up and make himself look presentable enough for dinner. He was dressed in a black dinner jacket, neat slacks, and a pressed white shirt. The final product was a bit dishevelled, at best, but one could see that Giles could fix up nicely if he were aware of the social importance of such things.

Without saying a word, Giles plodded over to the lone empty chair sitting at the end of the table nearest the foyer. He grabbed his napkin, placed it in his lap, and then proceeded to eat the salmon mousse cup as if he were raised by wolves. The guests pretended not to notice and quickly averted their eyes upon seeing Giles handle his food in this manner. Only Mrs. Flaherty kept staring at Giles who, as if returning dialogue in a silent conversation between the two, stared back while eating his appetizer.

"What about you, Ms. Crawford?" Mr. Powell asked. "What is it that you do?"

Oh, bugger. I had been so keenly interested in everyone else's story that I completely overlooked the fact that they would soon come for mine.

"Who me?" I tried to delay. I thought of my large typewriter box that Mrs. Flaherty had seen upon our arrival. What else could have been in that box? A sewing machine? I found myself replying without much thinking, "Seamstress. I am a seamstress. I brought my sewing tools with me to work on a gown for my assistant's wedding," I said, gesturing toward Anna.

Now, I am not sure if it was the fact that I am not the stereotypical seamstress type or if our fellow guests just had a difficult time believing that Anna could ever be engaged, poor girl, but the faces around the table were clearly unconvinced.

"Oh, my! A seamstress with an assistant! You must be quite important in England," Mrs. Powell said as her eyes lit up.

"*Mais non*, I am sorry, but you are most certainly *not* a seamstress," Ms. Lavoie piped in. "As a fashion designer, I can assure you I know a seamstress when I see one."

"Oh, is that so," I retorted.

"How can you tell?" Mr. Rossini asked.

"By the *feet* of her clothing," Ms. Lavoie responded.

"I'm sorry, the feet of her clothing?" Mrs. Powell repeated.

"Oui, the *feet*. You know, if it is loose or tight in the right places," said Ms. Lavoie.

"Oh, the *fit*. My clothes don't *fit* right, I see," I said, joyful that I figured out what Ms. Lavoie was trying to say before realising that her comment was actually quite insulting.

"*Ce n'est pas grave, madame*. Your clothes are fine but not perfect because you are no seamstress," Ms. Lavoie said. Then, she looked directly at me, squinted her eyes a bit, and said, "Ah, *oui*, but I think I *do* know who you are."

I could see Anna grow a bit tense and nervous across from me almost as if she were not sure if she should attempt to interrupt and save the cover story or just follow my next move.

Figuring I could try and call Ms. Lavoie's bluff I simply asked, "And who might that be?"

"If I am not mistaken, I believe you to be Dame Margaret James," Ms. Lavoie announced.

"Dame Margaret James? The famous author?" Miss Finley added.

Brilliant.

"Oy! You don't say! I have a famous fashion designer *and* a famous author staying here at Raven's Point Manor?" Mrs. Flaherty said, standing slowly in her chair. "Why, I would have prepared a nicer feast if I had known!"

"Is it true, Ms. Crawford? Er, Ms. James?" Mr. Rossini asked.

Figuring we were well past the point of preserving my anonymity I gave in, "Indeed, it is true. I am Dame Margaret

James, famous author and British socialite. I asked my assistant to book our stay under a false name in order to keep a low profile so I could work uninterrupted, but I had not anticipated Europeans staying here at Raven's Point Manor this week," I said, looking toward Ms. Lavoie.

"My apologies, Madame James. I know the importance of having some privacy in this world, believe me," Mademoiselle Lavoie said. "It is just that I spend a lot of time in London with my work, so from the moment I saw you in the library I thought you looked quite familiar."

Well, at least that explained what I thought was a critical second glance from Miss Lavoie when we first met. Still, whatever privacy I was hoping to have up to that point quickly evaporated. I just hoped it would not affect my writing.

*     *     *

The main course went by with much less ado than the starter, probably because everyone was still digesting all the new information while simultaneously attempting to digest Mrs. Flaherty's third salmon-themed dish of the evening.

Although the main course was relatively uneventful, dessert was anything but. Perhaps it was fitting that Mrs. Flaherty had prepared a pineapple upside down cake for dessert, you see, because the evening itself was about to get turned upside down in the most peculiar way.

Just as soon as Kath set the serving plate on the table there was a knock at the front door. Three knocks, actually. One. After. Another...but with a brief enough delay between each tap as to be noticeable.

"Why, who might that be?" cried Mrs. Powell.

"Were you expecting someone, Mrs. Flaherty?" Mr. Rossini asked.

"Expecting someone? At this hour? And in this weather? Not at all," Kath answered as she stood, wringing her hands on her napkin and heading toward the foyer.

"Giles…Giles, join me, please," Kath commanded.

Giles stood and followed Kath to the foyer. The rest of us, not invited to be a part of the welcoming party, strained our necks as we leaned toward the foyer to see the source of the knocking. It did not help that Giles was standing between our eyes and the mysterious visitor once the door opened, so we did our best to listen to what was being said.

"Aye, yes, I see," Kath could be heard saying. "Well, how many rooms would you need then? Two? You are in luck."

There was a bit more murmuring among the group of people now standing in the foyer, but the sound seemed to travel upward instead of over to the dining room. As such, we all resumed small talk as to not be thought of as eavesdroppers.

When Kath returned to the dining room, she was joined by two unfamiliar faces. A petite blonde woman in her late 20s and a fit blond man in his 30s entered the dining room from the darkness of the foyer followed by Giles who stood behind them awkwardly. The two strangers were soaking wet, presumably from the rainstorm, and the young woman was wearing what appeared to be a nurse's uniform under a trench coat. They were dripping so much water on the floor that I would have believed you if you told me they had just taken a swim fully clothed.

"Ladies and gentlemen, may I introduce Ms. Betty Simmons and her brother, Walter," Kath announced. "Their car got stuck in mud near the access road, and they walked all this way for help! In this tempest! Can you imagine?!"

"Good evening, everyone," Ms. Simmons spoke. "We are so very sorry to spoil your dinner. My brother and I were just on our way from the city to visit our parents when the weather hit. It is absolutely dreadful outside, isn't it?"

As the woman spoke, her brother seemed to shiver as if frightened, like he had just encountered a ghost. Judging by how drenched he appeared to be and how cold the temperature had dropped due to the winds he was probably in the early stages of hypothermia.

"It is dreadful outside, indeed!" Kath responded. "Let us get you two upstairs to your rooms where you can take a warm bath and change into something more comfortable." As she said this, Kath looked down at the visitors' hands and then out into the foyer before realizing that they had no luggage.

In a flash, Ms. Simmons started, "Oh, dear! We left our trunks back in the car! I suppose it just slipped our mind in our hurry to find shelter, but I imagine it would have been too much weight to carry in this treacherous rain in any case."

"Not to worry, love! I am sure we have some spare clothes for you and your brother here. Now, follow me so we can get you two all settled in," Kath said, leading the Simmons siblings out of the dining room into the foyer.

"Come now, Walter," Betty said softly to her brother, grabbing his arm and leading him toward Kath.

And, with that, the new guests left the scene as quickly as they had arrived leaving just Giles standing in the arched doorway between the dining room and the foyer, staring blankly at the painting hanging on the opposite wall of the dining room.

Like spectators watching a horse race at Epsom Downs, all of us watched as an invisible horse leapt from Giles' mind, galloped across the dining room table, passed the uneaten pineapple upside down cake, and then leapt off the table to the painting that was now the centre of Giles' attention. There, painted in dull colours, was a conspiracy (or group) of ravens, perched onto the treeless limbs of a stately, twisted oak tree.

"Captain Liberty," Giles began, "Captain Liberty. Captain Liberty."

The room was silent. Everyone glanced around the room at each other making eye contact with the other guests seated around the table. Finally, Mr. Rossini grabbed the dessert serving tray and announced, "So, dessert in the parlour, then?"

Everyone assented, stood up, and made their way to the parlour leaving poor Giles standing alone, staring at the painting, now whispering softly to himself…

"Captain Liberty. Captain Liberty."

$*$ $*$ $*$

The warmth of the parlour's fireplace was welcome on what felt increasingly more like a winter evening. One would have had a difficult time guessing it was early June with the chill in the air, so I positioned myself as close to the fireplace as possible without making it appear as though I was doing so (as that would be selfish). We had finished enjoying Mrs. Flaherty's delicious pineapple upside down cake and were engaging in conversation when one of the two strangers, Ms. Simmons, entered the room.

"Hello again, everyone," Ms. Simmons began. "I just wanted to apologize again for interrupting your dinner this evening."

"Not a bother," said Mr. Powell as he stood to gesture her into the room. "The more the merrier I say."

"And I say so, too," agreed Mrs. Powell. "I do believe Mrs. Flaherty has extra servings of tonight's dinner in the kitchen should you and your brother be hungry. It is not much good if I am to be honest, but I am certain she would be happy to serve you."

I was not as convinced as Mrs. Powell that Mrs. Flaherty would be happy to do *any* extra work this evening. Giles and Kath stayed behind in the dining room and kitchen, presumably to clean up the dinner mess and start preparing for tomorrow's breakfast. The last we saw of them, Kath was scolding Giles for not cleaning the grime off the golden dinner bell (as she had now asked "three times already") and informing us that tomorrow morning's breakfast would be a delicious, fresh-baked salmon quiche.

"Oh, I am not particularly hungry this evening," Ms.

Simmons went on, "my brother and I had just eaten at our parents' home before heading back to the city."

"That is just lovely," Mrs. Powell responded. "You know good people when they still manage to find quality time with their..."

"I thought you said you were just coming *from* the city to visit your parents," Anna spoke up from out of nowhere.

Almost on cue, everyone in the room turned slowly to see Anna, standing in the farthest corner, holding her tea and saucer in front of her chest, gently lowering her teacup from her lips after taking a sip of hot Earl Grey.

"I'm sorry?" Ms. Simmons asked, cocking her head to one side.

"Earlier, when you arrived, you said that you and your brother were on your way from the city to visit your parents. I was just confused as to whether you and Mr. Simmons were coming or going," Anna continued.

Perhaps I had underestimated Anna. She seemed to fancy herself a bit of a detective.

"Oh, I did?" Ms. Simmons laughed. "Sorry about that. I am *quite* exhausted. You see, I am a nurse at the nearby hospital and this week has been particularly demanding. And, of course, on top of that, I am the primary caregiver for my brother, which often feels like a job unto itself. Perhaps I should have just gone to bed instead of coming down here to..."

"No, dear, never you mind," Mrs. Powell interrupted. "Poor thing!"

"Yes, well, I do apologize if I am a bit out of sorts. My brother's condition requires that he has constant supervision and medication always at the ready should he get too excited," Ms. Simmons went on, "he is upstairs sleeping now, but should he begin to wander or disturb you in any way this evening or tomorrow before we depart, please just let me know."

There was a long pause while everyone thought of the same question.

Then, Mrs. Powell just asked it, "What's wrong with him?"

The rest of us cringed. For someone who spoke so highly of etiquette, Mrs. Powell seem to lack any hint of sophistication, class, or nuance.

"My brother? The doctors are not entirely sure," Ms. Simmons began. "They think it is neurological, but poor Walter just gets very animated and starts spouting nonsensical things. It would be harmless if he merely said words, but he can become quite physically aggressive sometimes, which is why he requires some light tranquilizers every so often."

"Tranquilizers?" Ms. Lavoie exclaimed. "You speak of him like he is a horse or some kind of wild animal!"

"It is not so uncommon," Mr. Richter chimed in. "Sometimes the brain's chemistry is just a bit off. It is like a recipe where one of the ingredients is too strong or too weak. The worst part," the young scientist continued, "is that it can happen to anyone at any time. That means that you could live for decades with a perfectly functioning brain and then BAM!" He slapped his hand on the desk, startling everyone, and said, "You're more of an animal than a man."

We experienced what felt like our hundredth moment of extended silence of the evening. This group had a certain flair for both the dramatic and quiet thinking time.

"Mr. and Mrs. Powell," Miss Finley started, "I do not believe we had the pleasure of hearing your occupation over dinner?"

"Ah, well, that is because there is not so much of an occupation to discuss," Mr. Powell responded.

"Oh, my poor man!" Mr. Rossini interjected. "You are unemployed? Of course, of course. This explains your clothing and your cheap cigars!"

A bit flabbergasted, Mr. Powell responded, "Um, not exactly, Mr. Rossini," as he looked down at his clothing likely wondering what was so wrong with them. "I am actually retired, see. The wife and I owned Powell Family

Farms for several years. We provided crops, meat, and feed to stores throughout most of New England. We made a tidy sum, sold the farm a few years back, and have just been enjoying retirement ever since."

"And you, Mrs. Powell? You said you wanted to be a schoolteacher, but did you also work on the farm?" Miss Finley asked.

"Who me? Oh, heavens no!" Mrs. Powell responded. "Far too dirty a job for my liking! Why, each day when Mr. Powell would come home, I would make him take *two* baths before he could give me a kiss hello."

"Surely, she is joking?" Mr. Richter asked.

"I wish, my good man," replied Mr. Powell, "I wish."

"I was a homemaker. I tended to things around the house," Mrs. Powell went on.

"You mean children and the like?" asked Mademoiselle Lavoie.

"Oh, no. No children for us," said Mrs. Powell. "I always found babies to be adorable, but children are snotty, dirty, smelly little imps. We had plenty of filthy living creatures outside the house. We had no need of any more inside the house."

She tidied up her dress, brushing off some crumbs or some lint that found its way to her lap. Feeling the silence in the room, she added, "Unless any one of you has children, of course, in which case I am sure they are just lovely and the rare exception to the rule."

"None for me just yet," Miss Finley responded.

"*Moi non plus*," Mademoiselle Lavoie answered.

"Nope," Mr. Rossini replied as he refilled his brandy.

"Not interested," Mr. Richter said putting his hand in the air.

"No, thank you," Anna said as if turning down an hors-d'oeuvre.

Ms. Simmons just shook her head no, smiling with her eyes closed, and then everyone looked my direction.

"Sadly, no," I replied with a heavy sigh. Not having

children was always one of my biggest regrets. I would have given anything to have a reminder of Harry to have around, to keep me company. Alas, I was far too busy with writing to think about motherhood when the time was right, and by the time I was more available, my "window of biological opportunity," let's call it, had passed.

"Children can be such a gift," I offered.

"But don't the very best gifts come with the greatest costs?" Mr. Richter added.

"I suppose so," I said. "I suppose so."

The hour was growing late as conversation began to fade. Eyes grew heavier. Sighs grew longer. I admit that I nodded off a few times thanks to the warmth of the fireplace and the rather dull conversation I found myself having with Mr. Rossini and Mademoiselle Lavoie regarding the latest fashion trends in New York.

"Anna, dear girl," Mrs. Powell's voice boomed across the room, "you are always so quiet in these conversations, but I am curious: what was it that you did before becoming Dame James' assistant?"

Anna fidgeted a bit, shifting the balance from one foot to the other while standing near the fireplace.

"A housekeeper," I said, "at least that is what she put on the application. Otherwise, I would say she is quite a good professional liar," I teased.

The room had a good chuckle over my small joke, but then a voice spoke up.

"Librarian," Anna said, "I was a librarian in Birmingham before I moved to London. I loved it, and I quite miss the work. However, for reasons far beyond my control I was forced to leave Birmingham suddenly, which is how I wound up in London cleaning houses."

"A librarian?" I asked. "But that is wonderful work! I am surprised you would not list this on your application or at least mention it during your interview. The skills of a librarian are so wonderfully relevant to assisting an author!"

How lucky for me!

"What, may I ask happened that required you to leave Birmingham so quickly," Mrs. Powell asked, again lacking any hint of social tact.

"Mrs. Powell," Anna began, "librarians are adept at preserving silence, right?"

"I suppose that's true," Mrs. Powell responded.

"Well, then let us just say there are some things that are better kept quiet," said Anna.

And with that mysteriously chilling reply, the convivial air of the room vanished, leaving just an awkward stillness in its place.

"Would you look at the time?!" Mademoiselle Lavoie commented, smartly shifting the subject.

"Indeed! The hour has grown so late," Miss Finley added.

It was not so late. Just 10:30pm, actually. Still, the out was offered.

The group exchanged their "good nights" and "pleasant dreams" as, one by one, each guest went up to his or her respective room for the evening. As we passed through the foyer, much commotion could still be heard from the direction of the kitchen and dining room, presumably Kath and Giles cleaning up from today's meals or preparing for tomorrow's meals. I thought about stopping off in the kitchen just to say, "Thank you," or to wish them both a pleasant evening, but Kath's nagging could be heard between the clanging of metal and the clinking of porcelain dishes. I opted not to interfere, which is a decision I would later come to regret.

*  *  *

I must have fallen asleep more quickly than I normally do, as I do not remember much between the time I readied myself for bed and the moment I slipped into a deep sleep. Perhaps the full day of travel took more out of me than I realized. I suppose that is what happens when we age.

Just as quickly as I fell asleep, I also awoke much earlier than I thought I would considering how sleepy I had been the prior night. I reasoned that my unplanned two-hour nap the previous evening might have had something to do with it. Still, I awoke by 6:00am, and by 6:30am I had grown too restless to stay in my room. I figured I would make my way downstairs to the kitchen to make a pot of warm tea and, if I am being honest, to have a look at the biscuit selection.

When I opened my bedroom door, I realized just how silent the manor was so early in the morning. The air felt still, and the consistent tick-tock of the grandfather's clock was a metronome keeping time despite an absence of music.

I made my way downstairs, seeing not a single soul, before arriving to the kitchen. There, on the counter, I saw a jar of salt, several large eggs, fresh salmon waiting to be sliced, some flour, and a few other ingredients for what was to be Mrs. Flaherty's salmon quiche. I continued on toward the pantry where I found a wonderful selection of tea and, importantly, a fair amount of biscuit options. I proceeded to grab a kettle, heat some water, and grab a teacup and saucer for my morning tea. It was not until I returned to the pantry to find some sugar that I realized I had not yet seen— nor, more surprising in her case, *heard*–Mrs. Flaherty in the kitchen.

"Odd," I thought, but then I figured she was just tending to morning chores and gave it no more of my attention. I took my tea across the foyer into the parlour where I had a wonderful view of the yards in front of the manor. The ground still appeared to be wet, but the torrential rain had stopped leaving just an overcast grey sky in its stead. From where I was sitting, I could see Giles, shovel in hand, already digging the loose ground in his attempt to redirect some of the standing water. Poor fellow.

Upon finishing my tea, I began my walk back to the kitchen to tend to my dishes, but when I entered the foyer, I saw that the door to the cellar had been left open. Figuring Giles must have accidently left the door ajar, I thought I had better give it a good close lest Mrs. Flaherty see it swinging open then use it as more ammunition against poor Giles.

I walked over to the door and stepped up on the little landing just in front of it. As I reached for the handle, something caught my eye from the depths of the cellar. Although the cellar was still dark, enough light was trickling in from the foyer to catch the strands of fiery red hair at the base of the stairs. Kath's fall must have been quick; simply missing the first step of the stairs was enough to send her tumbling down to the cement floor of the cellar. Her lack of movement, at least as seen from the top of the stairs, was cause for alarm, but it was possible the fall was not fatal.

I hurried down the stairs, careful to hold on to the railing on both sides (lest I wind up like Mrs. Flaherty). As I approached Kath, I did my best to look and see whether or not she was breathing, inhaling and exhaling to show signs of life. Honestly, I am not certain I would have been able to tell because my own heart was beating through my chest, my own breathing had become so exaggerated that I was essentially hyperventilating.

I could not bring myself to touch Kath's body, so I reached for a broom near the base of the stairs. I poked her back first. No response. I poked her once more. Again, no response. As sort of a last resort, I positioned the broom like a lever to turn her over at her chest. That is when I saw the first sign of blood, but thankfully not enough blood to suggest her head had been split open on the cement.

"Oh, thank God," I thought, assuming the worst had not occurred.

I continued to roll her body over with the broom, and that is when I saw where the blood was coming from. Kath's face was blue with crimson red blood trickling down her pale skin. There, in the place where her right eye used to be, I found the grimy golden dinner bell—the same bell Kath had used to summon all of us to dinner—sticking out of Mrs. Flaherty's skull.

She was dead.

# 4 | THE FIRST DEATH

"I guess someone grew tired of eating so much salmon," I heard a male's voice say above me.

I must have fainted upon seeing the grotesque sight of poor Mrs. Flaherty, because when I opened my eyes, I looked up to see Mr. Rossini and Mr. Powell standing over me at the bottom of the cellar stairs. The lights had been turned on, which illuminated the cellar, including Kath's fatal injury.

"I reckon it is too soon for such joking, Mr. Rossini," said Mr. Powell. "Besides, I believe what happened to Mrs. Flaherty was nothing more than a freak accident."

"An accident?" Mr. Rossini responded.

"Yes, an accident. The poor woman must have tripped on the stairs in the darkness and fallen, face first, onto the dinner bell upon hitting the ground," Mr. Powell explained.

"I suppose that could be the case," Mr. Rossini replied. "It's just so very unfortunate."

I sat up and tried to speak, although what came out of my mouth was truly mere mumbling. Apparently, my body was still a bit startled from my own recent tumble to the ground.

"Oh, Dame James," Mr. Powell said as he reached down to help me from the ground.

"Slowly, slowly," advised Mr. Rossini. "You do not want to stand too quickly or else you will be back on the ground before you realise."

The two gentlemen helped me stand slowly.

"We heard you screaming and raced down," Mr. Rossini

said. "Once we saw poor Mrs. Flaherty here, we sent Mr. Richter back upstairs to prevent the ladies from seeing this tragic sight."

"That was kind of you," I replied. "Although I wish I did not have the misfortune of seeing this myself. Poor Mrs. Flaherty!"

I looked down at the innkeeper's twisted, contorted body, trying my best to avert my eyes from her face. Such a horrific way to die!

While looking at Mrs. Flaherty's body I noticed that she barely had any bruises or scratches on her arms or legs, which seemed odd if she had just fallen down a flight of stairs. Not wanting to alarm Mr. Rossini or Mr. Powell with any wild speculation, I said nothing. After all, it could have been that Kath made it down the stairs perfectly well and only tripped near the bottom…just in the most unfortunate possible way.

"We need to do something with the body," Mr. Rossini said, breaking the silence.

"I imagine it would be best to keep it cold until the authorities arrive," I suggested.

Mr. Rossini gestured skyward with his hands and, to himself, muttered, "*Accidenti. Nel mese di giugno.*"

Mr. Powell and I stared back at him blankly.

"Ah, sorry. I mean, it will be difficult to keep her cold in the warmth of June, no?" Mr. Rossini pointed out.

"I suppose the coldest place is actually right here," I offered, looking toward the door to the wine cellar.

Just a few metres away was a small arched doorway leading to a room that housed the manor's wine collection. Prohibition had made it illegal to purchase alcohol in America, of course, but homes were permitted to retain their existing supply. It appeared that Raven's Point Manor was well stocked.

"Of course," replied Mr. Powell, "the wine cellar is sure to be the coldest place in the home. Let us carefully move the body in there for now and then ring for help."

Part of me hesitated. I found it perfectly plausible that Mrs. Flaherty was the victim of the most unfortunate accident, but had she been the victim of some attack, moving the body would complicate an investigation. No, no, she most certainly fell down the stairs; that was the simplest explanation.

I was too lost in thought to notice that Mr. Powell and Mr. Rossini had already started lifting Kath to move her to the wine cellar. I surveyed the scene a bit to see if there was any evidence of how Kath could have fallen. The cellar stairs were old, wooden stairs that creaked with each step. I could see Mrs. Flaherty missing a step in the dark or having her apron snag on a splinter, but one could not be certain. There was a small bit of blood on the concrete floor of the basement from where Mrs. Flaherty had been lying, face down. Otherwise, nothing seemed out of sorts. The open shelves were still fully stocked with canned food on one side, cleaning supplies on another. The half-finished brick wall that was being built, presumably to section off a new room, was as far along as when I last saw it the day before. The door at the far end of the cellar, likely to Giles' room, was still closed. Boxes and crates were strewn about in the cellar that was very much under construction.

Almost instinctively, I grabbed one of the blue tarps that was covering a pile of boxes and followed behind Mr. Powell and Mr. Rossini. The two men looked at me curiously.

"For respect," I offered, "she deserves to be covered."

"Of course," Mr. Powell replied, "we can take it from here, Dame James. You have seen enough for a lifetime. If you feel up to it, why don't you go ahead on upstairs and ring the authorities."

I nodded without saying a word, took one last glimpse at Mrs. Flaherty, and headed up the stairs into the foyer, holding onto the railing for dear life the entire way up the stairs.

\*          \*          \*

I found the other guests huddled together in the library, speculating about what could have been taking place downstairs.

"Did you hear that scream?" Mrs. Powell asked. "That is not the scream one makes when she sees a spider or a mouse. No, it was much more severe."

"Maybe there was an intruder?" Ms. Lavoie proposed.

"Maybe she saw a ghost?" Anna offered before crossing her arms and rolling her eyes.

"Oh, a ghost! I had not even thought of that," Mrs. Powell continued. "Of course! Houses like this one always have stories to tell of previous inhabitants. Mysterious deaths, curious disappearances, strange noises in the middle of the night! Why, I bet there could even be a ghost in here with us right now!"

It was at this unfortunate silence that I spoke up.

"Good day, everyone," I said.

Everyone jumped in a panic. I suppose it was the talk of ghosts and the fact that no one saw me enter the room that made my introduction so startling.

"Good heavens, Dame James!" Mrs. Powell exclaimed, putting her palm on her chest.

"Ah, you gave us a good fright, madam," Miss Finley said, her breathing clearly heavy. "We had just been talking of…"

"Ghosts. I heard," I said, entering the room. I quickly debated whether or not I should apprise the group about the situation downstairs. Realizing they would hear me discussing it on the phone unless I cleared the room anyway, I began, "I am afraid that my scream was the one you heard this morning."

"It was horrific! Like a banshee," Mrs. Powell replied.

I held my hand to silence her and continued, "I apologize for waking you in such a frightening way, but, well, it is with great displeasure that I must tell you there…has been an accident."

"An accident?" Miss Finley asked.

"What kind of accident? Was it Giles? You were in the cellar," Ms. Lavoie asked.

"No. It was…it was…" I found myself unable to go on.

Mr. Richter stood up and continued in my stead, "Mrs. Flaherty. It seems she took a fall down the cellar stairs and, most unfortunately, landed on something that punctured her skull."

Mrs. Powell, Miss Finley, and Ms. Lavoie all gasped. Mrs. Powell even covered her face with her hands, as if staring into her palms would make reality go away. Anna had a shocked expression on her face, as well, but otherwise showed very little emotion. This, of course, seemed typical for Anna.

"How did she puncture her skull?" Ms. Lavoie asked.

"Was it with a knife or a weapon of some sort?" Miss Finley added.

"No," I found myself saying. "It was the golden bell she used to call us to dinner. I imagine the poor girl was going to get supplies for breakfast or maybe getting something with which to clean that blasted little bell, but just one wrong step and…and…"

I again found myself unable to continue.

"Mr. Powell and Mr. Rossini thought it best we not expose you all to the scene," Mr. Richter continued. "So, that is why I asked you all to join me in here."

"And Giles? Does he know?" asked Miss Finley.

"I imagine he does not," I replied. "Judging from the freshness of the blood, it is possible that he was already out working the grounds. It would have been impossible for him not to notice if she had fallen before he ascended from the cellar."

A curious silence hung in the air.

"You don't suppose *he*…" Mrs. Powell began.

"Mrs. Powell, don't you *dare* finish that sentence," Miss Finley interrupted. "The poor man may have some mental limitations, but he is as kind and gentle as any of us here!"

"Well, it is just that Kath, Mrs. Flaherty, was not very kind to the boy. We *all* saw it. It is not like I am…"

"That's enough, Mrs. Powell!" Miss Finley yelled.

After a moment of silence, Mr. Richter began, "I saw Mrs. Flaherty at the base of the stairs, and everything I saw suggests that a simple fall could have led to her untimely death. Still, we should let the authorities be the ones to…"

Ah, yes! The authorities! I almost forgot the reason I came into the library in the first place.

"Speaking of the authorities," I began, "Mr. Powell and Mr. Rossini asked me to ring for help, so if you will please excuse me," I walked over to the corner of the room where the telephone sat on a small table.

The others sat in silence as they digested the morning's information. Miss Finley maintained a cross stare at Mrs. Powell who, somewhat absentmindedly, was picking pieces of lint off the terrycloth robe she must have thrown on to come downstairs in such a hurry. Even her silk scarlet sleeping mask was draped around her neck. It appears she had no time to dress properly but enough time to put a strawberry red lipstick on with a fresh coat of powder. Mr. Richter had a severe, concerned look on his face, while Anna still looked very worried. Ms. Lavoie had found a bowl of candy and was eating piece after piece perhaps to calm her nerves. Curiously, it was only then that I realized the latest guests to Raven's Point Manor, Betty Simmons and her brother Walter, were not among the group.

I grabbed the phone, raised the earpiece to my ear and held the handpiece in my left hand, which I was surprised to see was still trembling a bit from the shock of the morning's news. Not even 24 hours before I was just meeting the vivacious, bubbly, if not overbearing Mrs. Kathleen Flaherty, and now the woman lay lifeless, a bell sticking out of her eye socket, in the wine cellar of the manor that served as her place of employment for decades. Life is cruelly unpredictable.

"Hello?" I said to the operator, "This is Dame Margaret James at Raven's Point Manor, and I…hello? Operator?"

There was no reply.

"Operator? Are you there? Hello?" I tried again.

Still nothing.

I readjusted the phone, checking the wires. "Hello?" I began again, "Hello?"

I turned around to see the room full of people staring right at me, each with the same curious expression.

"It is disconnected," I said. "The phone is disconnected."

\*        \*        \*

"The storm must have taken out the phone line," Mr. Richter said, pacing back and forth in the library.

"Rather terrible timing," Mr. Powell added. He and Mr. Rossini had returned from the cellar and joined the group in the library. Betty Simmons had also emerged from her bedroom to join the group. Walter Simmons was still sound asleep upstairs.

"Well, I suppose Mrs. Flaherty is as good down in the cellar as she is anywhere else," Mr. Rossini said. "If we have to wait for someone to come get her, well, *sono cose della vita*."

"Ugh! I cannot fathom the thought of leaving that poor woman down there in a cellar full of bugs, dirt, and God only knows what," Mrs. Powell gasped dramatically. "I would rather die 1,000 deaths than to be subjected to that kind of substandard care."

"Do you think she cares? I mean, she *is* dead," Ms. Simmons said coldly.

"Such nerve!" Mrs. Powell said, glaring at Ms. Simmons. "I just think we ought to find some way to get Mrs. Flaherty to a proper resting place sooner than later."

"I agree," Mr. Richter added. "Even if we keep her as cold as we can, her body is likely to start the decomposition process, and I imagine we would not want to keep a decaying corpse anywhere in the house, even in the cellar. The smell alone would…"

"I say, good sir, you are speaking about a human being," Miss Finley scolded. "She may be dead, but need we refer to her as a 'decaying corpse.' She had a name, you know."

I watched this spectacle of odd human behaviour playing out before me. Some guests were clearly very sensitive and frightened of death whereas several others were as cold and indifferent to the topic as if we were talking about the day's weather or holiday plans.

Finally, someone said something sensible. Surprisingly, it was Anna.

"The access road," she began. "If we are unable to ring the authorities then perhaps we can flag down a car on the main throughway that connects to the estate's access road."

This was a reasonable idea, of course, although the amount of effort required was not minimal. Once the trying nature of this daunting task sunk in, the protests began.

"The access road?!" Mr. Rossini said. "But that is a good 15 kilometres away and through such hilly terrain!"

"It would take at least six hours, three each way," Mr. Richter added.

"But what choice do we have, really?" Miss Finley went on, "If it were one of you lying down in that cellar, you would hope we would do whatever it took, right?

"And if we walk out to the main throughway then certainly we will find Ms. Simmons' car, which will then provide us with a vehicle should we be able to fix it easily," Mr. Powell added.

Ms. Simmons interjected, "Oh, I am not sure that should be a priority at the moment. Poor Mrs. Fogerty should really be the focus of such an important trek."

"Mrs. Flaherty," Mrs. Powell corrected.

"Nonsense! Two birds, one stone," Mr. Powell replied.

Ms. Simmons backed down a bit and said, "Very well! It *would* be nice to have my own luggage. These clothes make me feel like some sort of medieval wizard!"

Betty Simmons began twirling in her robe, quite oddly, almost oblivious to the fact that there were eight other people in the room watching her.

"Well, I do not intend to walk outside in this weather," Mrs. Powell complained. "You know, they say that the day after a rainstorm is the worst for people with allergies. The rain opens up all the blooms, and the moisture keeps the allergens hanging in the air, unable to blow away."

"And you have severe allergies?" Ms. Lavoie asked.

"Do I ever! I was actually going to complain to Mrs. Flaherty about the level of dust at Raven's Point Manor, particularly this room and our bedroom, but I did not want to come across as one of those annoying types who just complains about everything," Mrs. Powell replied.

Everyone stared at her dryly.

"No, I do not imagine that we all need to go on this little adventure. Perhaps the gentlemen can make the trip and we ladies can stay behind," Mrs. Powell suggested.

"That does seem like a good idea," Mr. Rossini added. "Someone has to cook our meals now that Mrs. Flaherty is down for the count anyway."

Miss Finley shot daggers toward Mr. Rossini before saying, "I think I much prefer to join the expedition than to cook meals, thank you."

"Same for me, as well," Anna replied.

"Suit yourself," Mr. Rossini responded, glancing every so often at Miss Finley.

"I will be staying here, but I will not be cooking," Mrs. Powell stated. "I am quite sensitive to spices. Their mere presence will send my sensory system into a frenzy!"

"Fine," Mr. Richter said. "Let us determine this rather simply. By show of hands, who would like to join the group walking to the throughway to get help and to potentially fix the Simmons siblings' vehicle?"

Five hands raised into the air. Those hands belonged to Mr. Rossini, Miss Finley, Mr. Richter, Mr. Powell, and Anna. I surely wanted to go even if just to get some fresh air, but at 65, well, six hours is a bit too long of a walk.

"Great. And, again by show of hands, who would like to stay here at Raven's Point Manor?" Mr. Richter asked.

Four hands raised into the air this time: Mrs. Powell, Ms. Lavoie, Ms. Simmons, and my own.

"Wonderful, then it is settled," Mr. Richter concluded.

"Wait!" Mrs. Powell screamed. "What about *Mr.* Simmons? And Giles?"

"What about them?" Mr. Richter asked.

"Well, shouldn't they be given the option to join the trek to the throughway?" Mrs. Powell asked. "I am not sure I am comfortable with these men being present while the rest of the men are away."

"What, exactly, is that supposed to mean?" Miss Finley asked.

"Well, it is just that...well...you know...it is nothing against their mental well-being, but..." Mrs. Powell stammered on.

"I will be here to take care of my brother," Ms. Simmons offered. "His doctor requires that Walter is heavily sedated, so I will stay here to administer his medication."

"And Giles?" Mrs. Powell went on.

"And Giles is busy working the grounds," Mr. Powell responded to his wife, likely an attempt to quiet her impolite questions once again.

"Poor Giles," Miss Finley said. "He does not even know about Mrs. Flaherty yet. Someone really should tell him."

Everyone looked around the room, avoiding eye contact with one another in an attempt to deflect responsibility.

"I will do it," I found myself saying. "The young man deserves to know his colleague is no longer with us. Plus, it seems prudent to tell him there is a deceased body being stored just down the hallway from his room. I am certain *I* would want to know that information if I were him."

"I wouldn't," Mrs. Powell whispered.

"Great," Mr. Richter said. "Thank you, Dame James, for volunteering. That just leaves one other small item for discussion: who is going to make breakfast? It is important the walking group has a meal before departing."

Everyone had been so distracted by the morning's disturbing news that it was only at this moment we felt the hunger pangs in our stomachs. It was already 11:00am.

"I saw the ingredients for Mrs. Flaherty's salmon quiche are all out in the kitchen," I offered after a bit of silence.

"I will make breakfast," Ms. Lavoie offered.

"*You*? But you are a fancy fashion designer," Mrs. Powell said. "*You* can make a quiche?"

"I am French," Ms. Lavoie answered. "I can make *anything*."

*       *       *

Breakfast was a silent, sombre affair. Being in the dining room without hearing the clanging of pots and pans or the loud exclamations from Mrs. Flaherty made the setting feel like a new, different place.

The quality of the food also made breakfast feel different albeit in quite a good way. Pardon me for speaking ill of the dead, but Mrs. Flaherty's cooking could not hold a candle to the feast prepared by Ms. Lavoie! In addition to making a delicious salmon quiche, Ms. Lavoie managed to serve rosemary roasted potatoes, a fresh fruit medley, and even blueberry muffins! She clearly knew her way around the kitchen. But, then again, of course she did: she *was* French.

Following breakfast, the group convened in the foyer. Although it was no longer raining, a chill persisted outside, with grey clouds casting sort of a dreary feeling on the day. It was terribly fitting, however odd a forecast for early June.

"Are you certain you should be going, Albert?" Mrs. Powell asked her husband. "Your doctor said…"

"Never mind what the doctor said, Doris. I will be fine," Mr. Powell responded.

The walking group began putting on their jackets to face the blustery, chilly day awaiting them. At this point I found myself extra glad to be staying back at Raven's Point Manor.

"It is approaching 1:00pm now," Mr. Richter said. "If we make good time then we should be back well before sundown."

"Still, we should take these flashlights just to be safe," Mr. Powell advised, handing Mr. Richter one of the torches he had procured from the cellar storage.

"I will have a dinner prepared for everyone by 8:00pm," Ms. Lavoie offered. If breakfast had been any indication, this dinner would be something to look forward to.

"And, Ms. Simmons, whereabouts would you say your vehicle stalled so we know where to look?" Mr. Rossini asked.

"Ah, yes. Well, let's see. We had pulled off the main throughway and drove for just about ten minutes before the car stalled."

"Excellent. We shall have a look then. I'm taking a few tools along with us just in case," Mr. Powell said, lifting a toolbox in his hand.

The group staying behind wished the traveling group well, and with that, the group of five was off to get help. After the front door of the manor closed, the lingering silence was a bit awkward, as no one quite knew what to do at that moment. We all sort of stared at each other for a minute before Ms. Lavoie broke the tension.

"I had better see what ingredients are in the pantry," Ms. Lavoie said as she marched off toward the kitchen. "There's no way *I* am going anywhere near that cellar for supplies. If it is not in the pantry, it will not be on our dinner plate."

"I had better go check on my brother," Ms. Simmons replied. "He is likely to be waking up and may need some medicine."

Betty Simmons turned and started ascending the stairs to the second floor. This left just Mrs. Powell and me.

I waited, sort of on purpose, to see what Mrs. Powell intended to do with the rest of *her* day.

"Well," she sighed, "I best be off to…um…I really

must…no, let's see…I have to go…I have to go straighten my bed linens. Yes, that's it. With Mrs. Flaherty out of commission, someone will need to be fluffing the bed, no?"

And, with that, Mrs. Powell plodded her way across the foyer and up the stairs. I was certain she was simply going to go take a series of naps throughout the day. She had a difficult enough time coming up with *one* activity to keep herself occupied.

That left just me, standing in the foyer, the ticking and the tocking of the grandfather's clock counting down the minutes and the seconds until my next obligation: telling Giles about Mrs. Flaherty.

*     *     *

What follows next is an account of the journey from Raven's Point Manor to the throughway connected to the access road of the Radcliffe estate. My trusted assistant, Anna, provided me with all the information you will read in this section upon her return, which I immediately took note of in the event that it might be relevant for explaining the delay in getting Mrs. Flaherty's body to the authorities.

Per Anna's account of the journey, nothing particularly exciting took place on the way *to* the throughway. Mr. Powell regaled the group with off-colour jokes until Miss Finley insisted that he stop, which led to Mr. Rossini entertaining the group with old Italian love songs. This sounded absolutely miserable and made me ever so glad I stayed behind at the house.

As the group approached their third hour of walking, they saw the end of the access road…from a distance. Just as Mrs. Flaherty had predicted, the water surrounding the land of the Radcliffe estate had flooded a considerable amount. The base of the access road was at the lowest elevation of the property, which meant that the road, itself, was under a considerable amount of water. The valleys in these parts of New England were beautiful, indeed, but they did create some challenging landscapes for modern travel. The access road continued under the feet of the traveling group straight ahead for another half-kilometre or so, then disappeared under a flood of water, only to emerge at least another kilometre or kilometre-and-a-half away. The flood was too deep through which to wade and likely too dangerous with the current of the natural waterway now ripping through the flooded area. Nor would it be possible for a car to drive through water this deep without getting waterlogged itself.

Speaking of cars, Anna reported how the group's extreme disappointment about the flooded access road was only temporarily forgotten when Miss Finley made a curious observation. Ms. Simmons had mentioned that they had driven at least ten minutes on the access road once turning from the throughway. However, the group had not yet seen a vehicle of any kind parked along the access road.

"Maybe it washed away in the flooding?" Mr. Richter suggested.

"Impossible," Mr. Rossini replied. "Unless Ms. Simmons miscalculated her estimate, the car should have been much closer to Raven's Point Manor's front gate than here."

"Well, it *was* dark and quite miserable outside," Miss Finley offered. "If I were caring for a sick sibling and trying to get to safety, I am not sure I would be anywhere near accurate in making such an estimation."

This answer seemed to satisfy the group for the time being, and the group decided it would look more carefully for the sign of a parked vehicle or tire tracks in the mud off the road that might lead to the vehicle on the way back.

The return trip proved to be more agonizing than the walk out. Mr. Powell, already coughing and wheezing on the trip out, had to ask the group to stop several times so he could catch his breath. He mentioned something about his heart, but his mumbling and shortness of breath made it hard to understand. Mr. Rossini and Miss Finley were clearly cross with each other about something. Anna assumed it was regarding their differing position on the status of the Simmons' vehicle, but it seemed like a silly, small thing to have a row about. Mr. Richter was positively obsessed with the nature they passed on the return, stopping every so often to collect particular flower petals, insects, and even some tree bark, which he placed into little jars he brought in a bag. Near the end of the trip, everyone on the trek was hungry, exhausted, and a bit on edge. Importantly, Anna pointed out, they never came across any vehicle or tire tracks to suggest where the Simmons siblings' car could have been parked away from the road.

The group arrived back to the manor around 7:15pm and had just enough time to wash up from the journey and join the rest of the guests for dinner in the dining room. It was during this time that Anna recounted their journey to me and I took these notes. As peculiar the story was about that car, the bigger concern seemed to be the access road: without a working phone or road, we were completely cut off from the rest of the world. The very idea of it gave me such a chill.

*     *     *

After the walking group had left the manor, I gave myself some time to think about how I would broach the subject of Mrs. Flaherty's death to Giles. I wanted to be as sensitive as possible, of course, but I had also been told once that it is important to be direct and straightforward when sharing sad news, as this prevents the listener from dreaming up even worse scenarios in his mind, which could sometimes be even more devastating than the truth.

By the time I was ready to share the bad news, I found Giles downstairs in the cellar working on the brick wall that was to be the last wall of a room being constructed. I watched as Giles applied the mortar to each brick, set each brick on top of the prior row of bricks, straightened it, and then cleaned off the excess mortar. For as critical as Mrs. Flaherty had been about Giles' work tending to the estate grounds, he seemed to be quite methodical and precise while building this wall. It was impressive, actually, the speed with which he managed to complete the section he worked on as I watched from the stairs. It was as if he had a rhythm in his mind that kept the process moving along without missing a beat.

Mesmerized and lost in the rhythm of the wall's construction myself, I came to my senses again and called out to the young man.

"Giles," I said, "Giles, it is me, Dame Margaret James."

Upon hearing my voice, the groundskeeper stopped, lowered his arms, and turned his head ever so slightly, not enough to see me standing at the base of the stairs, but enough to signal that he was listening.

"Odd," I thought, but I kept going.

"Giles, I hate to be the bearer of bad news, but it seems there has been an accident," I went on, "it seems that this morning, Mrs. Flaherty...Kath...well, she suffered a severe accident, and is no longer with us."

The man stood motionless, like a display mannequin one might see at Harrods.

Worried he did not understand, I tried again, "Giles, Mrs. Flaherty has died. It was a tragic accident, and we shall all miss her terribly."

Still, nothing. The man just stood still, unmoving.

Trying once more, third time being the charm, I said, "Giles, Kath is dead. She's dead, Giles. Do you hear me? Mrs. Flaherty is dead!" I was practically yelling at that point.

Just then, Giles turned his head back toward the wall, grabbed a brick, put some mortar on it, and returned to laying the bricks as if nothing had ever happened, as if I had said nothing at all.

"Good talk, Giles," I said, ascending up the stairs even more carefully than I had that morning.

\*　　　\*　　　\*

Dinner began promptly at 8:00pm and was a glorious feast of onion soup, coq au vin, and a mouth-wateringly rich chocolate gâteau for dessert. Ever the one to make an inappropriate comment, Mrs. Powell said something along the lines of, "I know it is a shame Mrs. Flaherty is no longer with us, but this may very well be the best thing to come from her absence." Charming, that Mrs. Powell.

Aside from the typical offensive comment from Mrs. Powell and Ms. Simmons going on and on about some peculiar ability she felt she had in which she could communicate with animals, nothing was too out of the ordinary during dinner. Following dinner, the group proceeded to the library where Mr. Rossini again played bartender for everyone.

Walter Simmons had been brought down to dinner by his sister, which was a first for the group. He also "joined" us in the library, although I hesitate to use that word because that would imply that he was altogether there with us in the first place. Quite heavily sedated, it seemed that Mr. Simmons lived an existence of painkillers and sedatives. Ms. Simmons had said something about her brother's chronic pain, but it was unclear what the cause of that pain had been.

I found myself in a conversation with Ms. Simmons, Ms. Lavoie, and Mr. Richter when I took the opportunity to find out more about our curious guests, particularly after Anna had told me about the absence of any car along the access road.

"Tell us more about your family," I began. "You mentioned that you were on your way to your parents before your car broke down, yes?"

"Oh, yes. The poor things are probably worried sick about us," Ms. Simmons replied, tracing the rim of her wine glass with her finger. "Do you hear that? It is like music," she said, focusing on the wine glass.

"Where exactly is it that they live?" Ms. Lavoie asked,

seeming to follow my lead with respect to ironing out the prior inconsistency in the Simmons' story.

"Just outside Aspen Valley," Ms. Simmons responded without a moment's hesitation. "It is absolutely lovely there this time of year. Have you ever been?"

No one answered.

"Do either of your parents suffer from the same affliction as your brother?" Mr. Richter asked bluntly. Given that he was a man of science, I appreciated his focus on obtaining a solution in the most parsimonious manner. However, as a human being, I found his question to be cold and uncaring, even if I was delighted that he asked it.

"The same as Walter? Well, that is unclear," Ms. Simmons began, "you see, our parents, the parents we were going to visit, are our adoptive parents. Walter and I were both adopted but from different parents, so we are not actually blood relatives."

"How interesting," Mr. Richter replied, as he then daydreamed off as academics often do.

"I imagine, sometimes, what our respective parents must have been like," Ms. Simmons went on, "I like to think mine were performers, a famous stage actor and actress," she said as she stood and pantomimed a dramatic performance.

"So, you never knew them a child?" Ms. Lavoie questioned.

"I did not, no, but Walter did. My parents put me up for adoption when I was just an infant. Walter spent the first several years of his life with his birth parents before he was put up for adoption, so he probably has at least *some* memory of his birth parents, but..." she gestured to her brother, sitting in an armchair, just staring toward the fireplace.

Walter let out a gentle moan, which prompted Betty to pat his hand and console him.

"There, there, sweet brother," Ms. Simmons said. "Everything is fine."

As Ms. Simmons comforted her brother, Mr. Rossini broke into the conversation bringing a tray of drinks with him.

"Another Old Fashioned, Ms. Lavoie?" Mr. Rossini asked.

"*Ah, oui! Merci,*" Ms. Lavoie said as she grabbed a glass off the tray.

"And a gin Giblet for you, Mr. Richter," Mr. Rossini offered.

Mr. Richter went to grab one of the two cocktails still on the tray.

"No! Not that," Mr. Rossini said quickly. "That is Mr. Powell's Corpse Reviver! He'll be ever so sore if you take it!"

Mr. Powell, overhearing the commotion, jokingly responded, "Don't you dare, Richter, unless you want that drink to be your last!"

The small talk continued until the hour grew late and then, one by one, people began peeling off to head upstairs for bed. First, the Simmons siblings excused themselves, followed by Mr. and Mrs. Powell on account of the former being "dreadfully exhausted" presumably from the day's long walk. Ms. Lavoie left next, followed by Mr. Rossini and Miss Finley in close succession. Anna and I left at the same time, leaving Mr. Richter to tend to the fire before retiring. Giles had joined us for dinner, sitting quietly as usual, staring straight ahead to the seat where Mrs. Flaherty would have been. He went straight to the cellar following dinner, however, and did not join the group for post-dinner drinks in the library.

As I readied myself for bed, I took note of how long the day felt. It was only hours ago, not even one full day, that I discovered poor Mrs. Flaherty's body at the foot of the stairs. That felt like *ages* ago, like an entire lifetime had passed in just one day.

I climbed into bed and turned off the lamp on the nightstand. I had barely laid my head upon my pillow and shut my eyes than did the most curious sound emerge from the hallway.

Scrape. Scrape. Scraaaaaaape.

"Surely you must be imagining things after such a stressful day," I thought to myself, but then I heard the sound once more, louder this time.

Scrape. Scrape. Scraaaaaaape.

It sounded as if whatever was making this dreadful noise was getting closer. I stood up from my bed and made my way to the door.

Scrape. Scrape. Scraaaaaaape.

For a moment, I thought about opening my door and looking into the hallway to see what the source of this noise happened to be. Fear, however, got the best of me, and I found myself quickly reaching toward my key in the door with nervous, trembling hands, turning the key to make sure the door was locked, and then leaving the key in its place to ensure nothing outside could see into my room.

I slowly backed away from the door. First one step, then two, back toward my bed. After a minute or so of no scraping sound, I let out the biggest sigh I had been holding in without realizing.

"Phew," I said to myself. "That was most peculiar. It was probably just a branch scraping the side of the house in the wind."

I turned over in my bed, looked out the window into the moonlit sky, and saw the tree branches on the trees were absolutely still. The wind was not blowing at all.

# 5 | TWO IS A COINCIDENCE

I was in a deep sleep, dreaming a dream that felt so incredibly real. I was sitting on a bench in Belgrave Square Garden near our home in London. The sky was as blue as the ocean, the sun was shining brightly and felt warm on my skin. I could *feel* the warmth of the sun in my dream. Children were laughing and playing in the grass nearby, and straight ahead of me was Harry, *my* Harry, walking toward me along the paved path. He had aged a bit, looking as he might look if he were still alive today, but in my dream, he was very much alive! He walked closer and closer before stopping right in front of me, the sun behind him, his silhouette making it difficult to see his features or make out the expression on his face. He reached his right hand out as if to grab mine and help me stand from the bench. So, naturally, I reached out my hand to grab his, barely making out a beautiful smile on his face. When our hands touched, I felt as if I had grabbed a piece of ice. His hand was so cold, freezing cold, the sort of cold one feels in winter upon plunging a hand into freshly fallen snow. My hand reeled back from the surprise of this frigid temperature, but Harry did not let go. His grip grew firmer as I tried to pull my hand away. The sunny sky gave way to a cloudy, thunderous grey sky, which allowed me to see Harry's face. His eyes looked worried, concerned even, and I swear I saw a single tear streaming down his cheek. Just then, he opened his mouth to say something, so I leaned forward to hear what he had to say, and that's when he started screaming at the top of his lungs…

\*     \*     \*

The sound of a woman screaming jolted me awake.

The screaming coincided with Harry's scream in my dream in that strange way where dreams seem to predict what is happening in reality a split second before they actually happen. My adrenaline was already flowing, my heart already pumping, from my horrifying dream. I sprang into action, grabbing my robe and racing into the hall. Several of the other guests had already emerged from their rooms and had started running to the source of the scream.

"The Powells' room!" Mr. Rossini yelled.

We all stumbled into the room where we found Mrs. Powell sitting at the edge of her bed, her face buried in her hands, sobbing. She looked up upon hearing the commotion of so many of us barging into the room and pointed toward the washroom.

"There," she managed to get out, "he's in there!"

The men led the way into the bathroom where Mr. Rossini yelled, "*Dio mio!*"

Once we all managed to enter the washroom, we saw what had caught Mr. Rossini by surprise. There, lying in the bathtub, was Mr. Powell; eyes open, skin shrivelled, water ice cold.

He was dead.

\*     \*     \*

We left the men to take care of Mr. Powell's body and escorted Mrs. Powell out of the room down to the dining room. She was hysterical at first, unable to form a complete sentence without breaking down mid-word to start crying. I took it upon myself to prepare some tea for her, and by the time the tea kettle whistled, Mrs. Powell had calmed down enough to speak.

"I am sorry to be so emotional," Mrs. Powell began, "it

is all just so shocking."

"There is no need to apologize, Mrs. Powell," Miss Finley reassured her. "This is a natural, normal reaction."

It was at that moment I noticed Miss Finley was wearing a beautiful golden kimono, not unlike the one I saw my first day at Raven's Point Manor.

"I know, I know," Mrs. Powell responded, "it's just...oh dear...is my makeup running?"

Sort of an odd concern at a serious time like this, but contradictions were sort of Mrs. Powell's specialty.

"Mrs. Powell, if I may, when did you first notice that Mr. Powell had...passed on?" Ms. Lavoie asked.

Between sniffles, Mrs. Powell managed to tell her story of what happened the night before.

She began, "Shortly after we left you all in the library to come upstairs, I drew a bath for myself while Albert read a bit in the sitting chair in our room. When I came out of the bathroom, I noticed that Albert had dozed off, so I woke him up to let him know the bathroom was free. He seemed a bit groggier than usual, but I figured that the six-hour walk he took likely exhausted him. He has a heart condition, you know, which had made me worried, but he was so adamant about joining the walking group anyway. In any case, he insisted on washing up before bed, and I, thinking nothing of it, kissed him goodnight and climbed into bed to read for a bit. I cannot remember exactly when I fell asleep, but I could have *sworn* Albert came to bed. You can imagine my surprise, then, when I woke up to find the light still on and Albert's side of the bed empty. I reasoned that Albert must have gotten up to use the toilet or perhaps even to go make a tea, so I went back to sleep for beauty purposes..."

One might have been surprised at this strange detail, but those of us in the room already knew Mrs. Powell too well to be surprised by anything she said.

"I woke again about half an hour later and decided to get up for the day. I remember being particularly motivated by the thought of seeing what Ms. Lavoie intended to make for breakfast. I hurried into the bathroom to start getting ready, fixed my hair and put on my makeup. I spent a considerable amount of time on my hair, more than usual, because the increasing humidity had made it nearly unmanageable. I also had a difficult time determining what colour combination for my eyes, cheeks, and lips would serve me best in the overcast lighting we have been having."

At this point, it might have been easy to forget that Mrs. Powell's husband had just died. She certainly had a strange way of emphasizing unnecessary details when telling stories.

"I finished my makeup, topped it off with a generous dusting of powder, and then turned around to see Albert in the bathtub. I told him to hurry up or else he would be late for breakfast, and I was not about to be late on his account, particularly not for a delicious breakfast."

"That reminds me: I should probably start getting things ready for breakfast," Ms. Lavoie said, breaking away from the conversation at the dining room table. I was not sure if Mademoiselle Lavoie actually thought she needed to go to the kitchen to start preparing breakfast–she had already done some prepping the night before–or if she simply wanted to get away from Mrs. Powell's rambling story.

"When he did not respond, I thought he was playing some sort of joke. I again told him to hurry, and he had no reaction. I walked over to the bathtub and noticed his eyes were not following me as I approached him. I reached down to grab his arm hanging over the side of the tub, and it was limp. That is when I screamed and ran back into the bedroom," Mrs. Powell began to sob again, "I just could not bear the thought of being in a room with a *dead* person. And worse yet, I had just touched a corpse! A corpse!"

I found this last point to be a strange concern considering that the corpse was that of her beloved husband, but I also knew enough to understand that people say very silly things when they are in a state of shock and grief. For Mrs. Powell, a woman who very quickly established a reputation for saying nonsensical things even when she was *not* grieving, well, this just intensified the level of absurdity.

"There, there," I said, doing my best to console her. "Have some tea. It will calm your nerves."

It was about that time that a loud commotion could be heard in the foyer.

"You are moving too fast," I could hear Mr. Rossini's voice say.

"Well, it is not as if I have a choice, my good man," Mr. Richter replied. "This is not exactly a light load."

"I told you we should have asked Giles to help us," Mr. Rossini snapped back.

Thump.

"Don't drop him!" Mr. Richter warned.

"Relax! It was just one of his legs," Mr. Rossini replied.

We could hear the men struggling to carry Mr. Powell's rotund body down the foyer stairs, presumably to the cellar to be kept cold. Upon hearing the commotion in the next room, Miss Finley tried to distract Mrs. Powell so she would not pay attention to the gentlemen's struggle with her husband's heavy corpse.

"You know, I have heard that it is very helpful to recount positive times with a loved one in moments like these," Miss Finley said, standing and positioning her body between Mrs. Powell's line of sight and the foyer. "Would you be so kind as to tell us how you and Mr. Powell met, Mrs. Powell?"

A bit confused by a request like this at such an odd time, Mrs. Powell cocked her head to the side looking at Miss Finley and said, "No, strange child! Can you not see that I am in grief? Why should I add entertaining you to my list of painful activities to do today?"

From the foyer, Mr. Richter's voice rang out, "I am stuck, I am stuck! Mr. Rossini, lift! Lift!"

I sat back in my chair to see what was unfolding in the foyer. Mr. Rossini and Mr. Richter had managed to get Mr. Powell's body down the stairs, wrapped in a bedsheet. It appeared as though Mr. Richter had been pinned between

Mr. Powell's body and the landing near the cellar door. My guess was that Mr. Rossini had let go of Mr. Powell with one hand to open the door, which led to Mr. Richter stumbling backward with the weight of Mr. Powell falling on top

"Ugh, I cannot breathe! Hurry!" Mr. Richter managed to eke out.

Then, as if rolling a hay bale, Mr. Rossini pushed the side of Mr. Powell's lifeless body, getting it to roll off Mr. Richter successfully but having the unintended consequence of landing with an enormous thud on the floor of the foyer.

The thud was so loud and powerful that I swore the china on display in the dining room rattled.

"What was that?" Mrs. Powell asked.

"That? Probably thunder," Miss Finley responded.

Betty Simmons, who had mostly been staring outside this entire time, responded, "Thunder? It is not raining, silly!"

Miss Finley gave her quite the look.

"If it was not thunder, then what was it?" Mrs. Powell asked again.

"Perhaps it was Ms. Lavoie in the kitchen?" Anna offered. "You know what they say: the best cooks are not quiet cooks."

No one says that.

"No, it sounded as though it came from the foyer," Mrs. Powell insisted.

At this point, Ms. Simmons stood from the window, walked over to the arched doorway of the dining room and foyer, observed what was happening, and said, "See! I was right! It was *not* thunder. It was just Mr. Powell's fat, dead body falling onto the ground!"

Some things are better left unsaid or, if said, said a bit more delicately.

Whatever powder Mrs. Powell had put on that morning could not hide the dark shades of red that started filling her face. She pushed back her chair quickly, leapt from her seat at the table, and darted to the foyer where Mr. Rossini and Mr. Richter were trying their best to pick up Mr. Powell's heavy body.

"Is this any way to treat the deceased?!" Mrs. Powell raged.

"Ah, Mrs. Powell, forgive us. It is just that…" Mr. Rossini began.

"Save your breath, Mr. Rossini! I do not need to hear any excuses because this is perfectly inexcusable," Mrs. Powell said, kneeling down next to her dead husband's body.

"Oh, poor Albert! I am so sorry these two dolts have treated you so poorly," she said, patting where she thought his head was.

"Mrs. Powell, we are sorry, it is just that your husband is so…" Mr. Rossini began again.

"Enough! If you are too weak to move my husband then just admit it," Mrs. Powell said. "He deserves to be treated with respect, placed in a proper container in a nice, cool place that will keep him as fresh as possible so the medical examiner will be able to figure out what happened to him. He does not need two nincompoops dropping him here and there, adding bruises where there were none. Why, if he were not already dead then he would most certainly be dead now!"

After a beat, Mr. Richter said dryly, "Maybe *you* would like to move him yourself then?"

Mrs. Powell thought for a second, looked at the large body hidden by the bedsheet before her, looked down the stairs to the cellar, and then looked back at Mr. Rossini and Mr. Richter.

In a much softer, quieter voice, Mrs. Powell began again, "Perhaps I should just let you continue." And then, almost singing like a bird, she said, "Proceed!"

She stood up and moved out of the way as Mr. Rossini and Mr. Richter attempted to get a good grip on Mr. Powell's body, the rest of us watching on.

From that point on, Mrs. Powell became more of a director than a dictator, still calling the shots albeit in a slightly more polite manner.

"Careful, careful!" Mrs. Powell said. "He may be dead, but spirits can still feel, you know!" When the two men set Mr. Powell's body down on the cellar floor, Mrs. Powell gasped and asked, "If it would not be *too* much trouble, perhaps you can set his body on the stairs where the wood is cleaner instead of on this dirty, filthy floor?"

Mrs. Powell's concern for her dead husband's body was as admirable as it was annoying. The body was completely enveloped by the bedsheet, which would have prevented any of the cellar floor's dirt from contaminating the body. Mr. Rossini and Mr. Richter were visibly annoyed by the woman's unnecessary commands, but whether out of exhaustion or respect, decided not to protest.

Mrs. Powell was, herself, quite disgusted by her surroundings. She coughed quite dramatically and then took the handkerchief in her hand, which she had been using to collect her tears, to fashion a makeshift face mask that covered her nose and her mouth. She reminded me of the women Harry and I saw at the bazaars in the Ottoman…only much louder.

Finally, the men were able to get Mr. Powell's body into the wine cellar.

"Well, that should do it," Mr. Rossini said, clapping his hands to indicate a finished job.

"Wait, what?" Mrs. Powell asked. "You intend to leave him out here in the open where insects and bugs and rats can get at his body?!"

Mind you, we had yet to see any insects, bugs, or rats in the cellar, but Mrs. Powell had a very wild imagination.

"And next to this other dead body with no privacy?!" Mrs. Powell went on, "Absolutely not! Not on my life!" Mrs. Powell folded her arms and put her nose up in the air.

Mr. Rossini and Mr. Richter exchanged a knowing glance and then began looking around the cellar for a solution. Perhaps it was good fortune that the cellar happened to be under construction, as various crates of all shapes and sizes were scattered about.

My eyes caught one particular crate at just about the same time as Mr. Richter's who said aloud, "What about this, Mrs. Powell?" gesturing toward the large, oversized crate that could have, at some point, held a concrete pourer given its size.

"Yes, I suppose that will have to do," Mrs. Powell responded, never fully satisfied.

Mr. Rossini and Mr. Richter dragged the large crate into the wine cellar near where they had set Mr. Powell's body. To be honest, I pitied the poor men once I observed the look of recognition on their faces that they would have to lift the very heavy Mr. Powell once more. The men counted to three and then, straining every muscle they had, lifted Mr. Powell over the top of the crate and lowered him inside. I should point out that, despite the crate's large size, Mr. Powell *barely* fit inside.

Mr. Rossini placed the lid on top of the large crate, struggling to lift it due to its heavy weight. As soon as he set the lid in place and began walking way, Mrs. Powell started again, "You cannot just leave it like *that!*"

Mr. Rossini hung his head, sighed, and asked, "Whatever do you mean, Mrs. Powell?"

"Well, there are cracks! How is that supposed to protect him from the bugs? And the rats? I read somewhere that rats can flatten their bodies down to nothing. That is how they get under doors and into pantries!" Mrs. Powell rattled on.

Somewhat defeated by this point, Mr. Rossini asked, "And what, pray tell, do you expect us to do about…"

Mr. Rossini was unable to finish before Mr. Richter appeared holding a hammer and some nails. "Problem solved," he said with an almost sinister expression on his face.

"Yes, very well then. Make sure it is sealed nice and

tight," Mrs. Powell insisted. "I cannot bear the thought of little roaches and rats eating at my poor Albert! Ugh. It makes my skin crawl just thinking about it!"

As Mrs. Powell stood in the centre of the room, arms folded, rubbing her limbs with her hands as if to warm herself up from a chill, the two gentlemen began nailing the lid of the crate to better preserve Mr. Powell's body. Mrs. Powell watched on with a sad, worried look on her face, standing in the middle of the room careful not to brush up against anything that might get her dirty.

When Mr. Rossini and Mr. Richter hammered the last nail in Mr. Powell's temporary coffin, they pushed the crate as far against the wine cellar wall as possible. As they began to walk away, Mrs. Powell opened her mouth to speak one more time.

"What about Mrs. Flaherty?" she asked.

The two men looked confused.

"Well, it is hardly fair to do for one but not the other," Mrs. Powell commented. It is always so easy for one to criticize when he or she is not actually doing the work.

So, with that, the two men found a long, flat crate, grabbed Mrs. Flaherty's severely stiff body—surely rigor mortis had set in by now—and began the makeshift casket process again.

And to think: we had not even had breakfast yet.

*     *     *

The rest of the day was relatively quiet compared to the morning hubbub. Ms. Lavoie had cooked another delicious breakfast, but no one said a word as they stuffed their faces with Eggs Benedict and a potato hash. The thought of two people dying within 24 hours of one another under the same roof provides plenty for an individual to think about. Although both deaths seemed free of mystery or suspicious circumstance, how often is it that two people die within such a short duration of time in the same social circle? I had never experienced that in my 65 years, so even I found myself wondering what was at play. Coincidence? Curse? Conspiracy?

Around 2:00pm, a small group gathered in the parlour to socialize while Ms. Lavoie cleaned up the kitchen after a late lunch. Mr. Rossini and Ms. Simmons were engaged in a game of chess. Miss Finley and Mr. Richter were each reading a book. Anna and I sat sipping afternoon tea and enjoying the most delicious biscuits. Walter Simmons sat in a chair, sedated to the point of sleeping deeply.

"Such a curious painting," Anna said, staring at the painting of the Radcliffe family hanging over the room's large fireplace.

"Do you know who they are?" I asked.

"Not a clue," Anna replied.

"Mrs. Flaherty told me upon our arrival," I said, continuing to tell Anna the full story. "The Radcliffes were the original owners of this estate. Steel money, it seems. American royalty. Mr. Radcliffe was quite the adventurer, but it was on a safari that he and Mrs. Radcliffe died tragic deaths. The young child there, the boy, ran away upon hearing about his parents' deaths, never to be seen again."

"That's quite sad," Anna said, staring at the painting.

"Indeed, I felt quite the same as you," I replied. "Kath spoke fondly of the family, especially the young boy."

"How old was he when he ran away?" Anna asked.

"I believe he was a boy of only seven or eight per Kath's recollection," I added.

"So, per the year on the frame, that would make him…" Anna was doing the math.

"Late 20s, perhaps. Maybe early 30s?" I offered. "Depending on his actual age, I suppose. But Mrs. Flaherty said the authorities thought he drowned in one of the lakes or rivers nearby."

"Oh, that *is* tragic," Anna replied. "Did they find the body then?"

"Not that Mrs. Flaherty said," I said, lowering my tea

cup to its saucer.

After a brief pause Anna began again, "So, it is possible he did *not* drown then?"

Quite surprisingly I had not thought of that alternative, having just taken Kath for her word. "Why, I suppose that is possible, indeed," I said, finding my gaze lost in the painted eyes of young Elliott Radcliffe.

At that moment, Walter Simmons jolted awake from his slumber, eyes wide in a full panic. The poor fellow must have been having a nightmare. Ms. Simmons went to her brother's side and soothed him back to sleep, surreptitiously injecting him with one of his medicines to help. As she walked back over to her chess game, Ms. Lavoie entered the parlour and made her way to the sofa where Anna and I were sitting. After glancing around the room at the other guests, Ms. Lavoie leaned in and started in on a bit of gossip.

"Did either of you find it curious how indifferent Mrs. Powell seemed about her husband this morning?" Ms. Lavoie whispered.

"I did," Anna replied. "What person is so vain that she tends to her hair and makeup before saying, 'Good morning,' to her husband?"

I sipped my tea and listened.

"Well, there's more. Last night, I heard arguing taking place from my room. Now, I cannot be certain of who it was, but I definitely heard a man's voice and a woman's voice," Ms. Lavoie went on.

"But there are a lot of male, female pairings that it could be," I offered. I did not write mystery stories for nothing. Possibilities mattered. Details mattered.

"Certainly, and I have thought of this," Ms. Lavoie went on, "it could have been Mr. and Mrs. Powell, of course, but it could have also been Ms. Simmons and her brother or maybe even Mr. Rossini and Miss Finley."

"Mr. Rossini and Miss Finley?" Anna asked. "What makes you say that?"

"Oh, come now," Ms. Lavoie responded. "You do not

know?"

Anna and I shook our heads. I had a suspicion, but I would rather have Ms. Lavoie explain herself.

"Each morning I see Miss Finley coming from Mr. Rossini's room. This morning, did you notice that she emerged from his room and ran down the hall to Mr. and Mrs. Powell's room? Yet when asked to explain how they know each other, they are so very coy," Ms. Lavoie continued.

Miss Finley's golden kimono came to mind, as did the first day when I saw someone in said kimono making a run for it into a room, quickly closing the door behind her.

"You do not think they are…" Anna did not finish the words, but Ms. Lavoie knew well what she intended to say.

"*Je ne sais pas*," Ms. Lavoie responded, "but I do know that they are not married, for Miss Finley wears no rings. Well, I should correct myself: I know that *she* is not married."

Aha! There it was. Of course! Mr. Rossini, a successful, older businessman from the city. Miss Finley, a young, charming schoolteacher. A holiday out of the city into the country during the first week or so of the academic summer recess. It would seem that Mr. Rossini and Miss Finley were either dating or…

"Gasp! They are having an affair!" Anna exclaimed, raising her voice just a bit too loud.

At that moment, Mr. Richter and Miss Finley looked up from their books toward our trio. I could not tell if Miss Finley actually heard what Anna said or had any idea what it was we were discussing, but we made eye contact before she raised her brow, looked at Ms. Lavoie, and then resumed reading.

"I do not know whom I heard," Ms. Lavoie began again, returning to a whisper, "but it was late. The next thing I know, Mrs. Powell is screaming from her room and her husband is dead."

"It is all so peculiar," I added. "Two deaths in not even

two days. What are the chances?"

"Unfortunate timing," Anna said. "Or so it seems. An unfortunate accident. A weak and aged heart. If you would have seen Mr. Powell panting and struggling on our journey yesterday, I imagine it would make much more sense."

"Indeed, I suppose you are right," I replied. "Just a truly unfortunate coincidence, I suppose."

About that time, Mr. Rossini could be heard raising his voice, "That is not a fair move, Ms. Simmons!"

"But why isn't it?" Ms. Simmons asked, sounding a bit like an impetuous child.

"Because that is not how chess is played," Mr. Rossini responded.

"Says who?!" Ms. Simmons demanded, raising her voice.

"Says hundreds of years of history," Mr. Rossini roared.

"Well, then we should just make our own rules," Ms. Simmons replied.

"That's not how games work!" Mr. Rossini said, standing at the chessboard. "You cannot simply capture a pawn and a knight because you feel like it, Ms. Simmons. There are rules regarding movement of each piece, and I am quite certain you…"

"…but movement can be unpredictable," Ms. Simmons said, darting back and forth in place as she stood up as if to illustrate how unpredictable movement can be.

"Surely, but not in chess where each piece has very specific movement," Mr. Rossini said.

"Well, I wanted to capture your pawn, your horse person, and this lady right here," Ms. Simmons said picking up Mr. Rossini's queen.

"I say, good woman, have you even played chess before?!" Mr. Rossini asked.

"I play games by my own rules," Ms. Simmons responded, "and if you are displeased with that, Mr. Rossini, well, then you can just play this game by yourself."

Ms. Simmons stormed off, out of the parlour, and toward the stairs to the second floor leaving her brother behind in his sedated state.

Mr. Rossini, confused by this outburst, simply yelled to her, "That's not how chess works!"

Clearly the stress of the day had everyone a bit on edge.

"My, my," Ms. Lavoie began, "that was strange."

"Indeed," Anna replied.

"Well, let us look on the bright side," I started, "the access road will clear up soon, which will allow us to get in touch with the authorities. The sooner they get here, the sooner things will calm down for everyone."

"That would be a relief," Ms. Lavoie replied.

No sooner did she say the word than did the soft roar of a rolling thunder off in the distance rattle the foundation of the manor.

I looked outside the large window to the parlour. The winds were picking up, the sky was getting darker. This only meant one thing…

More rain was coming.

*    *    *

Mrs. Powell stayed in her room the entire day, not even leaving once to come down for lunch or dinner. Anna, kindly, took both meals up to the woman who simply stayed in bed, switching among her favourite pastimes: sleeping, crying, or complaining.

Unlike the previous two nights, none of the guests gathered for post-dinner drinks and socializing that evening, perhaps a function of our early wake-up call in the form of Mrs. Powell's bloodcurdling scream. Instead, everyone retired to his or her respective room earlier than usual save for Mr. Richter who appeared to be looking for something he misplaced throughout the manor. I could have sworn I heard him mumbling on about something to do with Darwin, but I had come to see him as the peculiar academic type by now and was not altogether surprised to see this behaviour.

Anna and I accompanied each other to our respective rooms where we bid each other goodnight and then locked ourselves inside for the evening. I thought I would take this quiet time to focus on what I had come here to do: write! Now that everything had settled down a bit with the unfortunate episodes of the past two days, I finally had the opportunity to engage in uninterrupted writing. I sat at the large desk in my room where I had set up the typewriter, and began typing, "The winters of Sweden are colder than most, and the nights among the longest and darkest..." I began. "A tale set at a Swedish ski resort," I thought, "with a murderous groundskeeper." This, of course, made me think of poor Giles downstairs who had not really been seen most of the day. There was a soft spot in my heart for the young man, so I found myself ripping that page out to start again. "The warm, sticky air lingered in the night, and a mysterious traveller in black appeared at the inn," I typed. A New Orleans mystery where a masked murderer kills someone in the middle of a crowded celebration during Mardi Gras. It must have been the mask that made me picture poor Mrs. Powell, confused and distraught over her husband's death, standing in the cold cellar wearing her makeshift face mask. At this point, it was becoming clear that the events of the past two days were in my subconscious, obviously influencing my ability to write.

That's when I heard the noise.

Unlike the previous night's scraping sound, this was more of a squeaking noise.

"Maybe Mrs. Powell was correct to be worried about those rats," I thought, standing up from my desk to see if I could determine the source of the squeaking.

I approached the door to the hallway. As I walked closer to the door, I realized that the sound was coming from outside my room. The sound grew louder and clearer as I approached, less of a squeaking sound and more of a shrieking noise.

"What on earth?" I asked myself aloud.

Almost on cue, as soon as I said those words aloud there was a roar of thunder that shook the entire house followed by an incredibly loud crashing sound from somewhere downstairs.

I thought about opening the door to go investigate, but I have written far too many mystery novels to take that sort of a risk. I reached down to make sure my door was locked, grabbed the chair nearby to barricade my door, and sat in silence for a good hour with just my heart pounding out of my chest.

"Thump, thump. Thump, thump."

# 6 | THREE IS A PATTERN

I awoke the next morning to the sound of a bird, presumably a fox sparrow, singing the most beautiful song. I must say that it was a pleasant departure from waking to the sound of screaming, which had been the manor's wake-up call the past two days: first my own scream at the sight of poor Mrs. Flaherty and then Mrs. Powell's scream upon discovering her husband dead in the bathtub. Such a lovely time I was having on this writer's retreat!

I finished getting ready and then went to exit my room into the upstairs hall. I forgot I had not only barricaded my door with a chair but also put some luggage in the seat of the chair for extra weight once I finally decided it was safe enough to climb into bed. These things always have a way of feeling so absurd the next day when the sun is shining into your room but always make perfect sense at night when one is unaware of what creatures could be running around in the darkness.

I opened the door to the hallway and proceeded along, down the stairs to the foyer, the familiar "tick tock" of the grandfather's clock counting each second to the same rhythm as my walking cadence. As usual, I went to the kitchen to make some tea for myself and, also as usual, I appeared to be the only guest awake. A quick glance outside suggested that even Giles had not yet risen to tend to his work, which seemed peculiar but not altogether shocking.

Why, even Ms. Lavoie seemed to be getting a later than usual start that morning, as she was nowhere to be seen in the kitchen or the pantry and had not yet assembled ingredients for whatever delightful meals she had in store for us that day.

"Strange," I thought, taking a seat in the parlour where I had a marvellous view of the estate, the sun rising over the greenest trees and grass, extra radiant from the previous days' rain. For the first time since arriving at Raven's Point Manor I felt a sense of relaxation. Why, I do believe I even sighed a small sigh of relief!

I am not entirely sure how much time had passed before I saw that Miss Finley and Mr. Rossini had joined me in the parlour. Since Ms. Lavoie had told me her suspicions about these two, well, I could not help but picture them as a pair, a somewhat scandalous couple carrying on in private, worried that someone may discover their secret. I, for one, did not so much care about an affair even if there happened to be one taking place. I would have been crushed, of course, to learn my Harry was carrying on with another woman during our time together, but by my age I had also seen quite a bit and grown weary of old-fashioned tropes and rules. That was more Mrs. Powell's purview. I thought of myself as a bit more contemporary than that.

"Good morning, Dame James," Mr. Rossini said as he bowed a bit.

"*Buongiorno*, I believe?" I replied, attempting to revive a bit of basic Italian I once knew.

"Ah, *sì*!" Mr. Rossini replied. "I figured you would be a woman of many languages!"

"How did you sleep, Dame James?" Miss Finley asked, sitting next to me on the sofa.

"Quite well, surprisingly," I said. "Once I got to sleep, I slept like a baby."

"Oh, how lucky you were then," Miss Finley said. "I had an awful go at it. There was the strangest noise coming from what sounded like every inch of the manor. And then, in the middle of the night, I heard a loud crash after all of us had already gone to bed. I assumed it could have been a tree breaking through a window or maybe Giles even, but it gave me quite a fright it did."

Relieved to hear someone else heard the same noises I had heard, I confided in Miss Finley, "I heard those noises, too! It made my heart beat right out of my chest," I said. "I even barricaded myself in my room! It must have been such a funny sight!"

We had a good laugh over our shared concern about what seemed to be nothing in the light of day.

"I suppose the situation with Mrs. Flaherty and Mr. Powell has everyone a bit on edge," Mr. Rossini said.

About then, we heard the most curious sound coming from the foyer.

"Darwin? Darwiiiiin?" a man's voice whispered. "Darwin, where are you?"

You can imagine how surprised Mr. Richter was to see the three of us in the parlour.

"Oh, good morning," Mr. Richter said awkwardly. "I was not sure that anyone was awake yet."

"Ah, yes, well, here we are!" Mr. Rossini responded. "Tell me, Richter, are you looking for something? Or…someone?"

"No. Well, yes. Well, not exactly," Mr. Richter stuttered over his words.

"Well, which is it, Mr. Richter? Are you or are you not looking for someone? Darwin, was it?" Miss Finley asked.

"Yes, very well. I, uh, I am looking for my copy of Darwin's *Origin of Species*. I was reading it just the other day and seem to have misplaced it," Mr. Richter responded.

"And, so, you were calling out to it?" I asked, bewildered.

"Um, yes. I know that, uh, sounds a bit strange, yes," Mr. Richter said, "but I read in a journal once that inanimate objects can sense things like humans can. Much like how Mrs. Powell believes the animals she eats can still feel pain."

Strange.

At this moment we were all surprised to see Mrs. Powell standing in the doorway. No, to be more accurate, we were surprised to see Mrs. Powell *leaning* in the doorway as if too weak to stand.

"I suppose you are all surprised to see me up and moving around just one day after my husband departed his earthly body," Mrs. Powell performed ever so dramatically. "Alas, one simply cannot mourn forever, and I felt as though I had to return to the living…"

"And to a delicious breakfast," I whispered to Miss Finley.

"…and to a delicious breakfast to nourish my weakened heart," Mrs. Powell went on. She certainly did have a flair for theatrics.

Mrs. Powell moseyed over to the sofa and sat herself right between Miss Finley and myself, careful not to touch anything other than the sofa in the same peculiar manner I saw her sitting the first night at the manor. By now it was clear to me that Mrs. Powell likely suffered from some minor mental ailment involving germs or dust. She simply could not be bothered to breathe in impure air or to touch anything that might have a speck of dust or dirt. It was as if she had been taken care of for far too long and had grown to expect a certain level of protection. I only wish life were so simple as to provide us all with such protection, but I knew that not to be true, both in my stories and in real life.

Anna joined our gathering shortly thereafter, apologizing for having overslept. By this point I was certain Ms. Lavoie would have come downstairs to begin breakfast, yet she had neither stopped by the parlour to say good morning nor started baking anything that we could smell from where we were sitting. By the time Ms. Simmons and her brother made it downstairs, I began to grow concerned. Those two were *always* the last to rise, so if Ms. Lavoie was still not downstairs, well, something was off.

"Good morning, good morning," Ms. Simmons said with a chipper energy and a smile. She helped her brother make his way to one of the sitting chairs near the large, stone fireplace. One could not help but appreciate the stonework of the fireplace and its massive size. Walter Simmons was a decently built young man, standing roughly just short of 2 meters. Quite tall, indeed! The fireplace was so large that had Mr. Simmons squatted, just a bit, he could have fit within the fireplace himself. It was an odd design but was something that reminded me of picture books I had as a child showing Viking dining halls. There was something quite barbaric about it.

We all sat about the parlour, sipping on tea and chatting about how lovely the day looked, even making plans to walk around the estate's grounds, when the grandfather's clock in the foyer struck 10:00am.

"My word!" I said. "Are we certain Ms. Lavoie has not snuck into the kitchen while we were chatting?"

"I have not seen her," Mr. Rossini said, "but I will run to the kitchen to check."

He returned moments later, but said nothing, instead offering a shrug and an expression suggesting he was clueless as to where Ms. Lavoie might be.

"Maybe we should go up and check on her, you know, to make sure she is okay?" Miss Finley offered.

"That seems like a great idea," Mrs. Powell began. "I am starving, so the sooner we can get her down here the better."

"Perhaps it is best if you go, Mary Jane," Mr. Rossini suggested. "I am not sure it would be proper for Mr. Richter or me to barge in on Ms. Lavoie."

"Certainly," Miss Finley responded. "Dame James, would you care to join me?"

"Of course!" I said, rising to my feet. "I would be happy to."

When we left the group sitting in parlour, Mr. Rossini, Anna, and Mrs. Powell were sipping their tea, Mr. Richter was searching behind the furniture for something, Walter Simmons was staring at the large, captivating painting of the Radcliffe family hanging above the fireplace, and Ms. Simmons was touching all the expensive curiosities scattered about the room. Miss Finley and I made our way up the stairs, turned left, and walked to Ms. Lavoie's door.

"Mademoiselle Lavoie?" Miss Finley called out. "*Es-tu là? C'est moi, Mary Jane.*"

We listened for a response but heard nothing save for a slight squeaking sound.

"Ms. Lavoie?" I asked, knocking on the door. "Are you awake?"

Again, we listened hard for a voice to respond, but the only noise we heard was a bit of movement and that same squeaking, slightly shrieking sound.

"Claudette, if you could please respond and let us know you are okay?" Miss Finley tried once more.

Hearing no response, Miss Finley looked at me and asked, "What should we do?"

"Well, given the events of the last two days, I suppose we should go in and make sure the poor girl is alright," I responded.

Miss Finley reached down to turn the door handle leading to Ms. Lavoie's room. Much to both our surprise, it was *unlocked*. We pushed open the heavy door and stepped into the room. The room was dark; the curtains had been pulled closed preventing light from entering and the lamp near Ms. Lavoie's bed was off making it difficult to see too far in front of us.

"Here," I said, "let me pull back the curtain."

I carefully felt my way through the darkness of the room and swore I felt something, or someone, brush past my body on my way to the window.

"Did you hear that?" Miss Finley asked. "It sounds like there's something moving in here. Oh, please do be careful, Dame James!"

Finally, my palms felt the familiar fabric of the window curtain, identical to the one found in my room. I pulled back the curtain and let sunlight flood the room. Not even a second after doing so, I heard Miss Finley's piercing scream.

I turned to see what had startled her so. There, in the

blinding light of the morning sun, was Mademoiselle Claudette Lavoie, sitting at her vanity, neck bent to the side, with a jade-handled dagger protruding from her neck.

My heart sank. Not only was I gutted to see Ms. Lavoie in her current state, but I also knew what this most likely meant: there was a murderer nearby.

I had barely registered this thought when Miss Finley let out a second bloodcurdling scream. I assumed she was just having another reaction to the horrific scene before us, but when I turned in the direction of her gaze, that is when I saw what had startled her a second time: standing in the middle of the bed, with blood all over its fur, was a small monkey.

It was at precisely the moment I locked eyes with the small primate that the door to the bedroom flung open again. In ran Mr. Rossini, Mr. Richter, Anna, and Ms. Simmons. Mrs. Powell followed soon after mumbling something about not wanting to be left alone with Walter downstairs. Mrs. Powell screamed at the sight of poor Claudette Lavoie and Anna covered her eyes in shock, while Ms. Simmons just stood still staring at Ms. Lavoie with her jaw to the floor. Miss Finley ran into Mr. Rossini's arms, while Mr. Richter did the most curious thing of all: he approached the *monkey*.

"*There* you are, Darwin!" he said, as the monkey jumped onto his shoulder. "I've been looking *everywhere* for you."

\*     \*     \*

"There is a murderer in this house!" Mrs. Powell screamed at the top of her lungs. "One of you killed Ms. Lavoie!"

A group of us had assembled in the parlour trying to make sense of the horrific scene in Ms. Lavoie's room.

"Let's not jump to conclusions, Mrs. Powell," Mr. Rossini said. "It could have been any number of things."

"Oh, really? Like what, Mr. Rossini? Like what?!" Mrs.

Powell asked.

"Like that little circus monkey did it," Mr. Rossini suggested.

"The circus monkey? Have you gone mad, Mr. Rossini? Well, have you?!" Mrs. Powell fired back.

"I can assure you that Darwin did no such thing," Mr. Richter responded, having returned the monkey to the cage in his room.

"Can you, Richter? Can you *really*? Did you see the blood covering its fur?" Mr. Rossini asked. "How can you prove to me that your demented little monkey did not take the dagger from this room, run upstairs with it, and murder Ms. Lavoie in cold blood?!" He was shouting by the end of the sentence.

"How can you prove to me that he *did*?" Mr. Richter asked calmly.

After a beat, Ms. Simmons offered another alternative, "Maybe she did it herself?"

"Suicide, you mean?" Anna asked.

"Yes, suicide. Happens all the time, right?" Ms. Simmons went on, "Maybe the stress of the past two days was just too much for her. See it all the time in patients, really. No big deal."

"But why would Ms. Lavoie commit suicide?" Anna asked. "She was very successful and had all sorts of future aspirations and amazing things planned?"

"It is always the ones you least expect," Ms. Simmons said, simultaneously shrugging and smiling.

"Well, the only thing about which we can be certain," Miss Finley began, "is that we cannot be certain of any of these explanations! And with the phone out and the access road flooded, we cannot hope the authorities will be here to figure it out for us."

"What are you suggesting, Mary Jane?" Mr. Rossini asked.

Miss Finley stood up from her chair, walked over to the sofa, and sat next to me. "Dame James, it will be incredibly important and helpful if the police are provided with a detailed summary of what has taken place here the past several days," she said.

"That is true," I said. "The more we can recollect and commit to paper, the better it will be for the authorities."

"If you do not mind, given that you are quick with the typewriter being an author and all, would you mind spending some time today typing out the events of the past 48 hours?" Miss Finley asked.

"I do not mind at all," I responded without a moment's hesitation, "but what are we to do in the meantime supposing that Mrs. Powell is correct? What if there *is* a murderer somewhere on the estate or, even worse, what if…"

I could not bring myself to say the rest of the sentence, but I did not have to, for Ms. Simmons was ready to finish my sentence for me, "What if one of *us* is a murderer?"

If it were possible for groups of people to experience the exact same emotions at the same time, I think that group began with the same feeling of doubt, followed by a sense of possibility, and ended completely gutted by pure fear.

"What if one of these people *is* a murderer?" I thought to myself looking around the room. Mr. Rossini was certainly full of an unnatural energy and an odd tic that made him the type loathe to endure silence longer than he had to. Mr. Richter had so far proven to be an absent-minded, mad genius, of sorts, lacking the sociability of most normal people. Mrs. Powell was a walking contradiction, having shown such little regard for even her own husband's untimely death and was quick to get her own way. After all, it was she who dictated the temporary burials of both Mr. Powell and Mrs. Flaherty while others did the actual work. Ms. Simmons came across as controlling with respect to her brother but otherwise aloof and often childlike in the strangest of moments, first up, then down with that one. Mr. Simmons did not seem altogether there, but that was only because his sister kept sedatives pumping through his system. How could we be sure that, when left to his own devices, Walter was not the violent madman his sister suggested he could be? And Anna, as much as I had grown fond of her, had always been so secretive and distant as if she had been hiding something she wanted to keep secret all along. She even said as much herself the first night during cocktails in the library.

I was lost in thought, assessing each person in the room (as I am certain they were doing, as well), when Mrs. Powell blurted out, "What about Giles?!"

Giles! I had not even thought of Giles. We barely saw him the entire day before and he had not yet come up from the cellar today, which was altogether peculiar.

"Has anyone seen Giles recently?" I asked.

No one said yes or nodded.

"You don't think it's possible that Giles murdered Ms. Lavoie, do you?" Mr. Rossini asked.

"*Anything* is possible," I responded stoically.

"No, impossible," Miss Finley said, again coming to Giles' defence.

"Well, no one has seen the man," Mr. Richter said, "and you know what happens to the war types sometimes. They get a thirst for killing on the battlefield that they simply cannot shake once they are back to normal life."

"I know the struggles such men face," Miss Finley responded, "but I just cannot see Giles hurting anyone."

"Well, there is one way to find out," I suggested.

And, with that, Mr. Rossini, Mr. Richter, Ms. Simmons, Anna, Mrs. Powell, and I went downstairs to find Giles.

\*       \*       \*

When we opened the door to the cellar, the lights were still off. I must admit that while I had been in the cellar on a few occasions already, entering the cellar knowing there were two dead bodies downstairs was quite frightening. Instead of descending into the basement of a beautiful manor, going into the cellar now felt like descending into the mausoleum of an old cemetery.

When we reached the base of the stairs, Mr. Richter turned on the light. We all saw it at the same time: something was moving back and forth in the far corner of the large open room of the cellar.

"Who's there?!" Mr. Rossini's voice rang out. He grabbed a shovel that was lying near the construction tools. Mr. Richter, following his lead, grabbed a loose brick from the wall that was nearly complete save for the narrow doorframe of the new room.

Whatever it was that was moving was not in fear of being seen, as it did not attempt to scamper off, hide, or run away. No, instead, it appeared as though the large mass of dark fabric was simply rocking back and forth in place.

We stepped closer, letting Mr. Richter and Mr. Rossini lead the way. Miss Finley took a torch she had grabbed in her hand and pointed it in the direction of the rocking body. There, in the corner of the room, was Giles, curled up on the floor, rocking his body back and forth with a worried expression on his face.

Upon seeing us, Giles continued to rock back and forth but slowly reached out his arm to point in the direction of the wine cellar. A chill ran down my spine: that was the wine cellar where Mrs. Flaherty and Mr. Powell were currently being kept.

Miss Finley passed her torch to me as she knelt down to rub Giles' back to calm him. My hand was trembling so much by now that the light of the torch was flickering across the walls of the cellar. I pointed it in the direction that Giles had indicated, each of us in the group taking slow step after slow step toward the cellar.

"Be careful," Mr. Richter whispered. "There could be someone inside."

On that cue, Mr. Rossini raised his shovel in an attack position to be ready should anyone emerge from the darkness of the wine cellar.

As we got closer, I quickly moved the light around the wine cellar looking for any sign that someone might be lurking in the shadows. I was relieved not to see anyone and then found myself panting for the breaths that I had not taken while in complete suspense. The others joined me in this collective sigh of relief.

Then, suddenly, Anna screamed, "Wait! What is that?!" and pointed in the direction of Mr. Powell's crate.

I aimed the light of the torch toward the crate as Mr. Rossini and Mr. Richter stepped in to get a closer look.

"How in the world did…" Mr. Rossini began.

It took a second for it to register, but then I saw what Anna and Mr. Rossini had noticed. Mr. Powell's crate, which had been flush with the wine cellar wall when we last saw it, was pushed out several centimetres away from the wall. Even stranger, it appeared as if the entire crate had fallen over on its side, as the lid of the crate was no longer the top side of the cube but, instead, was now its right side. But, worst of all, the lid of the crate was not as securely fastened at it had been when Mrs. Powell insisted that the crate be sealed shut to prevent insects and rats form getting inside.

"Who did this?" I heard Mr. Richter say.

"Giles, perhaps?" Mr. Rossini responded.

"Or someone else on the estate we don't yet know is here?" I offered. Again, writing mystery novels can come in incredibly handy.

"We should see if they have damaged anything," Mr. Rossini suggested. "That would be important for the authorities to know and essential to include in your notes, Dame James."

"You certainly do not intend to open my dead husband's coffin, do you?" Mrs. Powell snapped.

"We have to, Mrs. Powell. It appears as though someone has tampered with his coffin already," Mr. Richter replied.

"Well, I never! Who in their depraved mind would think to disturb the deceased in this way?" Mrs. Powell mumbled under her breath.

While Ms. Simmons busied herself looking at the various wines nearby, Mr. Rossini and Mr. Richter grabbed a crowbar and started removing the lid from the top (now side) of Mr. Powell's crate coffin.

"It appears that Mrs. Flaherty's crate is untouched," I offered, hoping to provide some positivity.

"The light, Dame James," Mr. Richter commanded. I had inadvertently shined the light on Mrs. Flaherty's coffin when talking about it instead of holding it steady on Mr. Powell's crate.

After working each side of the lid, the two men were finally able to pull it away from the rest of the crate, and the picture that emerged was one of the most shocking, horrifying images I had ever seen. The sheet that had once draped around Mr. Powell was bunched up behind him. A terrifying expression was frozen upon his blue face. Blood that was not on his body before seemed to appear all over his fingers and hands. And, the worst part, the wood on the inside of the lid had scratch marks like those of a caged animal trying to escape his captivity.

"What *is* this?" Ms. Simmons asked.

Mr. Richter said aloud what I thought in my head at the same time...

"Mr. Powell was buried alive."

\*　　　\*　　　\*

Mrs. Powell's body had to be pulled up from the cellar and laid out on the parlour sofa. She was still alive, of course, but upon hearing that her beloved Albert had been buried alive, Mrs. Powell fainted and hit the floor of the wine cellar quite hard.

"I swear that Mr. Powell was dead when we buried him," Mr. Richter said, pacing back and forth in the parlour. "I felt for a pulse. *You* felt for a pulse," he said, pointing to Mr. Rossini.

"Relax, Mr. Richter. I agree with you: the man was most certainly dead when we buried him," Mr. Rossini went on. "I am convinced that was the case."

"What if he came back from the dead?" Ms. Simmons said, arms stretched out like a mummy.

"Now is no time for jokes, Ms. Simmons," Miss Finley rang out. "Let us not forget that Ms. Lavoie's body is still upstairs and needs to be brought down to the wine cellar, as well."

"Better make sure *she's* really dead first," Ms. Simmons quipped.

"This is all so peculiar," Anna offered from the corner of the room where she was deep in thought. "First, Mrs. Flaherty dies with a grotesque puncture wound to the brain. Then, Mr. Powell does not actually die in the washtub of natural causes but, instead, dies after being buried alive in a packing crate, most likely suffocating to death. And, this morning, Mademoiselle Lavoie is stabbed in the neck with a dagger that came out of this very room with only a small monkey as the primary suspect?"

To be honest, I was also convinced that something was afoot. The first two deaths *were* peculiar, certainly, but the death of Ms. Lavoie and the strange turn of events regarding Mr. Powell's death seemed to suggest something more nefarious than pure coincidence. Still, I wanted to hear what everyone had to say before influencing their thoughts, particularly if I were to be the one recording everything for the authorities.

"This house is cursed!" Mrs. Powell mumbled, coming to again. "I told you the other day that these old houses carry their secrets, and the energy here is something rotten! Why, my poor, dear Albert! I simply cannot bear the thought that he was alive in that crate. Alive!"

Mrs. Powell buried her face in the pillow on the sofa and started sobbing again.

"I do not assume anyone in this room is a murderer," Mr. Rossini began, "but I also cannot rule out the possibility that these deaths, particularly the death of Ms. Lavoie, were not the result of foul play."

"I think it would be best if we assumed that everyone here is on the up and up," Mr. Richter added, "until we are given reason to think otherwise. We must be logical and rational in this moment and not let emotions cloud our judgment."

"I agree," Miss Finley added. "We should work as a team until we have good reason not to. That said, gentlemen, would you mind bringing Ms. Lavoie's body down to the wine cellar to join the others?"

"Of course," Mr. Richter replied.

"Indeed," Mr. Rossini responded before adding, "but first it might be prudent to have someone have a look at Ms. Lavoie's injuries to determine if…well…you know, if she were…"

"Murdered?!" Ms. Simmons said with unnecessary drama.

"Yes, murdered," Mr. Rossini confirmed.

"But who among us has such experience?" Miss Finley asked.

Suddenly, everyone's eyes were on me.

"Oh, come now," I found myself saying. "I *write* murder mysteries; I do not *solve* them. And I certainly am no detective."

"I understand, Dame James," Mr. Rossini said, "but you have written about detectives. What is that one, the famous one? Al something?"

"Alastair Evans?" I asked. "Indeed, he was the lead detective in 12 of my novels, but *I* am not Alastair."

"But certainly you must *think* like Inspector Evans," Miss Finley added enthusiastically, "sensitive to clues and details that the rest of us probably overlook."

I sighed a heavy sigh. Writing about the investigation of a fictitious death was inconsequential. Investigating the potential murder of a real person, on the other hand, was quite serious. My heart ached at the thought of having to perform this task.

"Surely, I understand what you see in me," I found myself saying, "but I am not confident that I could truly…"

"I will join you," Mr. Richter offered. "I understand human anatomy as part of my work. Perhaps that will be of some use."

"But it might have been your stupid monkey that committed the crime," Mrs. Powell yelled, head rising up from the pillow. "How do we know you won't tamper with the evidence?"

"I will make sure of it," Anna said, stepping forward.

"Oh, that would be swell, Anna," Miss Finley said. "I do not know why, but I thought you had gone back to your room."

"As did I," Mr. Rossini said.

"Same," replied Mrs. Powell.

Ms. Simmons said nothing but did raise her hand in agreement.

Poor Anna.

*       *       *

Our group of three proceeded slowly to Ms. Lavoie's room, making it abundantly clear that none of us was eager to see the horrible sight again. Oddly, when we opened the door to Claudette Lavoie's room, the scene seemed more peaceful than it had earlier. Perhaps that had to do with the lack of screaming and the absence of a monkey running around the room.

Ms. Lavoie had not moved, of course, her neck still exposed with the dagger sticking out of it, handle skyward. Blood, copious amount of it, had trickled down her neck, staining her ivory robe before some of it pooled around the floor. Most of it had dried, I noticed, which suggested that the incident took place several hours before and not recently. I suppose my Inspector Alastair Evans experience *was* coming in handy.

"Could it have been suicide?" Mr. Richter asked, surveying the scene. "She could have simply stabbed herself in the neck, right?"

"Hmm, I do not think so," I said. "Look here, at her hands. There is no blood. If she had stabbed herself with the dagger then the hand she used to stab herself would most likely have gotten at least some blood on it before falling."

"True," Mr. Richter said, "and the robe has soaked up any blood trickling down, so none has gone down either arm."

"So, if she did not kill herself," Anna began, "then is it at least remotely possible that the monkey had something to…"

"*Nein!*" Mr. Richter said. It was the first time I heard him speak German, which I found curious, but he continued, "Darwin is a monkey from my laboratory and was raised by my hand. He is not a wild animal, and it is not in his species' nature to be violent. The idea that he could steal a dagger from the parlour, bring it upstairs, and stab a human is preposterous!"

"I agree, Mr. Richter," I said, "but Anna is right to consider every possibility. As far as we know, the monkey was the only other living being in the room with Ms. Lavoie."

"Which makes me think," Mr. Richter replied, "if Claudette did not kill herself, and Darwin did not suddenly become a homicidal maniac, then which one of us could have had access to Ms. Lavoie's room?"

"Well, we *all* had access to the room," I responded. "Any one of us could have come to Ms. Lavoie's room last night."

"Is that true, though?" Mr. Richter asked. "We are all fairly certain that Miss Finley likely stayed with Mr. Rossini in his room last night. Let us not pretend as if this is not a universally understood truth."

Anna and I just stared at Mr. Richter as to not give anything away regarding the relationship between Mr.

Rossini and Miss Finley.

"You two came upstairs together, isn't that right?" Mr. Richter asked.

"Yes, that's true," Anna replied.

"And you stayed inside your rooms throughout the night?" Mr. Richter went on.

"Indeed, I was attempting to make use of the time to write," I said.

"And I could hear her typing through the wall because it was actually making it difficult for me to fall asleep," Anna said.

"Oh, dear. Sorry!" I replied.

"And Mrs. Powell was shut up in bed all day long, so it is unlikely she found some motivation to get out of bed and murder someone, particularly following the death of her husband," Mr. Richter went on.

"That is most likely true," I agreed.

"Which leaves us with the mysterious Ms. Betty Simmons and her brother, Walter," Mr. Richter went on. "Might it have been possible for the two to work together to murder Ms. Lavoie?"

"How do you mean?" Anna asked.

"Well, assuming they wanted to do it, one of them could have played lookout to see if anyone was coming while the other snuck to Ms. Lavoie's bedroom. Had anyone come out in the hallway, the two could have pretended to be up to something else or the lookout could have distracted the interrupting party."

"Go on," I insisted. I quite enjoyed hearing Mr. Richter's thoughtful speculation.

"So, one of them sneaks down to Ms. Lavoie's room, sees her performing her evening ritual at her vanity, leaps from the darkness of night, and stabs her in the side of the neck!" Mr. Richter proposed.

"Interesting theory, Mr. Richter," Anna responded, "but have you *seen* Mr. Simmons? Hardly a reliable lookout or a coordinated murderer."

"I have seen him, Ms. Winthrop, and so have you...*during the day*," Mr. Richter emphasized the last word. "But we have not seen him at night. Ms. Simmons keeps her brother sedated all morning, all afternoon, and all evening, but does she keep him sedated at night?"

"I had not thought of that," Anna said.

"That might explain the strange noises I have been hearing at night," I added. "I was convinced that was simply your monkey, Mr. Richter."

"How do we know that Walter Simmons is as immobile as he seems?" Mr. Richter asked. "Could it not all be a ruse to throw off our suspicion?"

"But why would they bother to conduct such a dangerous act?" Anna enquired.

"Who knows? Maybe they are criminals? Thieves? It was no secret that Ms. Lavoie was a successful, wealthy woman, and the Simmons arrived here as complete strangers. Strangers with an unclear past, even. You, yourself, caught Ms. Simmons mixing up her story, Ms. Winthrop, and don't forget how we did not see any vehicle that was rumoured to have broken down along the access road," Mr. Richter added.

"But she has a nurse's uniform," Anna protested, "and access to all those drugs for brother. Certainly some of her story must be true?"

"Perhaps?" Mr. Richter went on, "but who is to say nurses cannot also be thieves?"

I had to admit, Mr. Richter's theory was quite compelling, even if there was no direct evidence tying Betty or Walter Simmons to the scene. I thought I would ask him an important question.

"Mr. Richter," I began, "that theory is well and fine, but how do we know that *you* did not commit murder in this room? After all, it was your monkey that was found running around Ms. Lavoie's room, and you had been roaming the halls well after we all retired, so you would have been keenly aware if anyone was up and about."

"My dear, Dame James," Mr. Richter smiled an odd, wry smile, "if I killed Ms. Lavoie, why would I volunteer to return to the scene of the crime with the woman who created one of the world's greatest inspectors and could likely poke holes in any fictitious alibi I offered?"

Fair point. I wanted to answer, "To throw off suspicion," but in times like these it is often important to hold one's cards close to the chest. Still, Mr. Richter had not cleared his name in my mind.

We continued to look around Ms. Lavoie's room but found nothing of interest that would point us in the direction of any potential suspect. I do believe we were all three in agreement that Ms. Lavoie's death did not come by her own hand and that Mr. Richter's monkey Darwin, although limber, was not very capable of planning premeditated murder.

"Well, I suppose that is it then," Mr. Richter said. "I will go get Mr. Rossini so we can take Ms. Lavoie's body down to the cellar."

Mr. Richter left the room, leaving me and Anna alone in Ms. Lavoie's room.

"It is such a pity," I said, staring at Claudette Lavoie. "She had such a promising life ahead of her, and she was such a delightful conversationalist, not to mention an outstanding chef." I gasped, "Anna, who will cook for us now? Anna?"

Either Anna did not hear my question or thought it was too insensitive to acknowledge. Apparently, Mrs. Powell's poor manners were rubbing off on me. I turned to see what Anna was doing and saw her staring at something on the wall.

"Anna? Anna what is it?" I asked.

Without moving her head, Anna raised her right hand and pointed straight ahead in the direction she was looking.

There, on the wall a few feet away, hung a painting of a raven much like the one I had in my guest room and similar to the larger painting featuring a conspiracy of ravens in the dining room. My eyes followed the winding, twisting branches of a dark, old tree, all the way to a single raven perched on a sharp, jagged branch of the tree.

I stepped closer to the painting to have a better look, and as I neared the canvas something bright stood out from the dark mélange of colours painted in the scene. There, painted over the raven's visible eye, was a blood red X.

"That does not seem right, does it?" Anna asked.

"Not at all, dear girl," I responded. "Not at all."

# 7 | AN INVESTIGATION COMMENCES

We called a meeting that afternoon for 4 o'clock. This provided everyone some time to relax, refresh, and restart after the horrific discovery of Ms. Lavoie's body that morning. Mr. Rossini and Mr. Richter wrapped Claudette Lavoie in her bedsheet and proceeded to take her body down to the wine cellar where she joined the others in her own makeshift crate coffin (unsealed, this time).

Anna and I had decided to keep the detail about the raven's eye just between us for now. We saw no use in frightening the group, especially someone with the theatrics of Mrs. Powell, with speculation that someone was making a game of murder even if that was what it looked like.

By the time Anna and I arrived in the dining room, the other guests were already seated around the large dining room table. Mr. Rossini, Miss Finley, and Mrs. Powell sat on my left while Ms. Simmons, Mr. Simmons, and Giles sat on my right. Mr. Richter sat directly across from me at the far end of the table, his head framed by the painting of three ravens sitting in a tree. The sight of it made me shiver with memories of the defaced painting Anna and I just saw upstairs. I refocused and addressed the assembled group while Anna took her seat near Ms. Simmons.

"Good afternoon, everyone," I began. "As you know, it has been suggested that I conduct an investigation to the best of my ability—despite not being an *actual* investigator and having barely *any* clue as to what I should be doing—on account of my history of writing murder mysteries."

Mr. Rossini and Miss Finley nodded enthusiastically as if to say, "You can do it, old gal!"

"Although I may not necessarily agree that I am qualified to design such an investigation and, if I am being honest, truly believe that I am completely and utterly *unqualified* for such an important position, I do believe it is my obligation as a friend to both the deceased and all those currently present to offer what I can by way of an inquiry."

As I looked around the table, I noticed that all eyes were on me, even Giles' eyes. Mr. Simmons was in an altered state, per usual, but even he seemed to be expressing interest in the plan in his own, special way.

"To start, I propose there shall be three phases of the investigation into the mysterious death of Mademoiselle Claudette Lavoie. Phase one, the collection of evidence and facts from the scene of the stabbing, has already been conducted by Mr. Richter, Ms. Winthrop, and myself," I said, gesturing to Fred Richter and Anna. "We initially proposed three theories. First, that the Pygmy monkey who had escaped his cage in the room of owner Mr. Fred Richter, managed to sneak downstairs unseen, obtain the jade-handled dagger from the parlour across the hall, and return to Ms. Lavoie's room to murder her in cold blood."

"Why, that is the craziest thing I have ever heard," Ms. Simmons scoffed. "A murderous monkey! What's next? A bank robbing bluebird? A larcenous loon?"

"Precisely, Ms. Simmons, which is why we also considered a second theory: that Ms. Lavoie committed suicide while seated at her vanity. She could have procured the knife at some point during the day, held onto it until the evening, and then plunged the knife into her neck as a way to take her own life," I said.

"But we have already acknowledged that Ms. Lavoie would have had no reason to take her own life," Mrs. Powell protested. "She was a successful woman with a bright future."

I raised my hand to silence Mrs. Powell, "Indeed, Mrs. Powell, but hypothetical conjecture is not scientific evidence. However, close inspection of the body by Mr. Richter, Anna, and myself concluded that suicide would have been highly improbable, as the woman lacked any hint of blood on her own hands, which would have almost certainly happened given the amount of blood that spews from a punctured neck."

Miss Finley covered her face in fear, likely from imagining the gruesome description.

"Which brings us to our third, and most distressing, theory: that someone in this room murdered Claudette Lavoie," I said, as I looked around the table for any hint of guilt or suspicion. "It is unclear whether Ms. Lavoie had kept the door to her room locked, but regardless of this fact, it is possible someone could have hidden in her room, laying low until the opportunity to strike presented itself. Furthermore, given that Ms. Lavoie had established a trusting relationship with everyone here, it is possible that she would have opened her door to any one of us paying a late visit to her room, suspecting nothing."

"But the way the girl was found," Mr. Rossini went on, "why would she be seated at her vanity if she were entertaining a guest?"

"Excellent question, Mr. Rossini," I replied. "That part is unclear. After some consideration, the three of us investigating the scene proposed that the body could have been positioned on the vanity following the stabbing, so it is altogether unclear whether Ms. Lavoie was murdered while she was seated at the vanity or killed elsewhere and placed in this position."

"So, it was probably a man," Mrs. Powell chimed in. Seeing the others looking at her with a confused expression, she continued, "Well, you all saw how difficult it was for two grown men to pick up a dead body and take it downstairs. How could a woman manage to lift a body and pose it in a particular position by herself?"

I thought this was a peculiar comment for many reasons, not least of which was the fact that the dead body of which she spoke, her husband's, was hardly what anyone would consider an "average" body.

"I am not so sure, Mrs. Powell," I contradicted. "Ms. Lavoie was quite petite. It seems possible that even a woman, with careful consideration, might have been able to move Claudette to her final position."

"So, what is it then?" Ms. Simmons asked impatiently. "Who killed the girl?"

"We still do not know, Ms. Simmons," I replied, "which is why, of course, there are three phases to this investigation."

"Well, get on with it then," Mrs. Powell whispered under her breath.

"Before moving on to phase two, there is one more theory that must be considered to round out phase one," I said.

"And what is that?" Mr. Rossini asked.

"The fourth theory is that there is someone else here with us on this estate, someone we do not know, who is hiding somewhere out there," I said as I gestured toward the large window of the dining room.

"You mean to tell me there could be a murderous madman running around out there?!" Mrs. Powell shrieked.

"Or madwoman," Ms. Simmons added. "Women can be mad, too, you know. I am a nurse. I know such things."

"Or mad*woman*," Mrs. Powell corrected herself.

"That is correct, Mrs. Powell," I said, "which leads me to the next parts of the investigation, phase two and phase three."

I noticed that several of the guests were now splitting their attention between my speech and the estate grounds outside, as if, at any moment, a murderer might go running from one side of the front lawn to the other.

"Phase two involves expanding our collection of evidence to the rest of the manor and the grounds of the estate. Now, I realize that this sounds like a daunting task. However, if we all work together as a team, we can easily search the other rooms of the manor outside Ms. Lavoie's, as well as the grounds of the estate in a systematic, expeditious fashion," I continued. I paused a moment and thought to myself, "Impressive, Dame Maggie James. You *do* sound just like Inspector Alastair Evans!"

"You mean a thorough investigation of Raven's Point Manor?" Miss Finley asked.

"Yes. Top to bottom, including the cellar," I said as I looked toward Giles, "as well as Mrs. Flaherty's room, the attic, and other spaces we have not yet explored."

"And the grounds? How do you propose we search this entire estate?" Mrs. Powell asked incredulously. "It would take *years*!"

"Well, *you* would not participate in a search of the grounds, Mrs. Powell," I said, not able to resist getting in a small dig at the old, naysaying bat. "Instead, only the most able-bodied among us would search the grounds on behalf of the rest of the group. Mr. Rossini, Mr. Richter, Miss Finley, Ms. Winthrop, Giles, and Anna, for certain, and Ms. Simmons should she feel comfortable leaving Walter alone at the manor to rest."

"No, I would not feel comfortable being just two old ladies in this manor with *him*," Mrs. Powell said gesturing toward Walter Simmons.

Although I took some offense to her referring to us as "old," I let it pass to move on with the proposed plan. I began again, "Whoever wants to join the estate search can do so while the rest of us remain here to keep watch of the manor. Whatever information and evidence we find will be summarized, and I will type up this summary for both our records and for the authorities."

"So, what is phase three then?" Miss Finley asked.

"Phase three," I said, choking up a bit and finding it surprisingly difficult to swallow, "is when we review our evidence and ask ourselves 'whodunit?'"

The group shifted uneasily in the dining room chairs, looking around at one another likely thinking the very same thought I was thinking, "One of you in this room might be a murderer."

\*     \*     \*

The group resolved to begin the search of the manor that very evening. We decided to do an early dinner, although I hesitate to call what we ate a proper "dinner." Instead, it was truly a free-for-all trip to the pantry to grab whatever food one fancied, no proper meal preparation or planning. Not only was there not much time for that, we also were without our resident chef de cuisine, Ms. Lavoie. Part of me wondered if no one volunteered to step up as chef was because the last two titleholders wound up dead.

I quite enjoyed my meal of a soothing, calming tea and, of course, biscuits. I found some wonderful little chocolate biscuits at the back of the pantry. I think Mrs. Flaherty may have hidden them there deliberately to enjoy all to herself, but now that she was gone, well, someone had to eat them.

The guests gathered in the foyer at the designated time of 7:00pm. At the last of the seven chimes from the grandfather's clock, I began to read from my typed instructions. I wanted to make sure everything was as clear, coordinated, and consistent as possible.

"Dear friends, for the next three hours we will conduct a comprehensive search of Raven's Point Manor. We will work in two teams of three and one team of two. The first trio—Mr. Rossini, Mrs. Powell, and Giles—will search the first floor. The second trio—Miss Finley, Ms. Simmons, and myself—will search the second floor. The final pair—Ms. Winthrop and Mr. Richter—will search the cellar and the attic. Each group is to search every room, closet, nook, and cranny of its assigned floor and to take note of anything significant or peculiar. If any evidence of interest is discovered, document its specific location but leave it in its place for the authorities to observe upon their arrival. Each group is to return to the parlour by 10 o'clock pm or whenever it is finished exploring its assigned area, whichever comes first. Finally, and this is of the utmost importance, no one is to be out of sight from the other members of his or her group for any length of time."

I lowered the typed page from my face and looked up to the other guests, "Any questions?"

Ms. Simmons' had sprung into the air.

"Ms. Simmons?" I asked.

"Is there a prize for finding something? Like a reward of some kind?" she asked enthusiastically.

It took a great deal of effort and self-control not to call out the immaturity of this question, but I definitely had a few choice words cross my mind. I simply looked at Ms. Simmons and responded, "No," through gritted teeth.

And with that, we divided into our groups to explore Raven's Point Manor.

My trio decided that we would begin our sweep of the second floor by starting in the first guest bedroom and then proceeding, in order, until we reached the tenth guest bedroom. Lucky for us, aside from a few stray closets with some cleaning items, the second floor consisted of only the bedrooms and their respective washrooms. It was agreed we would begin in the washroom of each guest room and, once convinced we were finished there, each start at one of the three walls not containing the door to the hallway and work our way to the centre of the room, searching every millimetre for information that might be useful. In this way, we could be certain that we would not miss any potential clue due to oversight or accident.

Now, I would love to tell you that this systematic search of the bedrooms was a thrilling investigation that yielded several important clues, but that would be untrue. Below, I will recount only the most notable discoveries from our search, which, coincidentally, were also the *only* discoveries from our search.

We began in Room 1, Mr. Rossini's room, which was largely free from anything suspicious save for a woman's handkerchief on the vanity, which I simply pretended not to see out of respect for Miss Finley, who surreptitiously grabbed the handkerchief during the sweep of the room. A white, talcum powder bottle had been spilt in the bathroom, as well, but aside from this mess, Mr. Rossini's room was kept rather tidy.

The second room was Miss Finley's. For the purpose of an objective search, Miss Finley agreed to sit in a chair while Ms. Simmons and I combed through the room. Aside from the golden kimono that I had seen several times before, some snacks Miss Finley must have procured from downstairs, and a small collection of what appeared to be romance pocket novels, there was nothing of note in Miss Finley's bathroom or bedroom. Aside from blushing a bit upon our discovery of her romance novels, Miss Finley also had no odd reaction throughout our search of her room.

The third room belonged to Mr. and Mrs. Powell, and, thus, had not changed too much since Mr. Powell's *almost* lifeless body had been discovered in the bathtub just days before. Mrs. Powell, it seemed, only went from the bed to sleep, to the washroom to clean up, and to the vanity to apply the thick layer of makeup she wore each day. We were about to leave the room when I noticed something peculiar. In the same spot where a painting of a raven hung in my room and a painting of a raven hung in Ms. Lavoie's room, a painting of two ravens was hanging in the Powells' room. Even more curious, just as was the case for the painting in Claudette Lavoie's room, I noticed that one of the ravens in this room's paintings had its eyes scratched out with Xs.

"Do you all see…" I began before remembering Anna and I had decided to keep this discovery secret for now as to not scare the guests or, more importantly I realized, tip off a potential murderer that we were wise to this clue. I stopped myself and changed directions, "…see how tidy Mrs. Powell is? Surprising for a woman who is so all over the place, don't you think?"

"Peculiar," I thought to myself, "that now two paintings would have ravens whose eyes were deliberately damaged and the location of those two ravens happened to be in the rooms of the recently deceased." We continued on to the next room. I wondered if Mrs. Flaherty had a raven painting in her room?

The fourth room belonged to Mr. Richter, so I suppose I should not have been so startled to find Darwin hanging about in his little monkey cage, which had a thin sheet covering part of it. I had come to realize that Darwin was likely the source of the scratching and shrieking I heard the few nights prior. It dawned on me at this moment that he was also likely the source of the noises Ms. Lavoie had heard and questioned Mr. Richter about the first night at dinner. Although clean by way of dust and dirt, Mr. Richter's room was a bit cluttered, much like I imagine his mind must have been with all his theories and ideas bumping into one another in his curious brain. Academic papers were strewn about the desk with indecipherable symbols and mathematics scribbled upon them. Near his luggage was a bag full of natural items, like mushrooms and spores, it seemed. This coincided with Anna's description of Mr. Richter's behaviour on their walk to the throughway the other day, stopping and picking up odds and ends from the flora along the access road. Aside from this, some snacks he had procured from downstairs (presumably to feed Darwin), and a few books on his nightstand, nothing seemed too out of the ordinary for a man who had been hiding a monkey in his room.

Ms. Lavoie's room was next and, as such, was searched very quickly considering that Miss Finley and myself had already given it a good once over with Mr. Richter earlier that day. Nothing of significance was found, so we proceeded to check one of the small closets dividing the second floor only to find some cleaning supplies and linens that I am sure came in handy for Mrs. Flaherty when changing over the rooms.

Anna's room was next. I must say that while I had formed an informal partnership with my assistant over the past few days on account of our shared origin and pre-existing relationship prior to arriving at Raven's Point Manor, the girl was still a relative stranger to me. Her room was quite tidy, everything in its place, which I much appreciated. Her clothing in the wardrobe was all black and grey, just like her usual daily outfits, which gave one the impression she was constantly in mourning. She had some books on her nightstand, a pen and paper on her desk on which she had written various tasks to complete (mostly for me, I admit), and the photo of a young man, roughly her age, in a small frame. She had not mentioned any family or a husband, and to the best of my knowledge she was not being pursued by any gentleman caller, which, in all honesty, was not at all surprising. She hardly had any personality and, as you have likely realized by now, it was a great effort for her to stand out in even the quietest of rooms.

Satisfied with our search of Anna's room, we proceeded to my room. Following the protocol established in Miss Finley's room, I sat in my desk chair and watched as Ms. Simmons and Miss Finley searched through my room. I hoped I had not left out anything too embarrassing—undergarments, for example, or biscuits that I had collected over the past several days for snacking. The two women searched high and low as they were required to do and, satisfied that nothing of interest was found, indicated they were ready to move on.

The eighth room belonged to Ms. Simmons, so, again, the same protocol was followed. However, Ms. Simmons seemed a bit more anxious and agitated by our search of her room than either Miss Finley or I had been about our respective room searches. I would not say she was paranoid, but I would say that Ms. Simmons had a hard time staying seated as Mary Jane and I looked about the room.

"Lovely shade of red, isn't it?" Ms. Simmons asked just

over my shoulder as I opened the wardrobe to see what was inside.

"Aren't you supposed to be sitting in one place?" I reminded her.

Ms. Simmons walked back over to her chair to sit as I looked at the red dress hanging in the closet and searched through a few of the other garments hanging there. Having had to leave their luggage in their car, the Simmons siblings arrived with nothing other than Ms. Simmons' handbag that first night during the torrential rain. Mrs. Flaherty promised to provide clothing from the manor's collection, and I assumed these garments were from that collection. Meanwhile, Miss Finley was looking through Ms. Simmons' handbag, having dumped the contents onto the large desk near the window in the room. The contents were, quite literally, a mixed bag of junk. A hairbrush, a writing pen, some sort of toy contraption, a small metal statue of a dog, loose dollars and change, and, of course, vials of medicine of the sort used to keep Walter Simmons in a peaceful, sedated state.

"I am not one for organization," Ms. Simmons said standing just behind Miss Finley. The proximity gave Miss Finley a fright, as she gasped and dropped the vial of medicine she had been holding.

"Careful!" Ms. Simmons said. "We are going to need that to last if we are stuck here for a while!"

Miss Finley replaced the contents of Ms. Simmons' handbag, and we proceeded to explore the ninth room, the one belonging to Mr. Simmons. Walter's room looked as though it had barely been touched. Indeed, it seemed that the poor man just used the bed for sleeping and nothing else. Ms. Simmons kept him in such a sedated state that I could not imagine him doing anything other than sleeping when he was not sitting among us in the parlour or at the dining table where Ms. Simmons would spoon-feed her brother. Still, we were required to check every square metre of the manor, so we did. I found some clothing in the wardrobe that must have belonged to the Radcliffe family, as the fabrics were quite nice and expensive. Nothing was hidden under the bed, there was nothing to be found in the washroom, and poor Mr. Simmons had no possessions in his room, not even a single book. I could not imagine him being a murderer, but like Mr. Richter said, I had no idea what Mr. Simmons might be like if not sedated.

Although the tenth room had no guest staying in it, we thought we should explore the room for completeness so that we could rule out any suspicion. When we opened the door to the room, it was clear to see that it had not been used recently. The bed was perfectly made. The washroom was impeccably clean. The wardrobes and drawers were empty, and nothing of interest sat on the desk, nightstand, or vanity. If someone were hiding out in this room, well, he or she was doing a fabulous job keeping the place tidy.

"Looks like we're all done then," Ms. Simmons announced with glee.

"Not quite," I replied, pointing a bit farther down the hallway.

A small corridor led to a smaller door that I had not paid much attention to before.

"Mrs. Flaherty's room," Miss Finley suggested.

And, with that, we entered the room and turned on the light.

\*     \*     \*

The other guests began the search of their assigned areas at the same time we began looking around the second floor. I must admit, with full disclosure, that I do not know too much about the search that took place on the main level of the house. Mr. Rossini, Mrs. Powell, and Giles were assigned to explore the dining room, the kitchen, the pantry, the parlour, the library, the foyer, the orangerie, the lavatory, and a sort of makeshift music room featuring a piano, a Victrola, and yet another majestic fireplace. From that group I only later learned that the music room was covered in dust (suggesting no one had been inside for some time), the orangerie roof had sprung a bit of a leak (Giles noticed this and pointed toward it until the other two figured it out like a game of Charades), and the warm fireplace in the parlour had a hypnotizing effect, as Mrs. Powell fell asleep on one of the parlour's sofas halfway into the search, leaving Giles and Mr. Rossini to explore the rest of the main floor.

I do know more about what happened during Anna and Mr. Richter's search of the cellar and the attic, however, as Anna gave me the full debrief later that evening after we retired to bed. They started in the cellar, with Mr. Richter insisting they first turn on all the lights and take some torches to illuminate the areas of the cellar that remained in the shadows. They began in the vast, open room of the cellar that the stairs emptied into. The crates that had been there the past several days were undisturbed save for the one that had been recently repurposed to house Ms. Lavoie's corpse. Anna also noticed that the brick walls Giles had been constructing were finished with the exception of a thin cut-out for what was likely to be a doorframe. The interior of the new room was dark and without windows, which suggested it might be used as a storage room of some sort. Mr. Richter and Anna took a look in the deep wine cellar, saw the three crates containing Mrs. Flaherty, Mr. Powell, and Ms. Lavoie, and then quickly exited as not to disturb the deceased. I imagine it was also quite chilling to be in a room with three dead bodies, so I suppose I, too, would make my time in the room as quick as possible.

Three additional rooms were hidden within the stone masonry of the basement. One housed a boiler and small chute that allowed for coal to be deposited, but was otherwise empty save for a few shovels. The other was a small storage room that seemed to house excess furniture that could be brought up to the main level for hosting larger parties and gatherings. That left the third room, which belonged to Giles.

According to Anna, Giles' bedroom was a sad sight. The room lacked any windows or reminder of the outside world. The air smelled of wet, cool mould. His furniture was old and water-damaged, as if flooding had rotted away some of the wood over the years. His wardrobe consisted of the same work uniforms he had worn the past several days, one dinner jacket and nice shirt, and nothing more. Even more disturbing was the improvised toilet and wash basin situation in the corner of the same room where he slept. The man had very little by way of possessions, just some books strewn about, Anna said. It was Mr. Richter, however, who found a small notebook under Giles' pillow that was noteworthy. The notebook contained various drawings and pictures, it seemed, most of them rather rudimentary and simple, difficult to determine what it was they were attempting to represent. What was disturbing, however, was that starting somewhere near the middle of the notebook, a name was written. That, in and of itself, is not particularly alarming, of course, but it was the *particular* name that would cause one to raise an eyebrow and the fact that it was written time after time, page after page, in what must have amounted to hundreds to thousands of examples.

The name? Kathleen Flaherty.

\*       \*       \*

Upstairs in Kathleen Flaherty's room, we found ourselves rummaging through all sorts of odds and ends. Lots of Catholic relics from her Irish upbringing: an ornate Celtic cross statute, a necklace for Saint Michael (the patron saint of protection), and rosary beads sitting on her vanity. The room was clean but slightly cluttered given that it was much smaller than the guests' rooms on the same floor. That left Kath very little room with which to work, but she managed to make the room a cosy oasis from the rest of the manor.

Her personal washroom was spotless, as one might

expect for someone who had been a housekeeper for several decades, and her room was pretty dull in comparison to the other, more ornate rooms of the house.

"Look at me!" we heard Ms. Simmons say when searching through the room. When we turned around, Betty Simmons had thrown Mrs. Flaherty's apron over her clothes and positioned a fiery red dress on her head to look like hair. "I am Kathleen Flaherty!" Ms. Simmons said with a fake Irish accent.

"Ms. Simmons!" Miss Finley snapped. "It is bad luck to poke fun at the dead! You should stop that at once!"

Ms. Simmons, perhaps sore from being chastised, responded by mocking Miss Finley. There was something both oddly mature and often immature about Ms. Simmons. It was like a switch flipped off and on where she was concerned, and we had just witnessed one of her "off" episodes.

As we continued to search through Mrs. Flaherty's room, we found several photographs of her late husband, Mr. Flaherty, the former groundskeeper of Raven's Point Manor and the Radcliffe estate. As Mrs. Flaherty had indicated to me in the parlour, they seemed to get on well with the Radcliffe family, as there were photos of the two families together: Mr. and Mrs. Flaherty along with Mr. and Mrs. Radcliffe and little Elliott Radcliffe.

While going through the pictures, we came to several that consisted only of Mr. and Mrs. Flaherty and a young child, roughly the same age as the child who was in the painting downstairs. Everyone in the photo, all three of them, looked miserably sad. I imagined this was shortly after the demise of Mr. and Mrs. Radcliffe on that most unfortunate safari.

"I did not realise Mr. and Mrs. Flaherty had a son," Miss Finley said.

"Oh, no, that is not *their* son," I began. "He's the young child of the family who originally owned this estate." I proceeded to tell Miss Finley and Ms. Simmons the story that Mrs. Flaherty had shared with me. Mary Jane listened attentively while Ms. Simmons seemed rather distracted by something per usual.

"That is among the most tragic tales I have ever heard," Miss Finley responded when I had finished.

"I agree," I said. "When Kath told me the story, well, my heart just broke for the poor family."

"I cannot even begin to imagine the heartache of losing one's parents like that, and then for the boy to run off and die himself, well, that is just too…" Miss Finley kept going on about how sad the story was, but I found myself distracted by something else.

There, in the collection of photos, I found another, more formal photo of Mr. and Mrs. Flaherty doing a portrait sitting with another child. This child was a bit older, more like 10 or 11 would have been my guess. The child's haircut and clothes were a bit androgynous, making it unclear whether it was a boy or a girl posing for the photo with Kath and her husband. In some ways, the child even looked a bit similar to Elliot Radcliffe, but I believe it was the haircut of the time, as good for boys as it was for girls. A most unfortunate style.

"Strange," I thought to myself, "I could have sworn Kath said she had no children."

"…and to think that I used to complain about my parents or even my siblings for that matter, you know?" Miss Finley went on. "Dame James? Are you listening?"

I was not. As now, something else had captured my attention. While Miss Finley and I were going through the old photos from Kath's collection, Ms. Simmons had sprawled across Kath's bed, staring at a small shelf on the other side of the room. My eyes followed Betty Simmons' gaze to see what, exactly, it was that had amused her so for the last several minutes.

On the third level of the shelf, bending the wood from its heavy weight, was a black marble raven statue, wings outstretched as if frozen in flight.

And on top of the raven's two eyes, marked in blood red, were two Xs.

\*          \*          \*

The attic, according to Anna, was old and dusty. This, of course, was not surprising, as attics tend to be precisely that: old and dusty. Among the various boxes of the Radcliffe family's belongings were a child's toy collection, a lady's wardrobe separated by season, and some business papers from Mr. Radcliffe's steel enterprise. Nothing too out of the ordinary for a wealthy family with a stately manor on a massive estate.

As Mr. Richter and Anna carefully made their way to the far end of the attic away from the stairs that led to its entrance, they realized that a small art studio had been set up. Various cans of paint littered this corner of the attic, and canvases were leaning up against the angled walls, some three or four canvases deep. One canvas remained on an easel just a couple metres from a single chair sitting nearby. A large window in the attic framed the chair from behind.

"Mr. Richter! Have a look at this," Anna reported saying to her search partner.

The canvas sitting on the easel was a partially completed portrait of someone both Mr. Richter and Anna knew, someone we all knew.

Sitting in the chair in the painting having his portrait painted was none other than…

…Giles.

\*          \*          \*

By ten o'clock, the three different groups reconvened in the parlour to discuss what they had found. No group reported anything altogether suspicious and certainly no group had identified any evidence that would suggest the murderer was someone among the guests.

"What a waste of everyone's time," Mrs. Powell spat out.

"Was it, though?" Miss Finley asked, coming to my plan's defence. "Remember that one possibility was that someone in this very room was a murderer. The lack of any evidence in our private bedrooms, or in any room of the house for that matter, suggests that this theory is not to be supported."

"Yes, but where does that leave us, though?" Ms. Simmons asked.

"Well, if it is true that no one here is a likely suspect," Mr. Richter began, "then it suggests that there may very well be someone else on the estate grounds that we are not aware of."

"Or it means that the poor girl killed herself," Mrs. Powell nagged on. "What is the use of working everyone into some frenzy if it is perfectly possible that Ms. Lavoie stabbed herself in the neck?"

"We have already established that the evidence found in Ms. Lavoie's room suggested that she did not kill…" Mr. Richter began.

"…blah, blah, blah. You are no doctor, Mr. Richter, at least not the medical kind. Nor is Miss Finley here nor Dame James. If there is no evidence of foul play anywhere in the manor, then why do we not just assume it was suicide and enjoy the remainder of our time here until the authorities can come and sort out this mess properly," Mrs. Powell suggested. "I, for one, am tired of these *theories*, and as such, I shall retire to bed."

Mrs. Powell began to leave the parlour and make her way toward the stairs.

"There's reason to believe your husband was murdered, Mrs. Powell," I found myself saying. Anna flashed a look in my direction, wondering if I was about to go back on my word to keep our secret about the raven's eyes.

"What?" asked Mrs. Powell, turning around. This had clearly captured her interest.

"There is reason to believe that Mr. Powell was

murdered and Mrs. Flaherty, too, for that matter," I went on. "Now, I cannot reveal the evidence suggesting this account of the past few days' events just yet," Anna nodded, nonverbally approving of my strategy it seemed, "but I assure you that there is reason to believe that Mrs. Flaherty's death and Mr. Powell's death were *not* accidents and did *not* occur naturally."

"So, if you cannot reveal this 'evidence,' Dame James, what is it, exactly, that you suggest we do with this information?" Mrs. Powell asked in a somewhat snarky tone.

I looked around the room seeing various expressions of concern, worry, doubt, and even fear on the faces of the guests assembled in the parlour.

"For now, I suggest we retire to bed and then continue with a search of the grounds tomorrow, the second part of phase two of our investigation," I said.

"But even more important than that, I suggest we all take this very seriously," I said to the group despite looking squarely at Mrs. Powell for her own good.

"Very well then," Mrs. Powell responded. "Very well."

The group stood, wished each other goodnight, and proceeded up the stairs to the second floor with the only exception being Giles who headed for his dungeon-like room in the cellar. As we reached our respective doors to go to bed for the evening, I called out.

"Oh, and just one more bit of advice," I said.

"What is that?" Mr. Richter asked.

"Lock your doors."

# 8 | ALLIANCES FORM

The next morning it was painfully evident that everyone was on edge. Although the night had passed without any screams or scratching sounds, without any actual deaths or near-deaths (as was the case with poor Mr. Powell), the tension in the air was thick. Unfortunately, so, too, was the humidity. I looked outside before heading downstairs to see if it was raining, as that would have certainly interfered with the group's plan to search the estate. Luckily, while the sky was a dark, ominous shade of grey, the rain had not yet started.

The group assembled in the dining room, as planned, at 8 o'clock. Once the grandfather's clock finished its eighth chime, I finished my sip of tea to wash down the biscuit I had eaten for breakfast. I pretended that I did not often make it a habit to eat biscuits for breakfast, but as a woman my age I also felt it was my place to eat whatever I wanted for breakfast without any judgment.

I read from my typed instructions for the group, "Good morning, ladies and gentlemen. Today we shall commence with the second part of phase two: an exploration of the Radcliffe estate. It is very well possible that an unknown assailant is hiding within the woods, in a makeshift shelter, or even within one of the existing structures of the estate. Today, the able-bodied among us will pair up and search as much of the estate as time allows. Those pairs will be Mr. Rossini and Ms. Winthrop, Mr. Richter and Ms. Simmons, and Miss Finley and Giles. Those of us unable to endure this physical endeavour—Mrs. Powell, Mr. Simmons, and myself–shall stay behind and keep watch of the manor should anyone unknown try to enter. The group is to return by 4 o'clock pm or when it has successful covered enough of the estate as to adequately rule out there is no intruder on the property."

I lowered the paper from my eyes, looked out to the group, and continued, "I also intend to use my time today to type up the notes you provided regarding your search of the manor last night. That way, the authorities will have the most accurate, detailed picture possible."

"*I* plan to use *my* time at the manor catching up on my sleep," Mrs. Powell responded, "and if you all insist that Mr. Simmons stays here with Dame James and me, well, rest assured that my door will be locked all day."

"It is always something with you, old lady, isn't it?" Ms. Simmons asked, standing up from her chair.

"Now, now, ladies," Mr. Rossini chimed in, "I am sure we could all use some release, but, for now, please let us try to keep it together." His sniffling seemed worse than before.

Ms. Simmons sat back down in her chair, never once letting her eyes off Mrs. Powell who, in return, was quite intimidated by Betty Simmons' glare. Everyone finished his or her respective breakfast, went back to their room to get proper attire for the potentially rainy weather, and returned to the foyer to plan.

"We have, altogether, three pairs searching the grounds today," Mr. Richter began. "If we think of Raven's Point Manor as the centre of a large circle, I would propose dividing the circle in thirds and assigning each pair to explore their third of the estate."

The others nodded in agreement. It did seem like a sensible plan.

"Mr. Rossini and Ms. Winthrop, you will take the third of the estate that includes the front yard and the area leading to the access road. Ms. Simmons, you and I will take the third of the estate that includes the parlour-side of the home and the corresponding area behind the manor. That leaves the final third for you, Miss Finley and Giles, who will take the third covering the land on the kitchen-side of the manor and the area behind it," Mr. Richter commanded. "Any questions?"

"Yes," Ms. Simmons replied. "What if we run into a murderer?"

Mr. Richter looked Ms. Simmons directly in the eyes and replied with a simple, "Then you scream."

And with that, the group was off.

\*        \*        \*

My day stuck at the manor was quite dull. I spent most of the day typing up the events of the previous days, writing and then re-writing the chronology of what took place as details popped back into my mind. I found it incredibly important to be as thorough as possible, describing what people were wearing, where they were standing, what they were doing, and, whenever possible, what *exactly* it was they had said.

Of course, while engaging in this very rigorous exercise, I could not help but think through the events of the previous days and speculate about what was actually happening around me. I did not *want* to believe that there was a murderer in our ranks, but I also thought the idea of a murderous madman freely roaming about the estate and popping in every so often to commit a murder seemed highly unlikely. Certainly, we would have seen someone by now. Giles would have surely encountered him out on the grounds at some point. It just seemed very far-fetched to imagine some rogue vagabond lurking in the shadows of the Radcliffe estate.

Adding to my suspicion had been the odd markings Anna and I saw on the raven paintings and the raven statue in Mrs. Flaherty's room. Now, I suppose it could have just been a bit of coincidence that ravens with their eyes crossed out were located in the rooms of the deceased, but that would be quite the most peculiar of coincidences. No, it was as if someone had been taunting us, leaving his (or her) mark either prior to or after committing murder. But why would someone take that risk? Why wouldn't a murderer just leave well enough alone after offing the victims? Did this person *want* to be caught?

As I typed up my notes, another thought entered my mind. What if there were more than one murderer? It could be two people working together—Mr. Rossini and Miss Finley, Ms. Simmons and her brother, Mrs. Powell and her departed husband? The Simmons siblings had already been raised as possible suspects by Mr. Richter during our search of Ms. Lavoie's room, but I had not given the other pairs any thought. We knew the relationship between Mr. Rossini and Miss Finley was suspicious, but did we *really* know the true nature of that relationship? And the same could be said of Mr. and Mrs. Powell. There was nothing to suggest one of them was *not* Mrs. Flaherty's murderer. And while it was a bit of a stretch, the near-death debacle of Mr. Powell could have been a planned, intended distraction to provide Mrs. Powell the cover of killing Ms. Lavoie without others casting too much suspicion in the direction of a grieving wife.

"Phew," I thought to myself, "you are overthinking this, Maggie."

I decided to stop hopelessly speculating and, instead, opted to continue typing up my notes from the previous few days. "I may not live to see the end of this," I said to myself, "but at least the authorities will have the most detailed story possible." And, with that, I resumed my typing.

\*       \*       \*

Anna and Mr. Rossini walked around the massive front lawn of the estate and ventured into the woods on either side of the main lawn until the water prevented them from going any further. Of course, spending hours with just one other person and not finding anything of significance by way of questionable evidence leaves a vast void best filled by small talk. Anna filled me in on much of the conversation that took place between her and Mr. Rossini.

"So how long have you and Miss Finley been carrying on?" Anna asked, quite boldly.

"Excuse me?" Mr. Rossini replied, feigning shock.

"Oh, come off it. Everyone knows," Anna said.

Mr. Rossini hesitated for a moment and then began, "Two years."

The two kept walking in silence for a moment before Mr. Rossini continued, "I met Mary Jane two years ago. She was in the city for a holiday, and we had a chance meeting at a show, an opera…"

"That makes sense," Anna joked, poking fun at the Italian.

"…and we kept in touch for some time," Mr. Rossini went on. "At first, the letters were discussing simple things, you know, of the sort friends discuss: work, family, hobbies. But then, well, the conversation…it *changed*."

The two continued to walk, scanning the vast patches of green before them for signs of anything unusual.

"You see, I never thought it would amount to anything but a little bit of fun," Mr. Rossini continued. "She lived all the way in Maine, and I was in New York. But then she started to visit the city more often, and things just became…convenient."

Anna was getting much more than she bargained for in this conversation, but, figuring this information could be helpful, she let him go on.

"A few weekends turned to a few weeks. A few weeks turned to a few months. A few months turned into a year, and now, here we are, two years later," Mr. Rossini continued.

"So, what is your plan then?" Anna asked, curious to know more.

"Plan? What plan?" Mr. Rossini replied. "I am a married

man with three children. There is no 'plan.'"

"And Mary Jane? How does she feel about everything?" Anna asked.

"Not so good," Mr. Rossini admitted. "Mary Jane, she likes to have a plan for everything. After the first year, she wanted me to leave my wife. Now that it has been two years, she keeps talking about wanting to get married. The more invested she gets, the more I am trying to get out."

"I see," Anna said.

"To be honest, Ms. Winthrop, this trip was intended to be my clean break, an end to this affair," Mr. Rossini said, stopping in his tracks.

"And does Mary Jane know this?" Anna asked. "Have you told her?"

"*Sì*, I have," Mr. Rossini continued, "and that was the yelling that Mrs. Powell said she heard the other night. But, such is the way of life and love, right, Ms. Winthrop?"

Anna did not respond.

"Ms. Winthrop?" Mr. Rossini looked behind him to see what Anna was doing. When he turned around, he saw her staring at something just ahead in the distance. "What is it, Anna?"

Anna squinted her eyes and took a few steps forward to see better. The steps turned into a brisk walk, and the brisk walk turned into a run.

"Ms. Winthrop! Wait!" Mr. Rossini said as he ran after her.

The two kept running through an opening in the dense, green forest surrounding them to where Anna's line of sight was directed. They had reached the large lake that surrounded the Radcliffe estate and, thanks to the rain, presently trapped them on this small island.

Mr. Rossini was panting and gasping for breath while Anna explored the very thing that had caught her eye from a distance: a small rowboat was sitting just metres away from the edge of the lake, resting on a small mound. No oars were anywhere to be found, presumably lost to the lake forever.

Anna climbed into the wooden rowboat and sat on the little bench connecting either side of the small vessel. She leaned down and looked under the covered areas of the bow and the stern, reaching her hand in to pull out something that was wedged into the boat's stern.

Mr. Rossini, watching this all unfolded, spoke out, "Ms. Winthrop, what is it? What have you found?"

Anna stood up, turned around to face Mr. Rossini, and helped up a small, plastic ring.

"It is a medical identification bracelet," Anna began, "from the Aspen Pines Mental Asylum."

\*         \*         \*

Mr. Richter and Ms. Simmons were about as odd a pairing as oil and water, both of them rather peculiar and yet completely unable to mix properly. Mr. Richter summarized his time with Ms. Simmons as "challenging," and "unnecessary," as he found her to be more of an unpleasant distraction than a helpful travel companion.

According to Mr. Richter, just as soon as he and Betty Simmons left the manor, she started grating on his nerves.

"So, what kind of science do you do?" Ms. Simmons asked.

"The difficult kind," Mr. Richter responded, hoping that would pre-empt any more questions.

"Do you enjoy it, though? The difficulty, that is," Ms. Simmons went on, "as in, do you appreciate the difficulty as a challenge that must be overcome as opposed to a burden that weighs you down?"

"I suppose I do enjoy it if I am still doing it," Mr. Richter went on. After a moment while searching through the woods, Mr. Richter continued, "And you do enjoy being a nurse?"

"Do I ever!" Ms. Simmons responded. "We get a free meal in the cafeteria each day, and the doctors mostly stay out of our way."

"I would *hate* being a nurse," Mr. Richter replied. "Dealing with sick people must be so defeating."

"But you, yourself, are a man of science, no?" Ms. Simmons asked. "I would think that you appreciate medicine."

"Oh, I do," Mr. Richter responded, "but I much prefer to be on the side of prevention and discovery than on the backend of reactionary treatments and therapeutics."

"I see," Ms. Simmons said while poking through some foliage with a stick she had procured from the forest floor. "Is that why you have that monkey, then? To test out some of your preventative discoveries?"

"*Nein!*" Mr. Richter snapped back. "I do not test my ideas on animals, Ms. Simmons. Besides, the same treatments we use for animals do not always translate well to humans. If you want to cure a human, well, you have to test with a human."

This comment was enough to stop Ms. Simmons cold in her tracks, but that was not the only thing that caused Ms. Simmons to freeze in place.

"Mr. Richter," Ms. Simmons began, "do you see what I am seeing?"

Fred Richter turned in the direction Ms. Simmons was looking. Straight ahead, almost completely covered by overgrown trees, grass, and other foliage, was a small cottage. The tiny house had clearly seen better days: the porch awning was caving in, some of the glass in the windows was broken, and the space where a front door used to be was wide open, letting whatever insects and animals inside.

"Did you know this was here?" Mr. Richter asked.

"Of course not," Ms. Simmons replied. "Did you?"

"Of course not!" Mr. Richter replied.

And, with that, the two oddballs walked slowly toward the small guesthouse, careful not to fall through the open holes in its floor, to see if anyone might be hiding inside.

\*     \*     \*

I had paired Miss Finley and Giles together on purpose, as I knew that while some of our fellow guests were afraid (or intolerant) of Giles and his quirks, Miss Finley had a soft spot in her heart for the man. For reasons you will soon discover, I was never able to ask Miss Finley or Giles for a detailed report on their third of the estate. The best information I was able to gather came from the other two duos. According to the others, Miss Finley and Giles began the search of their assigned grounds at the same time. After several hours had gone by, Mr. Richter and Ms. Simmons reported that they ran into Giles, but not Miss Finley, in a part of the woods behind the house where their two assigned areas overlapped. When asked about Miss Finley, Giles simply pointed back toward the direction of the house and continued looking around his assigned area. When asked about the mysterious, dilapidated cottage Mr. Richter and Ms. Simmons had just discovered, Giles seemed to indicate that he at least understood what it was they were talking about, pointing in the direction of the small cottage from where the trio was standing.

Mr. Richter and Ms. Simmons later reported being torn. Ms. Simmons assumed that Mary Jane Finley was safe and sound, having needed to use the lavatory or something simple that drew her back to the manor without her partner. Mr. Richter was a bit more sceptical. Indeed, he thought it might have been possible that Giles, if truly a cold-blooded killer, could have attacked Miss Finley and left her for dead somewhere within their third of the property, the rest of us being none the wiser.

"Oh, come now," Ms. Simmons reported saying to Mr. Richter. "Don't you think we would have heard her scream? Or that there would be blood on that dolt?" She had a point.

So, without worrying too much, Mr. Richter and Ms. Simmons continued the sweep of their assigned third of the estate and left Giles to explore his.

\*  \*  \*

In the course of typing my detailed retelling of the previous days' events, my eyes grew weary and my back began to ache. I decided that I would go get myself a fresh tea and, of course, some biscuits to nibble on as I completed my assignment for the sake of the group. I had just stepped my foot down onto the first stair to the foyer when my conscience got the better of me.

"I had better see if Mrs. Powell would like some tea," I thought.

So, much against my better judgment, I walked over to Mrs. Powell's room, knocked on her door, and waited for a response.

"Mm-yes?" Mrs. Powell asked. "Who is it?"

"It is I, Dame James, just checking to see if you would like some tea, Mrs. Powell," I said.

"Oh, yes. Please do come in," Mrs. Powell responded.

I found this direction to be quite strange, as Mrs. Powell insisted that she would be locking her door if Walter Simmons were to remain in the house with us, yet when I reached down to open the door, it opened. When I walked into the room, Mrs. Powell was lying under her covers, in bed, makeup fully done up.

"I thought you had intended to lock this," I said as I entered.

"Oh, indeed, I had, but then I climbed into bed and simply could not bring myself to go over to the door," Mrs. Powell whined. "It was simply too far and, I, simply too tired." She yawned.

"Ah, yes, well then," I said. "I am heading down to the kitchen to make myself some tea and was curious as to whether or not you would like some, as well?"

"That would be lovely! How kind of you," Mrs. Powell replied. "I shall take whatever is most convenient…but nothing too strong. You can prepare it however you like…but also with three lumps of sugar, no more, no less…oh, and if there is lemon in the pantry, I will take a spritz of lemon…and cinnamon if there is any. You may have to have a look in the cellar if there is none in the pantry. Oh, and if you don't mind, perhaps something to snack on, as well? A biscuit or some crackers even?"

I was very much regretting my decision to be polite.

"Of course," I replied. "Be right back."

I closed Mrs. Powell's door, instinctively looking in the direction of Mr. Simmons' room. I had not heard him leave all day, and the door to his room was still shut, so I assumed that he was either sleeping, heavily sedated, or both. It was a miracle that Ms. Simmons had managed to keep enough medicine for her brother for the amount of sedation he required.

I walked down the stairs into the foyer and made my way through the dining room into the kitchen. The manor was creepily silent given that everyone else was gone searching the grounds of the estate. I figured I would hurry, make the tea, and head back upstairs as quickly as possible. Even if I did not necessarily believe there was a killer in the house at that moment, the mind is able to play tricks such that it imagines phantoms where there are none and devils in the shadows of dark rooms. I was getting the creepy feeling that someone else was in the manor, a feeling that I was not alone.

The tea kettle whistled, and I poured the hot water in my tea cup and Mrs. Powell's tea cup. I went through all the necessary motions to create a cup of tea that I was still certain would not measure up to Mrs. Powell's liking. I put the remaining hot water in a tea pot on a small carrying tray so that I could take Mrs. Powell her tea while also taking mine to my room. I grabbed the tray and started to head out of the kitchen into the dining room when I remembered: Mrs. Powell wanted snacks.

I set the tray of tea on the dining room table, turned, and went back into the kitchen to grab some biscuits and crackers from the pantry. There were some stale biscuits that I thought about grabbing for Mrs. Powell, but my mother had raised me properly. So, I grabbed fresh biscuits and some crackers so that Doris Powell could have her choice of a snack, and I then went back into the kitchen from the pantry so that I could...

"Ahhhh!" I screamed as I stepped foot back into the kitchen. Between myself and the door from the kitchen to the dining room stood a very tall, very strong Mr. Walter Simmons. He was holding on to the doorframe for support, which had the additional consequence of him blocking my exit from the kitchen into the dining room where I set the tea tray. He was struggling to stand up and was attempting to speak. In that moment, I felt my heart racing. I pitied the poor young man for his condition, but I also found myself afraid for my life. What did he want? Why had he come all the way downstairs in his shape? What was he yelling?

I looked around the kitchen to search for something, anything I could use should Mr. Simmons lunge after me. He was trying to take steps toward me, barely able to stand even though he was making progress forward.

"Knob...immerse," he said.

"Why, hello, Mr. Simmons," I said, acting cool. "And how are you doing this afternoon?"

My eye caught a rolling pin nearby.

"North...western...cinnamon," Walter Simmons mumbled, still lumbering toward me slowly.

"Cinnamon, you say? Why, yes, I just got some for Mrs. Powell's tea. Would *you* like some tea, Mr. Simmons? I would be happy to make you some," I found myself saying, my eyes darting around the room for something I could throw at the man.

"Iambic...actors," Mr. Simmons managed to say, by now far too close for comfort.

"I, I..." I barely managed to get out before Walter Simmons was about to fall on top of me.

Just as Mr. Simmons started leaning forward, an arm appeared around his waist from behind and a hand sprang out from over his shoulder, jabbing a syringe into the side of Walter's neck. The man collapsed backward into the arms of the mysterious person behind him.

"Phew. That was close," Betty Simmons said as she let go of the syringe in her brother's neck and eased his body to the floor of the kitchen.

\*       \*       \*

After I delivered Mrs. Powell her tea (who complained that it took "far too long"), I returned to my room to finish typing up the rest of the notes from the prior evening's search. Ms. Simmons and Mr. Richter had already returned, and Mr. Rossini and Anna returned shortly thereafter. I kept my eye on the time to make sure that I, too, would be downstairs by 4 o'clock, as I hated to keep anyone waiting.

The group had assembled in the parlour. I was surprised to see that even Mrs. Powell managed to come down from her slumber to join the group. The only people not present were Mr. Simmons (thankfully), Miss Finley, and Giles. It was just 3:55pm, so they still had a few minutes to arrive.

"Well, I hope you all managed to find *something*," Mrs. Powell said between coughs. "I fear I have caught whatever it is Mr. Rossini has been sick with the past several days."

Mr. Rossini gave a confused look at Mrs. Powell before beginning, "Has anyone seen Mary Jane? Or Giles for that matter?"

"We saw him," Ms. Simmons replied. "Miss Finley was not with him, but he seemed to indicate she had come back to the manor."

"If she did come back then I have not seen her," Mrs. Powell responded.

"But did you leave your room at all today?" Mr. Richter asked.

"I am here now, aren't I?" Mrs. Powell snapped back.

"They still have a few minutes," I offered. "Perhaps they will walk through the front door any moment now."

The winds were picking up outside and sky was growing darker. It had rained every day since we had been at Raven's Point Manor with just a brief respite of sunshine on occasion each morning. Honestly, if I had wanted weather like this I would have just stayed in London.

The grandfather's clock struck 4:00pm, and there was still no sign of Miss Finley or Giles. Ms. Simmons volunteered to check the rooms of both Miss Finley upstairs and Giles downstairs but reported they were both empty. The group was growing visibly uneasy, no one more so than Mr. Rossini.

"They should be back by now," he insisted, pacing back and forth. "I knew it was a bad idea to let her pair up with that monster."

"Please, Marvin," Anna began, "I am sure they are just running behind."

"Maybe they got lost in the woods?" Ms. Simmons offered before Anna shot her a nasty look as if to say, "That is *not* helping!"

"I am going out to look then," Mr. Rossini said. "It is *my* fault for letting her go with him, so I should be the one to find them."

Mr. Rossini started toward the foyer to grab his coat and hat.

"But the weather, my good man," Mr. Richter said. "You will get soaked!"

"And what else should I do?" Mr. Rossini asked. "Leave Mary Jane out there?" he gestured outside, "With Giles? Giles could have killed Ms. Lavoie for all we know. And Mrs. Flaherty, too! You have seen the man!"

With that, Mr. Richter backed down. It was clear no one would be stopping Mr. Rossini.

"I will be back as soon as I can," Mr. Rossini said, "with Mary Jane."

And with that, Mr. Rossini stepped out to search for the

missing duo.

After a moment of reorganization, I found the group all staring at me. I was not so sure I enjoyed the authority bestowed upon me, as the recognition also came with a great deal of pressure.

"So, as you all know, the purpose of today's search was to determine if the grounds of the estate were harbouring some unknown person that could have potentially been the culprit of Ms. Lavoie's death," I began. "To keep this as orderly as possible, we shall go in order starting with Mr. Rossini and Ms. Winthrop. Anna?"

On cue, Anna stood and began, "Mr. Rossini and I were responsible for the third of the estate that included the front yard, the access road, and the surrounding area. I suppose it is good news that we did not find any person or evidence of a shelter in our search of the grounds. And I suppose it is bad news that the water near the start of the access road is still too high to pass," she paused. "However, there was one peculiar item we came across in our search. At the edge of the property, right where the surrounding lake hugs the estate, we found a small rowboat that had washed ashore."

A few gasps could be heard among the group.

"A boat? Well, that means someone else *could* be on the island!" Mrs. Powell screamed.

"Well, possibly, yes," Anna answered, "but if it is any relief, Mrs. Powell, there were no oars present anywhere near the boat, so it is likely that the boat broke free in the storm and simply washed ashore. For all we know it could have been there for months, years even."

"Interesting," Mr. Richter responded, "and there was nothing else of interest in or around the boat?"

"No," Anna lied.

"Wonderful. Well, thank you, Anna," I said. "And next we will hear from Mr. Richter and Ms. Simmons."

Mr. Richter stood to speak, but Ms. Simmons began, "We found a scary house!"

More gasps came from the crowd.

"The roof was caving in, the wood on the floor was rotting, and it seems like someone could have been living inside," Ms. Simmons went on.

"Now, now, that is not entirely true," Mr. Richter attempted to correct his search partner.

"A house?! Why, I bet someone has been hiding there this entire time!" Mrs. Powell screamed out again.

"No, Mrs. Powell," Mr. Richter said. "There was no evidence to suggest that anyone has been living in the abandoned guesthouse."

"But who knew it was there?" Mrs. Powell went on. "I am certain Mrs. Flaherty would have known about this house!" She paused as a flash of realisation crossed her mind, "And Giles!"

I suddenly became a bit more concerned about Giles' absence, particularly because his search partner, Miss Finley, was still missing, too.

"Listen," Mr. Richter began, "this small house is in no condition to provide shelter to anyone. There are holes in the ceiling, the wood is rotten, and the interior of the home is exposed to the elements. I believe its electricity is still working, but I highly doubt…"

"But you cannot *cough, cough* completely *cough* rule out the *cough* possibility," Mrs. Powell said while suffering a coughing spell.

"No, I suppose I cannot," Mr. Richter replied, "but it is just highly unlikely."

"Then you cannot say *cough, cough* that someone is not *cough* possibly," Mrs. Powell broke into a fierce coughing episode and was having difficulty catching her breath.

Everyone just sat and stared at the poor woman while she was gasping for air.

"Can someone please get this woman some tea with honey?" I demanded, surprised that everyone seemed too paralyzed to help.

At that moment, everyone but Ms. Simmons jumped up

and ran to the kitchen to get Mrs. Powell some tea. The woman continued hacking and heaving uncontrollably, her eyes now watering from all this commotion.

When she finally stopped and caught her breath, Mrs. Powell looked at me and said, "This is why I don't leave my room," she paused, "the world is a filthy, dirty place."

\*　　　\*　　　\*

The rest of the evening was spent waiting for Mr. Rossini to return, with everyone hopeful for a surprise reappearance of Miss Finley and Giles. Admittedly, as the evening grew late, my hope of any of them returning safely was dwindling.

I was sitting in the library reading near the fire when Anna sidled up beside me on the sofa and whispered, "Look at this."

I looked down and saw that Anna was handing me what appeared to be a hospital medical bracelet.

"What is this? Where did you get it?" I asked.

"It was hidden within the small rowboat I mentioned earlier," she responded. "I did not want to alarm the group, so I did not present it when you asked if there was anything else we came across. I apologize for that."

"No need to apologize," I said, as I extended the ripped bracelet in my hands. "Mabel Merriweather," I read aloud, "Aspen Pines Mental Asylum?"

I looked up and saw the fear in Anna's eyes.

"Now I definitely understand why you did not share this, my dear girl."

\*　　　\*　　　\*

The grandfather's clock struck 11 o'clock pm, and none of the three missing guests had yet returned.

"We should go to bed," Mr. Richter said to the group assembled in the parlour. "There's no use staying up to wait for what may never come."

Mrs. Powell had already retired about an hour before, which relieved most of us who had grown tired of hearing her dry cough. Mr. Simmons never came down, which was also a relief, but Ms. Simmons went back and forth to check and make sure he was sufficiently sedated. At the moment, it was just Ms. Simmons, Mr. Richter, Anna, and myself waiting for the others to return.

We all stood up and began the trek upstairs to our rooms when the front door opened. When I turned around, I was hoping to see all three of the missing guests standing safely in the foyer. However, only Mr. Rossini was there, drenched from the rain and shivering from the cold winds that had also picked up.

"Nothing," he said shaking. "I found nothing."

He was visibly upset. Mr. Richter and Anna ran down the stairs to grab the man's coat and hat before leading him to the parlour to sit and warm himself by the massive fireplace. Ms. Simmons and I walked back down to the parlour, as well, to be supportive. Mr. Rossini just sat in his chair, shivering, staring straight ahead.

"I walked everywhere," Mr. Rossini said, "*everywhere* I could go on the estate. I looked in the forest. I looked along the access road. I even used my flashlight to see if anything was floating in the water. Nothing. Absolutely nothing."

We all just sat still, uncertain of what we should say.

"It is my fault for bringing her here," Mr. Rossini went on. "She would not have been here had it not been for me." We all had some idea of what he was talking about, but no one pressed him to explain himself in this sad moment.

"What I do not understand is *where* they could be?" Mr. Rossini continued. "They certainly could not keep on the move in this weather. And they had not taken shelter anywhere that I could see. I even came across a small, old guesthouse, but there was no one inside."

I do not know what it was that sparked the idea in Anna's head, but something Mr. Rossini had just said prompted her to look at me with a knowing look in her eyes.

"Dame James," Anna began, "if Giles is not in his room and he is not out on the estate grounds, there is one other place he *could* be."

Mr. Richter, picking up on Anna's logic from his search with her the previous day, chimed in to say what I was also thinking, "The attic."

*      *      *

Despite typing up all the notes from the top-to-bottom search of Raven's Point Manor, I had almost forgotten that Anna and Mr. Richter had found the peculiar space in the attic where someone had painted portrait after portrait of Giles, even recently judging from the paintings. Although it may have seemed like a bit of a long shot, the attic was one place on the property that Mr. Rossini had not yet looked for Miss Finley or Giles. As much as I hated to think it, might it have been possible that Giles had done something to Miss Finley and then hid himself away in the attic?

Before I had much time to think, Mr. Rossini stood up, looked at Mr. Richter, and said, "Let's go. Now!"

Anna, Ms. Simmons, and I stood and followed the two gentlemen as they went up the foyer stairs to the second floor and then continued upward to the narrow staircase that led to the attic. Mr. Rossini and Mr. Richter led the group out of an abundance of caution. It was unclear, after all, if Giles was a victim in this mess or a murder suspect.

The attic was dark and quiet, as one might expect, and the flashes of lightening through the windows on either side of the long room made for an eerie ambiance. The pitter-patter of the rain on the roof and the howling of the wind in the rafters made us feel as though we were in the centre of the storm now raging outside.

As the group approached the far corner of the attic where the easel had been set up, we could make out the figure of a man about Giles' size, sitting in the chair near the window.

"It's him! He's here," Mr. Rossini whispered to the group.

"Giles? Giles, is that you?" Mr. Richter called out.

No response.

"Giles, we are not here to hurt you," Mr. Richter continued, "we just want to make sure you are alright."

Still no answer. Giles was sitting in the chair, which had been slightly repositioned such that he was now facing outward toward the window with his back facing the easel and our approaching group.

"Giles, can you hear me?" Mr. Richter began again.

The group stopped and let Mr. Rossini and Mr. Richter approach the young man sitting in the chair. Giles did not turn around, even as the men approached. The two gentlemen walked on either side of the chair, making their way toward the front before turning around to face Giles.

As they did this, my eyes were drawn to the easel, where someone had painted over the original image of Giles' portrait. Whoever it was wrote the same thing over and over again, "Kathleen Flaherty. Kathleen Flaherty. Kathleen Flaherty."

"Dear God," Mr. Rossini screamed.

Kathleen Flaherty. Kathleen Flaherty. Kathleen Flaherty.

Mr. Richter pointed his torch toward Giles' face, blinding the rest of us with the light.

Kathleen Flaherty. Kathleen Flaherty. Kathleen Flaherty.

"His eyes," Mr. Richter began, "they have been slashed!"

Kathleen Flaherty. Kathleen Flaherty. Kathleen Flaherty.

Mr. Richter turned the chair to face the group of us still standing in the shadows. Much to our horror, we saw poor Giles, tied to the chair, mouth stuffed full of paintbrushes, with four slashes forming two Xs where his eyes used to be.

Captain Liberty. Captain Liberty. Captain Liberty.

Giles was dead. Closer inspection revealed a deep

puncture wound in his back that likely pierced his heart. It was at that precise moment, seeing Giles dead in that chair and the repeated name on the painting, the same name scribbled time and time again in Giles' notebook, that it struck me: Giles had *not* been chanting "Captain Liberty" over and over again.

No. Giles had been repeating Kathleen Flaherty's name the whole time.

Captain Liberty. Kathleen Flaherty.
Captain Liberty. Kathleen Flaherty.

# 9 | ALLIANCES FALL APART

The discovery of Giles' dead body in the attic significantly changed our current situation. Although several of us had been convinced that Ms. Lavoie's death was no accident or suicide, we could not necessarily *prove* that it had been murder. The lack of any corroborating evidence from the searches of the manor and estate grounds actually spoke against the possibility of homicide.

However, now that Giles' body had been discovered, tied up and maimed, it was impossible to deny that something sinister was afoot. Even more chilling was the fact that someone had been *in* the manor while the rest of us were also present without our awareness. I did not want to think it, of course, but someone among us could potentially be a murderer.

Mr. Rossini and Mr. Richter took Giles' body down to the wine cellar before everyone went to bed. There were now four bodies—*four*—decaying slowly in the wine cellar. Now, I am normally not one to become frightened or scared easily, but I was starting to wonder whether *any* of us would make it out of Raven's Point Manor alive. I prayed the rain would die down so that the access road could reopen. I imagine those of us still living would make a sprint for it if it meant the difference between our survival or murder at the hands of an insane person.

The next morning, the search for Miss Finley began early. Mr. Rossini skipped breakfast altogether before starting out with Ms. Simmons who agreed to join him on the search. Mr. Richter had planned to join Mr. Rossini, but the gentlemen were worried about leaving the ladies alone in the manor without a man present. Mrs. Powell, stubbornly old-fashioned, found this charming, whereas I, much more forward thinking, found this insulting. In any case, it was determined that Mr. Richter would stay behind with Mrs. Powell, Anna, myself, and Mr. Simmons.

Shortly before she left with Mr. Rossini, Ms. Simmons asked Mr. Richter if he had within his resources some sort of sedative that would be alright to give to her brother. I imagine that her supply was now dwindling given that their extended stay here at Raven's Point Manor had not been planned. Despite my horrific encounter with Mr. Simmons in the kitchen the day prior, I felt for the poor man if his sedatives were wearing off and he was running out of medicine. The way Ms. Simmons described her brother's condition suggested he would feel a great deal of pain if not constantly sedated.

Before I could hear Mr. Richter's reply, a visibly worsened Mrs. Powell hacked in my direction and asked if I would make her "some of that tea [I] made yesterday." When I asked her for clarification about what that meant, she simply responded, "You know, that tea I liked."

Marvellous.

*       *       *

Mr. Richter, Anna, and I decided that we would spend most of our time that day in the parlour so we had a clear view of the front door should anyone return. We had been instructed to lock the front door and to open it for no one other than Mr. Rossini and Ms. Simmons.

Mr. Richter busied himself by reading some of the papers he had brought along for his trip, while Anna and I played some games of chess and read some books we found in the library. To help stifle the silence, Mr. Richter had put a record on the Victrola. The first song was the catchy tune "Sweet Georgia Brown," which, aside from bringing a bit of joy to an otherwise gloomy time, was just loud enough for Anna and I have to have a private conversation beyond earshot of Mr. Richter.

"So, I have been thinking," Anna began, looking back to Mr. Richter to make sure he could not hear. "There *must* be some relationship between Giles and Mrs. Flaherty, one that extends beyond their working relationship."

Admittedly, this thought had been weighing on my mind since seeing Mrs. Flaherty's name written all over the canvas where Giles' dead body was discovered.

"I concur," I said to Anna. "To think he had been telling us Mrs. Flaherty's name over and over again. And to think that she deliberately misled us into thinking he was saying, 'Captain Liberty,' the whole time!"

"Precisely," Anna replied, "which makes me think that Mrs. Flaherty was trying to hide *something*, but I just cannot quite figure out what."

"Well, don't forget, I found that photo of Mr. and Mrs. Flaherty with a child that was too old to be Elliott Radcliffe, yet Mrs. Flaherty never mentioned that she and Mr. Flaherty had a child," I added.

"So, perhaps it is possible that the Flahertys *did* have a child but kept it secret for some reason?" Anna went on, "maybe something was wrong with the child and they were ashamed? Lots of people do that, you know, leave their children at the steps of an orphanage at the first sign of trouble. Maybe they were just embarrassed to have produced a child with…problems?"

I saw what she was getting at.

"Do you mean to think that Giles was actually Mrs. Flaherty's son?" I asked.

"I do not know for sure, but it *is* possible, right?" Anna went on, "We do not know much about the man's history other than the fact that Mrs. Flaherty said he served in the war, which is what led to his mental deficiency."

"That's true," I replied.

"But one could just as easily argue for a reality in which

Giles was the disabled son of Mr. and Mrs. Flaherty, one whose needs she would have to tend to for his entire life, a *burden*," Anna went on. "I know that sounds harsh, and *I* would not see such a child as a burden, but you saw the way Mrs. Flaherty treated him, as if he were more an animal than her own flesh and blood."

I was quite impressed by Anna's thoughtful analysis of the situation. She was correct, and she approached the case like any one of the detectives in my books would have. Inspector Alastair Evans would have been so impressed!

Anna finished her thought just as "Sweet Georgia Brown" ended and "Dinah" began.

"I know we cannot be certain at this point," Anna went on, "but I do think it would be prudent to search for more information about Giles and Mrs. Flaherty. Something seems off."

*News is spreadin' about our weddin', I hear church bells ringin'...*

"It is funny you say that, Anna," I started, "because I have been having some strange thoughts of my own."

"Go on," Anna replied.

"Well, ever since Mrs. Flaherty told me the story of the Radcliffe family," I said, gesturing toward the painting of the Radcliffes above the large fireplace, "I could not help but wonder if Elliott Radcliffe were truly *dead*."

Anna sat back in her chair.

"To your point about a need for evidence, I must admit that I have none other than my own daydreaming," I continued, "but there was also no evidence that the young Radcliffe drowned as the authorities suggested he did. For all anyone knows, the boy ran away and lived a nice, long life and remains alive to this day!"

*Dinah, is there anyone finer, in the state of Carolina? If there is and you know her, show her!...*

"Huh," Anna began, "that *is* something. But how old would Elliott Radcliffe be now if he were to have survived?"

"Well, that's just it. If what Mrs. Flaherty said is to be believed, then the young man would be in his late 20s or early 30s by now," I answered.

Just at that moment, Mr. Richter stood from his chair, which made a bit of a commotion. Anna and I looked over, his eyes caught ours, and he gave a friendly smile before stretching, reaching for a different paper, and then sitting back down to read.

"So, it *is* possible that Elliott Radcliffe is still alive somewhere out there?" Anna asked.

"Very much so," I went on, "except that he may not necessarily be somewhere *out there*."

"What do you mean, Dame James?"

"Maybe it is that he is somewhere very much *in here*," I said, gesturing around us.

Anna gasped, which caused Mr. Richter to look up from his reading.

"Oh, I thought I had checkmate!" Anna pretended. She was a clever girl. I had clearly made the correct decision hiring her.

Once Mr. Richter was again lost in his reading, Anna began once more, "Do you mean to say that Elliott Radcliffe is the mysterious person stalking the manor?"

"I do not know," I replied. "I think it could be possible he is somewhere on the estate, maybe coming back to claim what is rightfully his according to Mrs. Flaherty's story. But another thought also crossed my mind."

"What's that?" Anna asked eagerly.

I paused for a second, glanced over to Mr. Richter, then leaned into Anna and said, "What if Mr. Radcliffe is someone we *know*?"

*Dinah, with her Dixie eyes blazin', how I love to sit and gaze in, to the eyes of Dinah Lee!...*

"But who? Mr. Richter? Mr. Simmons? Mr. Rossini?" Anna asked.

"Probably not Rossini," I responded. "He's a bit too old, I think. But the other two, well, perhaps it is preposterous, but stranger things have happened."

"But if it is Mr. Simmons, what about his sister Ms.

Simmons?" Anna asked.

"Well, Mr. Richter suggested that they could be working together," I responded. "Some sort of conspiracy perhaps? Maybe a ruse to gain entry back to the estate to claim what is rightfully his? A pretend sister? A fake illness?"

"There was no car," Anna added, "and it is strange they knew to walk along the access road in the dark to find the manor."

"Precisely," I responded.

*Yet, every night, my, how I shake with fright, because my Dinah might change her mind about me…*

"Well, and Mr. Richter seems to have had quite the nice upbringing himself," Anna added. "A learned man like him probably came from money. I wonder if he isn't Elliott Radcliffe himself. Even his initials are similar: Fred Richter, F.R., Elliott Radcliffe, E.R."

I had not even thought of that. Anna was good!

"This song reminds me," Anna continued, "you probably knew that Miss Finley and Mr. Rossini have been engaged in an affair for some time?"

I nodded.

"Well, during our walk about the estate I found out that Mr. Rossini was planning to end the affair during this holiday together," Anna said.

I gasped. "That explains the bickering Mrs. Powell claimed to hear from her room!" I realized.

"Yes," Anna confirmed, "and it also makes me worried about Miss Finley's whereabouts. Although she seemed to have her wits about her, I worry what the young girl might have done if she thought her relationship was coming to an end."

I did not follow Anna's logic.

"What I mean is, perhaps she was distraught over this unfortunate news and ran off," Anna suggested. "She could have harmed herself even or, worse yet, harmed someone else?"

"People have been known to do crazy things over love

and heartache," I added.

"Mr. Rossini seems genuinely concerned, but I wonder if he knows more than he is letting on," Anna said.

The song on the record player switched from "Dinah" to "Bye, Bye, Blackbird."

*Pack up all my cares and woes, feeling low here I go, bye, bye, blackbird...*

"I love this song," Mr. Richter announced, which caused Anna and me to jump. We had gotten so lost in our conversation that we forgot all about Mr. Richter.

"I am beginning to think that there *is* someone here who knows more than they are saying," Anna whispered.

"Quite possibly several people," I added. "We cannot rule out the possibility that two or more people are conspiring against the rest of us for some reason, whether that be the Simmons siblings, Mr. Rossini and Miss Finley, or anyone else for that matter."

"Well, I suggest we had better stick together then, Dame James," Anna said as she stood, placed her hand on my shoulder, and walked over to the fireplace to toss in another piece of firewood.

*Nobody seems to love or understand me, and all the hard luck stones they keep handing me...*

Perhaps it was just the lighting in the room or my old eyes playing tricks on me, but when Anna turned around from the fireplace with the painting of the Radcliffes just behind her head, an important detail came to mind.

When Mrs. Flaherty told me the story of Elliott Radcliffe, she only ever referred to the third Radcliffe as "the child." I remembered finding it odd at the time; so odd, in fact, that I took another glance at the painting that first night to see if I could not determine the gender of the young Radcliffe. Sure, Elliott tended to be a boy's name, but there were female Elliotts I knew. The child was so young in the painting that it was not possible to truly determine if it were a boy or a girl. In that moment, the dark features of the child contrasting with his or her pale skin bore a striking resemblance to the woman standing between me and the painting: Anna.

*Where somebody shines the light, yes, I'm coming on home tonight, bye, bye, blackbird...*

"*I suggest we had better stick together then, Dame James.*" Anna's words echoed in my brain.

*Bye, bye, blackbird.*

*     *     *

The sun had already started setting before Mr. Rossini and Ms. Simmons returned. We had not heard much from Mrs. Powell who seemed to be fighting an even more aggressive cough than she faced the previous day. I had taken her some tea with honey to help throughout the day, but I am not sure she was making any progress.

The search of the estate turned up nothing. No evidence. No sign that Miss Finley had been walking around the grounds. Mr. Rossini had convinced himself no foul play likely happened at the hands of Giles given the state we had found Giles in the night before, but he was clearly very concerned about Miss Finley's whereabouts.

"It just doesn't make any sense," Mr. Rossini said to the small group of us gathered in the parlour. "First, Mary Jane and Giles go missing. Then, Giles winds up dead but Mary Jane is still gone. And there are no signs of life anywhere outside this manor."

The group sat in silence, partly out of respect for the missing Miss Finley and partly because no one really knew what to say.

"There is one possibility I have not heard you consider," Ms. Simmons said, breaking the silence.

Mr. Rossini looked over to the woman who had laid herself out awkwardly on the sofa, perhaps tired from a day of walking the estate grounds with Mr. Rossini.

"All day long you talked about, 'Poor Miss Finley,' and what you would do if you found the person who took her,"

Ms. Simmons continued.

"And? What is your point?" Mr. Rossini asked.

"Well, what if Miss Finley is no victim of kidnapping? No victim of anything even?" Ms. Simmons went on.

"Do you mean you think she's playing some sort of sick joke? Like she is hiding somewhere?" Mr. Rossini asked.

"Maybe," Ms. Simmons said, standing up and shrugging indifferently. "Or maybe *she* is the one who killed Giles?"

At this point, Mr. Rossini was fuming. He started saying something in Italian, which I am probably happy I did not understand given the tone of his voice.

"You had better apologize, Ms. Simmons!" Mr. Rossini raged.

"For what? I am just proposing another idea," Ms. Simmons went on, "you do not have to get all bent out of shape about it. Besides, can you prove that she didn't?

"Didn't what?" Mr. Rossini asked.

"Kill Giles," Ms. Simmons responded.

"That seems outrageous," I found myself saying despite trying to stay out of such disputes if I could help it. "We all saw how much the girl cared for Giles, even coming to the poor young man's defence at every opportunity. Why would she kill the very person she fought to death to defend?"

"Why does *anyone* kill someone?" Ms. Simmons asked.

The group stared at her without answering.

"Maybe she was insane?" Ms. Simmons suggested.

Anna and I glanced at each other knowing about the bracelet she had found. Could it have been Miss Finley's?

"Maybe he tried to attack her?" Ms. Simmons continued.

No one said anything but, instead, watched Ms. Simmons circle around them in the room like an alpha predator circling its prey in the wild.

"Maybe she was a simple girl, jilted by her lover, and just found the easiest man to take out?" Ms. Simmons proposed.

This last suggestion was enough to rile Mr. Rossini.

"How dare you suggest…" Mr. Rossini began, but before he could finish there was a loud commotion in the foyer.

Someone was plodding down the stairs quite loudly.

"Mrs. Powell?" Anna asked. "Surely that cannot be her."

Within seconds, the source of the commotion appeared in the doorway of the parlour.

Walter Simmons, breathing heavily and leaning against the wall for support, raised his hand to point at his sister, Betty.

In between inhaling and exhaling large breaths, Mr. Simmons spoke, "Not...a...nurse..."

Betty Simmons, now across the room near the fireplace, began, "Walter? Walter, you have not had your medicine, have you?"

She walked toward her brother.

"Come now. Let's go upstairs and..." she said.

"Not...Walter...Simmons..." the man said to our group. "Ripley...Walter...Ripley."

The two were now circling the group opposite one another, like two sumo wrestlers about to begin a match.

"I am...a doctor," Walter was able to get out. It was clear that whatever sedatives had kept him in his strange, vegetative state the past several days were wearing off.

"Walter, you are imagining things again," his sister said in a soothing voice, trying her best to calm him down.

"She...is not...a nurse," the man said looking at Betty.

"Walter, that is enough," Betty replied, picking up her pace a bit.

Mr. Rossini, Anna, Mr. Richter, and I sat in shock in the middle of the room while Betty and Walter continued walking in circles around us. Admittedly, the whole charade was mildly entertaining at first, but then the situation escalated...drastically.

Grabbing a fire poker from near the fireplace, Mr. Walter Simmons—or Mr. Walter Ripley depending on whom you believed at this point—raised his new weapon like an épée and said, "Escaped. Escaped."

"That's right," Ms. Simmons said, also grabbing a poker

from the collection of fireplace tools. "We got you out of the hospital and need to get you home to mom and dad." Betty Simmons raised her fire poker, as well, until it truly felt like we were in the centre of a fencing match.

"No. Not right," Mr. Simmons/Ripley said, still struggling a bit but coming to his senses more and more.

"You need to snap out of it, Walter," Betty Simmons said, her voice a bit sterner. She grabbed a drink from the table and threw its contents in Walter's direction, drenching him in whiskey.

"Not nurse. I doctor," Walter said. It was either the case that the poor man had truly lost his senses or he was struggling to communicate something important to the rest of us about who the two of them were. At this point, I was not sure whom to believe or trust.

"Honestly, Walter, we have been through this a million times," Ms. Simmons went on. "We do not have any more medicine, so you are going to have to cooperate. Can you cooperate? For me? For mom and dad?"

Betty grabbed another drink from the table and tried to splash Walter's face with it, missing and drenching his clothing.

"Maybe it's…the weather," Walter said.

At this point, Betty seemed quite fed up. She grabbed a large decanter from the table and threw its stopper to the floor. She flung the contents toward Walter repeatedly. By now, Walter's clothing was drenched in alcohol and the rest of us also had a light misting of liquor, as well.

"Maybe it's…weather," Walter said.

"Walter, you don't know what you are saying," Betty laughed, trying to appease her brother's condition. "Come, now, let's just calm down and we can get you back to…"

"Mabel…Merriweather," Walter managed to get out.

Anna and I looked at each other and knew precisely what the name meant. Mr. Rossini, who had been with Anna when the medical bracelet was discovered, also stood up.

"Mabel Merriweather?" Betty laughed. "Who is that?

Silly, boy, let's just go upstairs now, and…"

"Mabel Merriweather. Insane," Walter continued. "Drowned children. I…doctor."

"What are you even saying right now, Walter?!" Betty asked the man. She looked at us and continued, "I am so sorry you all have to witness this. He's usually never this bad…"

Out of nowhere, Mr. Rossini spoke up, "We know, Mabel."

Betty Simmons stopped dead in her tracks. The colour left her face and her eyes widened. She began to clench her jaw tightly. Her nostrils flared as she began breathing heavily.

"What, exactly, do you know, Mr. Rossini?" Betty asked, fuming.

"We know you are *not* Betty Simmons," Anna said, rising in support of Mr. Rossini, "and we know that you *are* Mabel Merriweather, a patient of Aspen Pines Mental Asylum." Anna pulled the bracelet from her handbag.

"An *escaped* patient from what we gather," I said, standing in support of both Anna and Mr. Rossini.

"Well, congratulations, detectives," Mabel said. "To be honest, I cannot believe how stupid you were to let two complete strangers into a home, in the middle of a rainstorm, completely unannounced."

"To be fair," Mr. Richter said, standing up, "that was Mrs. Flaherty who was stupid enough to let you in. I imagine the rest of us would have been just as likely to leave you outside in the rain."

"Oh, the scientist is a comedian!" Mabel responded. "We would have probably been better off staying out in the rain. Look at this place! Four people dead. One missing. Is this supposed to make a person feel *safe*?"

Mabel and Walter were still circling the group, pokers raised in the air.

"How did you do it, Mabel?" Anna asked. "How did you kill Ms. Lavoie and the others?"

"And where is Mary Jane?" Mr. Rossini demanded.

"I don't know what you're talking about," Mabel replied, "I did not kill anyone."

"That's…not true," Walter said, staring at Mabel.

"Oh, okay. Fine. Yeah, I maybe killed a few of my children, so what?" Mabel went on, "What mother doesn't want to do that from time to time?"

"Three…children," Walter added.

"Walter, Walter, Walter. That really is enough out of you," Mabel said. "No one would help, you know? My husband left. My family had nothing to do with me. My real parents left me alone when I was just a child. It was just me. It was *always* just me. Then it was just me, and three hungry, crying children. It was the crying that got me," she stopped moving, "the constant crying, all day and all night."

She started laughing as Walter Ripley slowly crept closer and closer to her.

"I had no help. I had no other option, really. No other option. I mean, what would *you* do?" the woman said, pointing to me. "Would you suffer your whole life knowing your children are just as miserable? Would you?"

"No, I don't suppose I would," I said calmly, hoping my voice would soothe the woman.

Mabel grabbed a bottle off the table and took a drink. She continued, "He didn't tell you the full story, you know. I tried to kill myself, too. I tried to drown all of us. ALL of us, Walter. You didn't tell them that. Why didn't you tell them that?"

"I'm…sorry, Mabel. Calm…down," Dr. Walter Ripley said, still making his way toward Mabel.

The woman stood next to the large fireplace and began to stare at the flames. She went on, "I would have died with them. I would have. But because they got me out alive, then *I* was the crazy one. *I* was the one who needed help. *I* was the one who needed to be put in a home."

Mabel Merriweather started hitting herself in the head.

"I had to get out. I had to go see my children. They *needed* me," she said as she began to cry.

"Mabel...calm down...it's okay," Walter Ripley said. "Come...with me...now."

"Dr. Ripley, I didn't mean to," the woman started sobbing, "I just wanted out, and I...I just didn't..."

Mabel was now sobbing uncontrollably into her hands while the rest of us just stared on at the scene unfolding before us.

Dr. Ripley was now just upon Ms. Merriweather, and it seemed as though he would be able to calm her down enough to sedate her and get her to bed upstairs. It was amusing to me how we had thought, all along, that Mabel was the caretaker and Walter the one needing care. Not only were the roles reversed, but they also weren't even siblings to begin with!

"Funny," I thought to myself, "they *do* look so similar. I would have believed..."

As I was thinking this, Mabel raised her head up from her hands, grabbed the bottle of whiskey she had just set down on the table, and broke the bottle on the mantle just above Dr. Ripley's head. What took place next happened so quickly that I had to replay the scene in my mind, time and time again, just to make sense of it all. Dr. Ripley, drenched in alcohol from the repeated dousing from Mabel, lunged in to grab Ms. Merriweather who, whether the result of premeditated planning or animal instinct, pushed Dr. Ripley into the parlour's massive fireplace. Drenched in alcohol, the poor man's clothes caught fire at once.

Instinctively, the four of us in the middle of the room stood up to help Dr. Ripley, who was still in a weakened condition from the sedatives wearing off as it was. At that moment, Mabel turned to face us, swinging the fire poker she kept beside her.

"*Now* you want to help?" Mabel asked. "Where were you when *I* needed help?"

"Mabel, please," Anna begged, "let us just help Dr. Ripley from the fireplace."

"You'll help him before you help me?" Mabel whined. "Why does everyone else always get help before Mabel gets help?"

"Ms. Merriweather, please," Mr. Richter pleaded. "He will die if we don't save him."

"What about me?" Mabel asked. "What will happen to me if no one saves *me*?"

The woman had lost all sense of control at this point, but the rest of us felt the urgency of getting to the fireplace in enough time to save Dr. Ripley.

Without speaking the plan aloud, our group of four divided in two, Mr. Rossini and Anna on one side, Mr. Richter and I on the other. We approached the fireplace from either side, which forced Mabel to try to fend us off from both directions.

"You'll be sorry you saved him," she yelled. "You'll be so sorry!"

She raised the poker high in the air, which I was certain was going to come down squarely against my head or the head of one of my fellow helpers attempting to save Dr. Ripley. Instead, she brought the poker down and swung it against the bottles of alcohol on the table, creating a confetti of glass pieces in the room. At that moment, she sprinted from the parlour into the foyer and then out the front door into the rain.

"Go after her!" Mr. Rossini yelled to Mr. Richter as the former tried to reach into the fire to grab Dr. Ripley.

Mr. Richter ran to the front door as quickly as he could. Anna and I helped Mr. Rossini retrieve Walter Ripley from the fireplace, pulling a curtain down to help put out the flames on his body.

Dr. Ripley had only been in the fireplace for a moment, but the alcohol on his clothing and skin had clearly accelerated the burning. His face was barely recognizable, and his breathing had become more laboured. The three of us laid him down away from the heat of the fire, trying to avoid all the pieces of shattered glass now littering the floor.

"Dr. Ripley," Anna began, "Dr. Ripley, can you hear me?"

The lobes of the man's ears had been badly burned, but it seemed he was still able to hear. He looked up at Anna as she spoke her words, then his eyes moved to Mr. Rossini, before landing on me.

"Dame...James," the badly burned man managed to say, "so...sorry. Tried...to warn...you."

My mind flashed back to the day before in the kitchen when Walter was lunging toward me saying things that sounded like gibberish.

"Knob immerse," I said to myself. "Not a nurse?"

"North western cinnamon," I thought. "Not Walter Simmons?"

"Iambic actors," I repeated in my head. "I am a doctor?"

Of course, the poor man had been trying to tell me the truth just before Ms. Simmons—Mabel Merriweather—silenced him. If only I would have figured it out sooner. If only I would have been able to stay calm and understand him.

The man's body shook a bit, his eyes rolled backward, and the convulsions began. He looked to be in complete pain, with burns covering every part of his body.

"He's going into shock," Anna said.

And then, almost as soon as his movement began, it stopped.

No more shaking, no more convulsions, and no more breathing.

Dr. Ripley was dead.

As I tried to collect my thoughts from what had just transpired, I realized that this episode was more meaningful than we had yet realized. With Mabel Merriweather now exposed we may very well have identified the person who murdered Giles, Claudette Lavoie, and potentially the others, as well. As shocked as I was in that very moment, I found myself feeling an odd sense of relief, too.

That relief was short lived.

161

"She's gone," Mr. Richter yelled, appearing at the front door.

"She got away."

# 10 | A BREAKTHROUGH IN THE CASE

I imagine no one slept very well that night.

Ms. Merriweather was somewhere on the grounds of the Radcliffe estate and had become the top suspect in the murder of at least three people if not more. Before heading to our rooms, our group of four went to Mrs. Powell's room to make her aware of the situation. Finding her door locked, we opted to just let the poor woman sleep. She had not been feeling well anyway, and we could just tell her the update in the morning.

The rest of us vowed to stay locked in our rooms until 8 o'clock exactly. The grandfather's clock would chime, and we would open our doors simultaneously so that if Ms. Merriweather had returned in the night, there would be a group of us at the ready. We just had to hope Mrs. Powell would not wake up earlier than that, but if history were any indication, Mrs. Powell would likely stay in bed for some time.

Mr. Rossini, Mr. Richter, Anna, and I stepped into our respective rooms at the same time, promptly locking our doors behind us. As I had done the previous few nights, I placed a chair against my door's handle and placed some of my luggage in the seat of the chair to add extra weight. The window was too high to reach and the wall outside too difficult to scale to break in through the window, but I still made certain the window was latched and the curtain pulled just to be extra cautious.

As I readied for bed, my mind could not help but run through all the permutations of the previous days' events. I pictured Mabel hiding in a dark corner of her room at the asylum, waiting for her nurse to enter so that she could jump out and attack the unsuspecting woman. Once knocked out, Ms. Merriweather might have taken the nurse's uniform, grabbed some medicine vials, and proceeded to sneak out of the hospital. Just as she was about to make a clean break, she's found out, so she grabs hold of a doctor nearby and holds a syringe to his skull. She backs out of the hospital threatening to kill her hostage if anyone tries to follow her. She makes it out of the hospital and begins injecting Dr. Ripley with light sedatives to keep him mobile enough but otherwise incoherent. She runs, without a plan, until she happens upon a small boat along the lake. She paralyzes Dr. Ripley, puts him in the boat, and arrives to the Radcliffe estate, unaware of her location. She rips off her bracelet and hides it in the boat and throws the oars into the lake to prevent Dr. Ripley from escaping should he come to and break free from her control. The two of them then walk through the rain looking for shelter until they stumble upon Raven's Point Manor, and that's when her ruse begins. She will be Betty Simmons, nurse and caretaker of her disabled brother, Walter Simmons. As long as she kept him sedated, she would have nothing to worry about.

It was unclear whether Mabel murdered Mrs. Flaherty or Mr. Powell, as those deaths seemed just as likely to be accidental as deliberate, but jealous of Ms. Lavoie's success and irritated by her judgmental attitude, Mabel likely stabbed Claudette Lavoie during one of her trips upstairs to "check on her brother." Realizing that Giles would be an easy target because of his mental deficiencies, Mabel then lured the groundskeeper up to the attic, tied him to the chair, and slashed his eyes, the twisted mark of a mentally ill murderer. The cruel, calculated way Mabel murdered Dr. Ripley shed some light on the operations of Ms. Merriweather's twisted mind. Upon realizing she was trapped and that Dr. Ripley was going to reveal the truth, Mabel acted just like a cornered animal. Shifting into a flight or fight response, Mabel fought first by deliberately dousing the doctor in alcohol and pushing him into the fire before fleeing to the grounds of the estate. It was unclear what Mabel did to Miss Finley, but I was convinced that it was just a matter of time until we found poor Mary Jane somewhere outside on the Radcliffe estate, another unsuspecting victim of an uninvited madwoman.

I was a bit disappointed that I had not realised Ms. Simmons was a murderer until it was in front of my face. She had acted in such a peculiar manner from the moment she and her "brother" arrived, carrying no luggage in the rain and telling a story that had contradicting details. When Anna reported back that the walking group found no car along the access road, I should have pressed the strange woman further for details or at least some explanation. It might have saved so many lives, but who really knows for sure? Trying to predict the behaviours of an insane person is a futile endeavour.

As I replayed the events of the past several days, looking at them now through a different lens informed by Mabel Merriweather's truth, everything seemed clearer. I am not sure when I fell asleep, exactly, but my dream that night was extraordinarily bizarre. I suppose this should not be too surprising given the events of the evening, but the dream was *so* vivid. It began with Kath Flaherty, albeit a younger version of the woman, like the one pictured in the photographs I found during the search of her room. She opened the massive front door to Raven's Point Manor, and there, standing in order from left-to-right, were Ms. Lavoie, Mr. Powell, Giles, and Dr. Ripley. Beyond Dr. Ripley was a bit of a space and then, left-to-right, stood Miss Finley, myself, Mr. Rossini, Anna, and then Mr. Richter seated on a large throne that had been added to the foyer. Atop the throne was a single, jet-black raven, spreading its wings and ruffling its feathers every so often.

I realised upon seeing the group and myself, in particular, that I was not seeing the world through *my* eyes, but through the eyes of some stranger. At first, I was worried it was through Ms. Merriweather's murderous eyes, but my fear was assuaged when a glance into the parlour showed Mabel Merriweather handcuffed and talking to the local authorities. That was a relief, of course, but if I was not Mabel Merriweather, then who was I?

At that moment in my dream, I suddenly found myself in the cellar. The room was dark, as the overhead lights were not on, but I had a torch in my hand that I used to light up various parts of the cellar. As I moved the torch around, I saw something run by quickly in the direction of the wine cellar, the same place we had stored the bodies of Kath, Mr. Powell, Ms. Lavoie, Giles, and Dr. Ripley in reality. I walked over to the wine cellar slowly, worried that someone was hiding inside. I had just seen the deceased standing upstairs as if perfectly healthy, and I noticed there were no crates in the wine cellar as there were in reality. Still, I was convinced *something* had moved inside the cellar.

I stepped foot into the doorway of the wine cellar. The air around me felt so much colder, like I had walked from summer into a winter's day. I could see my breath forming in front of my face. And then I heard a noise. It sounded like breathing, but a deep breathing. A man's breathing. In the dream I became convinced that there was someone else in the wine cellar with me and that this person had been on the Radcliffe estate hiding the entire time.

I flashed the light of the torch into the far corners of the wine cellar. The first corner was empty, but in the second, I saw a figure wearing a dark robe. His back was to me, and it appeared as if he was bending over slightly. A rope was tied around his waist as if it were a makeshift belt or sash for the black robe.

"Hsss, air...hsss, air," the figure was making soft noises.

"Hello?" I called out to the figure. It didn't move.

"Hsss, air...hsss, air," the sounds got louder.

"Hello? I can see you," I said. "I am not going to hurt you. Please, turn around."

"Hsss, air...hsss, air," the figure seemed to start nodding its head up and down, up and down.

I finally got close enough to reach out and touch the figure, so I placed my hand on its shoulder and began to turn it around.

"Hss, air...hsss, air," the figure got louder and louder, "he's here...he's here...he's here!"

By now, the figure was yelling, "He's here!" but his face was still obscured by the hood of the robe. I grabbed either side of the hood with my hands and pulled the hood back to reveal...

...Harry, my dead husband, rotten and decayed with time.

"He's here!" Harry yelled.

And then I woke up.

\*       \*       \*

I awoke in a sweat, startled by the awful dream I just had, my heart beating rapidly. The sun was already shining quite brightly, as I managed to see it even through my closed curtains. Upon pulling the curtains back I found myself a bit worried, "Had I missed the 8 o'clock wake-up call?" I so hated being late for anything, but this planned meeting was of the utmost importance.

Breaking the agreed upon rules of the group, I unlocked my door and peeked into the hallway. No one appeared to be up just yet, and there was no sign of Mabel Merriweather. I tiptoed into the hallway, grabbing an oversized umbrella from my room for protection. As I walked down the hallway, I noticed that the manor was silent, deathly silent, which was not altogether unusual so early in the morning, but this felt different. As I approached the stairs down to the foyer, I realized what was different: the grandfather's clock, which usually provided its tick-tock as the morning metronome, was completely quiet.

"That's odd," I thought as I made my way down the stairs, step by step.

As I approached the last step, I looked in the direction of the large grandfather's clock and realized why it was not ticking: the clock had been opened and its parts disassembled. The gold pendulum that kept time was nowhere to be seen, and the clock face had been manually set to 8 o'clock. I was not entirely sure what it meant at the time, but it was strange enough that my body went into instinct mode. I hurried back up to my room, locked the door behind me, and looked for my pocket watch.

"9:37?" I said aloud. "How is it we *all* overslept?!"

Realizing I was too afraid to go back into the hallway alone, I walked over to the wall I shared with Anna.

I knocked on the wall three times. "Anna," I said, "can you hear me?"

I knocked three more times and then waited for a response.

At first, the lack of a reply worried me. What if Mabel had come back into the manor and attacked Anna? Or everyone for that matter? What if I were the only person still alive and now Mabel was waiting for me somewhere in the house?

As I was worrying myself with hypothetical possibilities, three knocks sounded on the wall. Anna had returned my call.

What a relief.

"Anna?" I yelled a bit louder this time through the wall, "can you hear me?"

"Barely," I heard Anna's voice yell. "Just open your door; I'm coming over."

I walked to my door to open it, but two ideas flashed through my mind quickly. The first was the pact that we had made to all open our doors together so that no one was ever alone with anyone else, especially not Mabel. The second was the image of Anna standing in front of the Radcliffe family portrait, looking as if she could easily be a member of the family.

Before I had more time to consider what to do next, I heard Anna just outside my door.

"Dame James," Anna said, "open up, hurry."

I decided I would open my door but only slightly. Just in case.

"I am not fully dressed, Anna," I lied in an attempt to justify my cracked door. "I just wanted to see if you were awake."

"I am, Dame James," Anna replied, "but it is well after 8 o'clock. You see, I knew it was time for us to open our doors, but the clock downstairs never chimed, and I was worried that my watch was broken."

That seemed plausible enough, I thought, but it could also be something that a murderer might say to get me to open my door. I was 90% certain that Mabel was responsible for the unnatural deaths that had taken place in the manor, but I was not 100% sure. Not just yet.

"And the others? Mr. Rossini? Mr. Richter?" I asked. "Are they awake?"

"I am not sure," Anna replied. "I have not left my room until just now."

"Well, then," I stammered a bit, "I suppose that, uh, I suppose that we should go check."

"Yes, let's. Hurry!" Anna said.

I took some time and pretended to dress for the day, and before I opened the door, I grabbed my umbrella once more.

When I opened the door, Anna looked at me, looked at my umbrella, and asked, "Is it supposed to rain today?"

"How should I know?" I responded.

Anna pointed to my umbrella.

"Oh, this? Well, one can never be too prepared," I improvised.

Anna seemed fine by this response, and we began our trek down the hallway, first to check on Mr. Richter and then to retrieve Mr. Rossini.

When we arrived at Mr. Richter's door we knew he was already awake because we could hear him talking to either himself or his monkey, Darwin. I found myself a bit apprehensive to knock on Mr. Richter's door following my nightmare, as well. It was as if the trust I had in this small group the night before had been challenged by my Harry's warning. "He's here." But who? *Who* was here?

"Who's there?" Mr. Richter asked upon hearing our knock.

"It is Dame James," I replied.

"And Anna," Anna added.

The door opened, and Mr. Richter hurried us into his room. "Do you have any idea what time it is?" Mr. Richter asked.

"It is after 9 o'clock, we know," Anna said.

I figured I should not tell anyone that I had already been downstairs and discovered the grandfather's clock in pieces, as they would probably wonder why I had broken our agreement to leave our rooms. So, I played dumb.

"Did you hear any chimes at 8 o'clock, Mr. Richter?" I asked, "because I certainly did not."

"No, which I found incredibly peculiar and more than slightly annoying," Mr. Richter went on, "I am of German heritage. We are not known for being late to anything."

That reminded me of Mr. Rossini who, by his Italian heritage, was likely late for everything (but only because Italians keep such good company at such delicious tables).

"We should see if Mr. Rossini is awake," I suggested.

The three of us turned slowly toward the door and opened it as quietly as possible. It was as if we were all convinced Mabel would be standing in the hallway waiting to murder us at the same time. Mr. Richter pulled the door open more, ever so carefully. He checked the hallway to make sure it was clear. Then, as we were about to step into the hallway, Darwin started shrieking.

"Darwin, *ruhig sein!*" Mr. Richter yelled.

Darwin stopped. When someone yells at you in German, you take them seriously.

"He does that sometimes," Mr. Richter explained.

The three of us stepped into the hallway and proceeded to the far end where Mr. Rossini's room was located. Mr. Richter reached out and knocked on the door.

"Mr. Rossini?" Mr. Richter asked in a loud whisper. "Are you…"

"Awake?" Mr. Rossini said as he opened the door.

We all must have looked genuinely surprised.

"You think because I'm Italian that I would not already be awake?" Mr. Rossini asked with a hint of sarcasm in his voice. "I think you have confused me for Mrs. Powell."

"We were just concerned," Anna went on, "none of us heard the grandfather's clock chime, so we were too afraid to leave our room."

"I noticed that the clock has not chimed," Mr. Rossini said. It appeared as though he was still in the middle of getting ready for the day, as his hair was uncombed and he had white talcum powder on his undershirt and face.

"Well, why don't you finish getting ready while we check on Mrs. Powell and then meet us here in the hallway shortly?" I proposed.

Mr. Rossini agreed and then closed his door to finish getting ready while Anna, Mr. Richter, and I went to check on Mrs. Powell.

When we knocked on the door there was a long delay between our knock and Mrs. Powell opening the door. The woman who opened the door looked much older than she had just days before. Her eyes had severe bags under them, her hair seemed greyer, and her body appeared weaker. She was clearly sick, but I am not certain we had a good understanding of just how sick she was. Still, despite her weak state, she had done up her hair and makeup, as always.

"I just cannot seem to shake this cough," Mrs. Powell said, struggling to breathe.

"Do you want some tea?" I asked.

Mrs. Powell nodded and continued, "I promise you, it's the dust and mould in this house. Ever since I went down in that cellar, I have had…" she could not finish her sentence but just kept coughing.

We told Mrs. Powell about the events of the previous evening to which she simply replied, "I knew that all along." Of course she did. We advised her to keep her door locked and not to open it unless there were two of us there together to deliver her tea and check on her.

She agreed and ushered us out of her room.

By the time we were finished with Mrs. Powell, Mr. Rossini had stepped out of his room and joined our small group.

"Okay, all ready," he said. "I propose we all go downstairs to eat a quick breakfast and then go out and look for Mary Jane. The weather looks like it will cooperate today."

He was correct. The sun was shining and the sky was blue. It was an absolutely gorgeous June morning and, from the hall window near Mr. Rossini's bedroom, not a single grey cloud could be seen. It would be a wonderful day to be outside.

As we descended the stairs, it was Mr. Richter who first noticed the grandfather's clock.

"Look," he said.

We all looked in the direction of the clock to see its door open, its pendulum missing, and its face set to 8 o'clock.

"Did one of you do this?" Mr. Richter asked.

We all responded to the negative.

"But how did someone know to set the clock at 8 o'clock exactly? That was our meeting time for this morning," Mr. Richter asked.

"Yes, but 8 o'clock was also when breakfast was ready every day," I responded.

"Mabel would have been very well aware of that," Anna replied.

"But how could she have gotten back into the manor,"

Mr. Rossini asked. "The front door is still locked."

"A window? The back door? The cellar?" Anna suggested. "There's any number of ways a rat can get into a house, Mr. Rossini. They *find* ways."

The group figured this mystery was not the most pressing issue of the day and continued on into the dining room and then the kitchen. I grabbed my usual breakfast of tea and biscuits, then made some tea for Mrs. Powell. As we were preparing our small meals and, in some cases, eating them, Mr. Rossini proposed a plan.

"I say the four of us stay together as much as possible," he began. "Ms. Merriweather is still out there somewhere, so it is important none of us is on his or her own. If we stay together as a group, she will have no way to hurt us, but if we go off on our own, well, she has already proven to be a vicious killer."

The jarring image of her pushing Dr. Ripley into the fireplace entered my mind.

"I feel like Mary Jane is still okay somewhere on the grounds, so we will use the morning and afternoon to find her," Mr. Rossini said. "We *must* find her."

My heart pitied the man a bit. Sure, he was a married man having an illicit affair, but it seemed clear that he cared for Miss Finley even if he had every intention of breaking off their relationship. He seemed doomed either way, really.

"Should we make a formal plan then?" I asked, thinking a systematic search would be best.

There was a brief pause.

"I do think there should be a plan," Mr. Rossini began, "but I wonder if it is best for you to stay here, Dame James, at Raven's Point Manor."

"Stay *here*?" I asked. "Did you not just say it would be prudent for us to stay together in the event that Ms. Merriweather returns?"

"Yes, that *is* true," Mr. Rossini proceeded cautiously, "but we also do not want to leave Mrs. Powell all alone, do we?

I saw what he was getting at, so I challenged him a bit.

"But Mrs. Powell will be locked in her room all day," I began, "I cannot imagine a safer place she could otherwise be."

After yet another pause, Mr. Rossini began, "Dame James, I think it is important for us to search the grounds as quickly as possible, and I wonder if that…"

"…if that means I should stay behind so I do not slow you down," I admitted defeat. "I may be a bit less spry than I used to be, but my mind is still sharp as a tack, you know."

"My apologies, Dame James," Mr. Rossini said. "I mean no offense."

"No, no," I said, waving him off with my hand, "none taken. I shall lock myself away in my room with some tea and biscuits to type up the events of last night for the authorities."

I could tell he felt a sting of regret for having insulted me on account of my age, but I felt digging into him further would be unkind given the man's precarious situation regarding his missing mistress. He had bigger problems on his hands, it seemed.

"I shall just help myself to my tea and biscuits before you go," I said, standing and heading into the kitchen, "and if you do not mind waiting to depart until I make tea for Mrs. Powell, as well. I would feel safer knowing you are all still here."

"Of course," Mr. Richter said.

I made tea for myself and Mrs. Powell, grabbed as many biscuits as I could (enough, I thought, to last the entire day should the group be gone long, yet I would soon realize only lasted me for about an hour), and then headed upstairs. The group accompanied me as I dropped off tea to Mrs. Powell, (who was looking worse for the wear than ever), locked her door, and stowed myself away in my room.

"Good luck and Godspeed," I said to the trio as I shut my door. I heard them say something about taking five to ten minutes to ready themselves for their search and then to meet back in the foyer. I heard the sound of the manor's front door closing when the three left for their search.

As much as staying at the manor all day sounded slightly appealing–working some on the record for the authorities in between naps and biscuit snacking–the truth is that I would have *much* preferred to be a part of the action. An author's life is a mix of extended periods of solitary quiet time writing a book followed by a period of time in which one is barely alone: galas, soirées, and appearances at various social clubs around the city to discuss your work. This balance grew to be important, particularly as my fame increased and I found less time to dedicate to my work. My social schedule became so full that I found myself wanting some quiet time to myself. I began to realize that the life I had once known, one of obscurity and free of expectations, was no longer and would never be again.

The fact that I had spent so much time working on the records for the authorities made me anxious to get out of the manor, not to mention the fact that I was at least somewhat concerned that Mabel Merriweather might make a reappearance while the others were away. Sure, the front door was locked, and yes, I had barricaded my bedroom door with as much furniture as I could, but I saw the behaviour of Ms. Merriweather the previous night. She was an animal. Certainly, my locked door, bedroom furniture, and oversized umbrella would be a poor defence against a woman who threw a man into a fire without flinching.

On the other hand, knowing that Mabel Merriweather was our primary suspect put me at ease, as well. I was reminded of that old saying–"better the devil you know"– even if Ms. Merriweather were still a threat, at least we no longer had to worry that someone else was roaming around the Radcliffe estate waiting to pounce on us one by one. I was still being cautious, even with the other guests, given the many unexpected surprises over the past several days. Perhaps it was the mystery writer in me, but the case was not closed until it was closed, and Ms. Merriweather was still on the loose.

I had managed to type up the events of the previous night and enjoy several of the biscuits I selected (they go better with tea when it is warm, which has the unfortunate consequence of eating them all very quickly instead of spacing them out over time) before climbing in bed to take what I figured would be one of several short catnaps of the day. After all, what else did I have to do?

So, you can imagine my surprise then, when I heard a commotion downstairs on the first floor of the manor. It sounded as if someone had broken down the front door with a battering ram and proceeded to enter the foyer with a small army.

"Dame James," I heard a familiar voice yell. "Dame James come quickly!"

I recognized the voice as Anna's and then realized that the small army was just Mr. Rossini and Mr. Richter chattering back and forth about something in a frenzied manner. The search group had returned and much earlier than I anticipated.

"Perhaps there is still someone out there?" I heard Mr. Richter say.

"Maybe someone was acting in self-defence? Do you think it could have been Mary Jane?" Mr. Rossini asked.

I began moving the furniture away from my door when suddenly there was a knock.

"Dame James, it's Anna," she began. "There is something you need to see. Hurry!"

As soon as I opened my door, Anna grabbed my hand and pulled me in the direction of the stairs. Sure, I was too old to explore the grounds with the group, but when something exciting happened I was expected to be an Olympic sprinter.

"What is it, Anna?" I asked. "Did you find Miss Finley?"

"No," she replied, "it is something much more curious!"

We ran down the stairs with such momentum that I half expected we would be unable to stop, like a boulder rolling down a steep cliff, and continue out the door into the front yard.

"Dame James!" Mr. Richter said. "Good! Come with us. There is something you have to see. We want your unbiased opinion."

"Can someone please tell me what is going on?" I pleaded.

"We would prefer you see the situation and give your objective assessment," Mr. Rossini added.

By this point, the group was walking out the front door into the front yard of the estate. On either side of the manor's massive front yard were forests of the lushest, greenest fir trees. I found myself being pulled quickly to the forest to the left of the yard when facing away from the manor. The flooding from the previous days' rains had mostly subsided, but there were still traces of standing water, which just served as evidence of how much rain the tempests had brought.

I noticed that there were large mounds of dirt all over, and next to each of the mounds was a similarly sized hole, the inverse of the mound. These must have been dug by Giles to help direct some of the flood water or at least catch it to prevent flooding the main yard. The mounds and holes were *everywhere*. I cannot imagine how much time it took the poor groundskeeper to dig so many holes everywhere and how frustrating it must have been for Mrs. Flaherty to be so unappreciative of his work. I did wonder what, exactly, the nature of their relationship had been. So peculiar.

We stopped near one of the larger mounds, which, of course, meant that this mound's corresponding hole was that much deeper. Sure enough, to our right was the rim of a massive hole in the ground, which appeared to look more like a swimming pool with muddy water filling the bottom third of the hole. The hole was two to three metres deep with steep sides that would likely be difficult to scale given the amount of water and moisture from the rains.

I was busy studying the dimensions of this hole when

something caught my eye. Although covered in mud, some of it dried on her skin, I recognized the blonde hair of Betty Simmons/Mabel Merriweather sitting atop a head that was partially submerged in the muddy water of the large pit.

"Oh, dear God," I gasped upon seeing the woman. "Is she? Is she…?"

"Dead?" Mr. Richter filled in my word. "Yes, she is."

"But how did she…," I went on, "did she drown?"

"That's what we thought," Anna started. "When we found her, we figured that when she ran away from the manor last night in the rain she veered left into the trees unaware that Giles had created so many pits."

"There was probably even more water in the holes last night given the rain," Mr. Rossini added. "That, combined with the darkness, meant that Ms. Merriweather could have fallen into the hole and been unable to get herself out. There were even some marks on the side of the hole here where she may have unsuccessfully attempted to climb out."

"What a tragic way to die," I said. Even if Ms. Merriweather were a murderer, the idea of drowning in a muddy pit, alone, during a rainy, dark night sounded like a terrible way to go.

"Well, that is what we *thought*," Anna said, putting special emphasis on the last word.

"What do you mean?" I asked.

"We wanted to make sure she was, in fact, dead," Anna continued, "so, we looked for something to poke her with, a stick of some sort, just to see if there would be a reflex or a reaction of some kind."

"And that is when we found this," Mr. Richter said, pulling out a rod that had been leaning against the back of a tree nearby.

The rod Mr. Richter retrieved was a peculiar item to find in the middle of a small forest. Golden in colour and slightly dented on its circular end where it had clearly been hit against something solid, the item Mr. Richter was holding in his hands looked just like a…

"Pendulum," Anna said aloud. "It's the pendulum from the grandfather's clock."

"I am not sure I understand?" I asked, quite confused.

"Look," Mr. Richter instructed as he reached down into the hole with the pendulum. He positioned the circular end of the pendulum against the side of Ms. Merriweather's head that was not visible. He flipped her head to the side, which revealed a massive gash and dried blood along the side of the woman's face.

"Ms. Merriweather did not drown," Mr. Richter offered. "She was bludgeoned to death…with this."

He held the grandfather's clock pendulum in his hands like he was making a sacrifice at an altar.

"But that would mean…" I started.

"That a murderer is still out there," Anna offered.

"That's right!" I said, suddenly more anxious to be among the three people nearby. My mind also flashed to Mary Jane Finley who had now been missing for quite some time. Could Mary Jane be a suspect? Or maybe she was working with Mr. Rossini? I had heard tales of Italian crime families of New York. I was not one for assuming types, but this discovery turned my thoughts about the past few days' events completely upside down.

I took a look back at the woman lying dead in the bottom of the muddy trench.

"What a gruesome death," I said aloud, "to be struck with a pendulum and then tossed into a muddy pit during a rainstorm with no one around to hear your cries for help."

"Well, it is not as if she were deserving of any help," Mr. Rossini responded.

"Wait one minute," Anna began.

"Now, now, Mr. Rossini, the poor girl was mentally disturbed," I offered in defence. "While I find what she did to be heinous, I dare say that she, herself, was suffering with…"

"The *pit*…" Anna said to herself.

"…her own demons and diseases, of the mental kind,"

I finished.

"A chemical imbalance most likely," Mr. Richter added. "It is the focus of some of my research: how the brain adapts to a deficiency…"

"The *pendulum*…" Anna mumbled.

"…or an abundance of particular elements and chemicals in the brain," Mr. Richter went on.

"Stop. Stop!" Anna shouted.

We looked at her somewhat surprised. She had not been taking part in the conversation among Mr. Rossini, Mr. Richter, and myself yet was insisting we stop talking to focus on her even though she had just been mumbling to herself. Why, at the time, I found it to be the rudest thing the girl had done since hiring her.

It was only later, after I realized the significance about what she said next, that I completely forgot about her uncharacteristic rudeness in this moment.

Anna looked at us with her sharp grey eyes, her face looked gravely concerned, and she uttered a completely chilling sentence.

"I think I know where Miss Finley is."

*     *     *

Anna started sprinting back to the manor with a clip I could simply not match. Mr. Rossini followed in hot pursuit, clearly very eager to see where Anna thought Miss Finley might be hiding. Mr. Richter, ever the gentleman (however socially awkward), waited patiently as I hurried myself along at a surprisingly fast pace. Despite what others might have thought, I still had a fair bit of pep in me yet.

Mr. Richter and I arrived at the front door of the manor in just enough time to see Mr. Richter and Anna escape down into the cellar. We hurried over to the cellar door where Mr. Richter let me advance before him. As I descended the stairs, I could see Anna scurrying about as if she were a mouse searching for cheese in the basement. By the time I reached the bottom of the stairs I could see that she had entered the wine cellar where the temporary coffins of our departed acquaintances were now piling up.

"Where is she, Ms. Winthrop?" Mr. Rossini asked impatiently. "Why are we down here?"

I watched as Anna ran her hands against the stone walls of the wine cellar. It was certainly a peculiar sight to behold, and I found myself wondering if all the stress and anxiety of the past several days might have thrown Anna into a bit of psychosis. Or, even worse, if whatever ailed Ms. Merriweather were somehow contagious and we would all be batty before the day's end.

Unsatisfied with her search of the wine cellar, Anna returned to the main room of the basement. She looked around with wild eyes before she focused her sight squarely on me. She stared in my direction for such a long, awkward moment in silence that I felt a social obligation to respond.

"Anna?" I asked. "Are you alright?"

I was seriously concerned for the poor girl's mental health and, in that moment, felt a bit of guilt for being the one who brought her into this affair, albeit unintentionally.

She started walking toward me, step after step, slowly. When she was upon me, she was close enough that I could feel her breathing, yet she seemed transfixed by something just beyond me. Behind me, actually.

I turned around to see what it was that had so captured Anna's attention.

The brick wall Giles had been building was the object of Anna's current fascination. I observed the craftsmanship—quite impressive, it was, and I found myself pitying the poor groundskeeper who had died such a horrible death. Why, it was just the other day I saw him layering brick after brick atop one another to finish the wall with only the doorframe remaining...

...the doorframe. As I replayed the scene in my mind, the one of Giles working on the wall, I *swore* there had been a carved-out area for what would become a doorframe allowing entry into the small storage room. Now, however, there was no such doorframe.

"Certainly, you must have imagined it," I said to myself, trying to think harder to clarify my memory of what the wall had looked like, but I was positive there had been a hole left in the wall.

"Here," Anna said without emotion, pointing to the brick wall. "She is in here."

"What on earth?" Mr. Richter said, sounding as if he were convinced Anna had gone mad.

Without a moment's hesitation, Mr. Rossini grabbed a hammer laying among the nearby tools and started chipping away at the brick wall. Even if Anna's apparent premonition had been nonsense, the stuff of travelling mystics, Mr. Rossini was taking no chances. He chiselled away at the brick wall, bit by bit, and then called for help.

"Mr. Richter, grab something and help me break down this wall!" Mr. Rossini yelled.

Mr. Richter did as he was told, and within minutes the two men managed to create a sizable hole large enough to let light inside. The smell of burned wood or fire of some kind seemed to emanate from the small room. Indeed, it was as if there were a fireplace in the cellar that had been burning all day, yet no such fireplace existed to my knowledge.

Mr. Rossini grabbed a torch, shined its light through the hole, and then yelled, "Mary Jane! Mary Jane!"

I will likely never forget the way Marvin Rossini yelled the name of his lover. It was an awful sound of despair, hope dwindling away, love that would never again be realized. Now that the man knew Miss Finley was just on the other side of the wall, he began hammering more furiously, choking back tears as he broke down enough of the wall to climb inside himself.

Mr. Richter held a torch up to the hole to illuminate the small storage room that was now accessible. Inside was the body of Miss Mary Jane Finley being held by a completely distraught Marvin Rossini.

Anna, Mr. Richter, and I looked at the horrific scene and then at one another before Anna broke the silence.

"It all makes sense now."

\*        \*        \*

Anna and I left Mr. Rossini and Mr. Richter to tend to the dear Miss Finley. I had grown quite fond of Miss Finley since arriving at the manor; smart, polite, and never one to suffer fools like Mrs. Powell or Betty Simmons/Ms. Merriweather. It was unclear how long she had been trapped in the bricked room, but our guess was that she had been stuck there since she had gone missing days before.

As soon as we made it upstairs to the foyer, Anna bolted toward the library and said, "Follow me."

A bit stunned by the revelation downstairs, I simply did as I was told. Now all bets were off. Who struck Ms. Merriweather in the head with a pendulum if not Miss Finley? And who bricked Miss Finley into the wall? Giles? Ms. Merriweather? An even more terrifying thought entered my mind: what if someone in the manor with me right now committed one, or even both, of these horrible acts?

In the library, Anna ran over to the shelves and started reading the spines of the books placed there. A bit more methodical in her approach than her hyperactive episode in the cellar just moments before, Ms. Winthrop scanned the shelves appearing to search for a particular volume.

Figuring I could help, I asked, "Anna, what is it that you are searching for?"

Either the girl did not hear my question or she was choosing to ignore me. In any case, she continued to search the library for *something*, it was just unclear what, exactly.

Figuring I was of no great use standing, I sat on the sofa in the middle of the room at complete attention. My posture must have very closely resembled that of Mrs. Powell on that first night, her overly formal, oddly uncomfortable contortion that allowed her to avoid touching the dust or germs of the couch. And now, despite all her efforts to stay healthy, she was bedridden upstairs with a terrible cough. Fate does play funny games, I suppose.

"Here!" Anna yelled, reaching for a large volume in the far back corner of the library.

"What is it, Anna?" I asked hoping that my query would not be ignored this time.

"Are you familiar with Poe?" Anna asked.

"Poe? As in Edgar Allan Poe, the 19th century author and poet?" I asked with a hint of judgment in my voice. What did this poor girl take me for, a bloody imbecile? "Of *course*, I know who Poe is. Why do you ask?"

"This morning, when we discovered Ms. Merriweather in the hole Giles dug up, I did not think anything special about her death; nothing other than the fact that she fell into a flooded, muddy hole in the rain and died trying to get out," Anna said.

"Go on," I encouraged.

"But when we brought you out to examine the scene, someone said the word 'pit' and someone said the word 'pendulum'," Anna continued. "I feel so ignorant for not seeing the connection sooner, but it struck me that I *had* heard those two terms together before. Many times, in fact."

It took me a second, but then I was able to impress Anna with my own trivial knowledge.

"Ah, *The Pit and the Pendulum*," I said, referencing the famous short story by Poe.

"Exactly," Anna said. "The tale from the Spanish Inquisition of a prisoner who manages to escape a trap room featuring a deep pit and a razor-sharp pendulum swinging overhead."

I was impressed by Anna's knowledge of the story. I suppose I should have expected as much from a librarian, but then I remembered she had failed to mention her previous experience as a librarian on her application. That background only became known over drinks the first night of our stay at Raven's Point Manor.

"Strange," I replied, "but how was that able to help you locate Miss Finley?"

Anna gave a look of judgment as if I should have already known the answer to my own question.

"*The Cask of Amontillado*," she replied.

"Ah, yes! *The Cask of Amontillado*!" I said. "I remember reading that disturbing story in school! It gave me nightmares, it did."

Anna recounted the tale with a crazed look in her eye, "Set in Venice during Carnival, a man tricks his drunk friend into following him into the catacombs connected to a wine cellar, where he proceeds to brick him inside and leave him for dead because the drunk man had insulted him."

"Just like Miss Finley," I realized.

"Down to the lit torch dropped inside," Anna added. That explained the smell of smoke and fire that escaped from the enclosed brick room.

"To ensure she suffocated," it dawned on me.

"Precisely," Anna said, as she combed through the pages of the collection. The book, *The Complete Works of Edgar Allan Poe*, appeared to contain countless stories, perhaps all of the man's work, in a single volume. Stillings & Sons Publishing House had been trying to get me to do a collection of this sort for years with an introduction penned by me. Now, I was not certain I would even live to have the opportunity.

"Of course," she whispered under her breath, seemingly to herself, as if she had temporarily forgotten I was still in the room. "It's *all* right here."

We both leaned over the large table where Anna had placed the book, and she began to spell out a story that I would have never expected *her* to piece together given her mediocrity (and I mean that in the kindest way).

"Look here," Anna began, "how was it that Mrs. Flaherty died?"

"Kath? Why, she fell down the cellar stairs and landed on her dinner bell in the most unfortunate way," I said.

"Indeed. Look here," Anna pointed to the title of one of the poems in the book, "*The Bells.*"

"Surely that is just a coincidence, Anna? Plenty of books and poems speak of bells, and that poem references church bells not dinner bells," I challenged.

"Who was next?" Anna asked, "Mr. Powell, right? Buried alive and then discovered under the lid of his crate, dead?"

I nodded.

"*The Tell-Tale Heart,*" Anna said. "The narrator murders an old man, dismembers his body, and hides it under the floorboards only to be discovered later by the authorities."

"My God, that is grisly," I said. "I believe you *are* onto something, Anna!"

"Who died third? Ms. Lavoie, correct?" Anna went on. She pored over the thick volume, flipping pages and scanning the titles to see which, if any, reminded her of Claudette Lavoie's death.

"Of course!" she replied, "*The Murders in the Rue Morgue!*"

This one was shocking. I knew the story well, as it was considered in literary circles to be among the very first detective stories, a precursor to my own literary works.

"That's the one where the two women are found murdered," I began, "and the detective figures out that they were actually murdered by an orangutan!"

"And remember how Mr. Richter's monkey, Darwin, was found in Ms. Lavoie's bedroom with blood on his fur?" Anna asked.

My heart dropped. "Anna," I began, "this cannot be mere coincidence."

The girl shook her head in agreement.

"Someone has been using the stories of Poe as a playbook for murder," I said, a chill running down my spine.

She continued paging through the book, "Giles, Giles…I know there was a story about a painting. A man made his wife sit for so long while he painted her that he did not notice as she gradually faded into death from a lack of food and water. Ah, here it is: *The Oval Portrait*."

"And Giles was found tied to a chair near all those portraits of him sitting in that same chair," I added.

"But who would have orchestrated such a maniacal plan?" Anna asked.

If I am being honest, that question had already crossed my mind. It was not lost on me that Anna, as a librarian, would be intimately familiar with the works of Edgar Allan Poe. She had also proven to be quite clever over the past several days, and certainly cleverer than I imagined she could be when I hired her. Was she leading me on at present by pretending to be discovering this horrific plot, or was she genuinely just now uncovering the work of a maniac?

And then there was Mr. Richter, the scholar. As an educated man he would have been very familiar with the classics, including the collection of Poe's stories. He had always acted a bit peculiar, and I wondered why he would have a monkey with him on holiday if not for some specific purpose. He was just as likely as Anna, in my mind, to have the intellectual prowess to pull off such an elaborate ruse.

But as a writer of mysteries, I could not help but think of an even more complicated explanation to this odd series of events. You see, Miss Finley was a schoolteacher, and we saw several books in her room when conducting the search of the house. There is no doubt she, too, would have been familiar with Poe's work. Perhaps she fell into a murderous rage upon learning about Mr. Rossini's intention to end their relationship and, fearing imprisonment more than death, bricked *herself* into that storage room in the cellar?

I was a bit lost trying to piece all the elements of the puzzle together, but then I heard Mr. Rossini and Mr. Richter walking up the wooden cellar stairs to the foyer.

"I am not sure, 'Who?' is the question we should be asking, my dear girl," I added with a concerned tone in my voice.

Anna looked at me curiously.

"There may not be time to answer that question just

yet," I said and looked down at the story Anna had inadvertently opened to in the book.

*The Masque of the Red Death.*

*       *       *

By the time we made it upstairs to Mrs. Powell's room, we figured she would already be dead.

Her coughing had become so violent over the past few days and her body emaciated. It was unclear how she got sick, but if Anna's theory about the mysterious deaths of the past several days had any merit, we could be certain that her illness was no accident.

In *The Masque of the Red Death*, a prince holds a masquerade ball in the middle of a plague after having sealed the doors to his palace, letting the commoners die outside. The guests of the masquerade dance from room to room, each represented by a different colour, but they all deliberately avoid one room—the black room—which has a darker ambiance. At midnight, a new guest appears at the ball, dressed in funeral shrouds and wearing a frightening mask. The new guest travels from room to room and eventually angers the prince who becomes mad that someone so severe and serious has infiltrated his carefree soirée. Finally, the prince encounters this masked figure and dies immediately, as do the other party guests, for it seems that no one could escape the plague no matter how much he tried.

The parallels to Mrs. Powell were readily apparent. A woman who feared dirt and germs more than pain and even death, a woman who went well out of her way to avoid illness only to have it find her in the end.

The door to Mrs. Powell's room was locked, but Mr. Rossini and Mr. Richter managed to break down the door with very little difficulty. There, lying in the bed, was Mrs. Powell: motionless, not breathing, and cold, but also wearing her bright red sleeping mask. The sight of it was chilling. It was at this point that I was convinced Anna's theory was correct.

As I stared at the terrifying picture before me, I felt someone tap on my shoulder.

"Dame James," Anna whispered. "The painting."

I turned to look at the painting of the ravens and saw what had concerned Anna: the eyes of the second raven in the room's painting had been crossed out with two red Xs.

# 11 | THE RED HERRING

If the murderer had been following a systematic, methodical plan, then whatever sense of order I thought *we* were operating under while investigating the deaths and keeping one another safe had completely collapsed upon discovering Mrs. Powell's dead body.

There was no way Ms. Merriweather could have returned back to the manor, killed Mrs. Powell, and placed the red mask on her if she were dead out in one of the trenches dug by Giles. That left Mr. Richter, Mr. Rossini, and Anna, or maybe someone who had managed to evade us during the previous searches of the manor and the Radcliffe estate grounds. Whatever relief I had when I thought Mabel Merriweather was the sole suspect had vanished. I was not sure I could trust *anyone* at this point.

Unsure of which mysterious illness killed Mrs. Powell, we decided it would be best to leave her body in her room lest we contaminate ourselves attempting to move her down to the wine cellar. The group also opted to leave Ms. Merriweather out in the pit, which I found a bit barbaric, but I was not about to protest as the lone compassionate one of our remaining group.

Mr. Rossini seemed terribly out of sorts, which I imagine was a consequence of finally knowing that Miss Finley was truly gone. He sat in the parlour, his head hanging in his hands, alternating between fits of anger and sadness.

"It is my fault," he kept repeating, "it is my fault she was here."

I did not disagree. From what I had gathered, it *was* Mr.

Rossini's idea to bring his mistress to Raven's Point Manor for the purpose of ending their little affair. Now, she was stuffed in a crate in the wine cellar downstairs, hardly the romantic weekend I imagine she had in mind.

If you had been a fly on the wall in the parlour that afternoon, you would have observed an odd dance of suspicious minds. Anna, Mr. Richter, Mr. Rossini, and I were still acting very friendly toward one another, of course, but we were sitting as far about as we could physically be in the room without making the entire experience too awkward.

I felt it would be best—safest, really—if we all four stayed in the same room with one another instead of separating and locking ourselves away in our respective rooms. I still had not quite figured out how the deaths fit together or who could have pulled them off alone or if there was some conspiracy among several accomplices at play. It was like attempting to complete a jigsaw puzzle where all the pieces were present but none of them fit together quite properly.

After sitting in silence for some time, it was Anna—easily forgotten, blends-into-the-background Anna—who spoke first.

"I suppose we are all working through the timeline of the past several days in our minds," Anna said, "and, if you are struggling the way I am, then you know that not everything makes sense."

"That is quite an understatement," Mr. Richter responded.

"But while I cannot piece together the logic of every episode that has happened," Anna continued, "I have come to realize the importance of motive."

Anna stood and started pacing about the parlour almost as if physically pacing through the timeline and logic she was describing.

"Who would find joy in murdering a series of strangers?" Anna began, "and why would he or she begin murdering in the first place?"

The rest of us watched the young woman walk back and forth, but no one offered an answer to either of her questions. One got the sense she was not actually seeking an answer.

"Opportunity," she stopped pacing. "Being isolated from the rest of the world. Being separated from any authorities who could stop a murderer. Having a house full of resources that one could exploit for personal gain and profit."

Motive was always central to any murder, or crime for that matter, but I was not exactly sure where Ms. Winthrop was headed with her narrative. Still, I was intrigued and leaned in to indicate my growing interest in where she was taking her logic.

"At one point in time, Raven's Point Manor played host to a successful fashion designer, a wealthy, even if simple, farm-owning couple, one of the world's most successful authors," Anna gestured in my direction, "and a woman who indirectly inherited the home and belongings of one of the wealthiest families in America: the Radcliffes."

I still was not following, but I was relieved to see that both Mr. Rossini and Mr. Radcliffe were equally as lost.

"Although these strangers seem completely unconnected, there is one person who ties them all together, one person whose profession could have benefitted greatly from them, one person who murdered them all, save one," Anna nodded in my direction once more as the lone survivor of her list of accomplished guests, although this time I wished should would not have done so given the topic.

"Mr. Marvin Rossini," Anna said, looking sternly at the man.

Mr. Rossini shifted in his chair uncomfortably before asking, "What are you getting at, Ms. Winthrop?"

"Mr. Rossini," Anna continued, "can you please remind us what line of work you are in?"

"Jewellery," Mr. Rossini responded. "It is a family

business, passed down for three generations."

"And how do you procure the jewellery that you sell in this family business?" Anna asked.

He hesitated a bit and then continued, "Various sources."

"Could you please elaborate, Mr. Rossini?" Anna asked.

"What?" he asked, visibly annoyed. "Fine. Okay. Sure. We have sources back in Palermo that provide some of our merchandise."

"*Some?*" Anna asked. "Some of your merchandise? What about the rest?"

Realizing she was not going to let up, Mr. Rossini continued, "And pawning. People bring us their jewellery and we give them money for it."

"And how much of your business would you say comes from pawning compared to sourcing jewellery from Italy?" Anna enquired.

The professionalism with which she was making her case reminded me of the assistant who often joined Inspector Alastair Evans in my novels featuring the latter. Lieutenant Henri Foussard was a little, wee man with an outsized personality. As I watched Anna, such a quiet, demure girl really making a go for it, well, I felt as surprised as I did proud.

"Uh, I am not sure," Mr. Rossini responded. "Maybe 80/20? Eighty percent pawn, twenty percent purchasing from Italy? I don't know. What are you getting at, Ms. Winthrop?"

"Might it then be of interest to you, Mr. Rossini, to consider ways to procure jewellery for your shop that you did *not* have to pay for, whether from Italy or by pawning?" Anna asked.

I could see where she was going.

"I am not sure what you mean, Ms. Winthrop," Mr. Rossini said, crossing his arms.

"What I mean, Mr. Rossini, is that you, yourself, commented extensively about the jewellery being worn by

Mademoiselle Lavoie, the Powells, and even Dame James," Anna went on.

"It is jewellery! It's what I *do*," Mr. Rossini pleaded. "I notice these things just as *you* probably notice the dull monotony of day-to-day life." Mr. Rossini's attempt at an insult fell flat.

"Then might it be possible that you saw an opportunity to obtain free merchandise for your store by stealing jewellery from the wealthy guests staying at Raven's Point Manor?" Anna charged.

"What?!" Mr. Rossini asked, standing angrily. "I have no idea what you are getting at, woman, but I am no thief!"

"No, Mr. Rossini, I am not standing here calling you a *thief*," Anna replied.

"Good," Mr. Rossini said, retaking his seat and crossing his arms once more.

"I am calling you a *murderer*," Anna said.

Mr. Rossini stood again, and Mr. Richter hurried to position himself between Anna and Mr. Rossini.

"Now, now. Anna, you are accusing Mr. Rossini of murder?" Mr. Richter began. "That is a serious accusation, no?"

"I realize that, Mr. Richter," Anna replied, "but I have given it considerable thought and realized that Mr. Rossini had motives aligning with his personal wealth and his private and professional life."

Mr. Richter was intrigued, "Go on."

"Well, beyond the obvious financial wealth Mr. Rossini could accrue by pocketing the jewellery of the wealthy guests present at the manor, not to mention the collection of jewellery likely to be part of the Radcliffe estate in Mrs. Flaherty's possession, Mr. Rossini also had another incentive to murder: infidelity," Anna continued.

I was hanging on every word Anna said, primarily because I found her story captivating but also because I knew I might have to type everything she was saying for the authorities' record I had been preparing.

"Everyone knew Mr. Rossini and Miss Finley were having an affair," Anna went on.

"They did?" Mr. Rossini asked, genuinely surprised.

"We did," Mr. Richter and I said simultaneously.

"But it is not the infidelity of the extramarital affair to which I am referring," Anna went on. "No. Instead, I am referring to the infidelity of an accomplice who, realizing she was too far into something that was not befitting of her moral fibre, wanted out of the arrangement."

"Miss Finley?" I found myself saying my thoughts aloud.

"Indeed, Dame James: Miss Finley," Anna said. "During our search of the grounds, Mr. Rossini deliberately told me that he had brought Miss Finley to Raven's Point Manor to end their affair, which I found to be an odd thing to discuss so openly. It was as if…"

"He *wanted* you to be aware of that information," I said my thoughts aloud again.

"Yes, Dame James," Anna said, a bit visibly annoyed that I stole her thunder. "Why would a gentleman openly discuss his extra-marital affair *and* his intention to end said affair with a perfect stranger, particularly a *female* stranger? I will tell you why…"

Mr. Richter was as keenly interested in the story as I was. Mr. Rossini had the most curious expression on his face; it was unclear whether he was angry or worried.

"Before she died, Ms. Lavoie revealed to me and Dame James that she heard a man and a woman arguing from her room," Anna went on, "and although she was not entirely certain whom she heard, she speculated that it might be Miss Finley and Mr. Rossini. She had already witnessed Miss Finley leaving Mr. Rossini's room early each morning, as had Mrs. Powell, and was onto the idea that the two were conspiring in some way."

"That does not prove anything other than a romantic relationship," Mr. Rossini shouted.

"But, Mr. Rossini, it was *you* who tried to throw us off the trail by providing a reason for the argument Ms. Lavoie heard," Anna went on. "You were trying to get me to think that Miss Finley was cross with you because you intended to leave her, yet your behaviour toward her this weekend suggested otherwise. No, the reason you and Miss Finley were engaged in a heated argument was that she was an accomplice in your plan, whether willingly or unwillingly, and had decided she wanted out."

"That's preposterous!" Mr. Rossini said, shouting from his chair.

"Is it? A young, innocent girl, blinded by love and romance, happy to be guided by an older, successful man, willing to do whatever she needed to do in order to keep his love," Anna went on, "Even if that meant *murder*."

"That is enough, Ms. Winthrop!" Mr. Rossini said. "Richter? Dame James?" Mr. Rossini looked our direction in a plea for help.

But we wanted to hear more.

"Between the two of you, one of you managed to trick Mrs. Flaherty to the cellar while the other hid in the shadows with the weapon that ultimately killed her. And need I remind you, Mr. Rossini, that *you* were the first person in the bathroom where Mr. Powell sat in the bathtub, *not* dead, although you claimed that he *was*, in fact, dead," Anna continued.

Mr. Rossini was steaming mad by this point.

"And poor Ms. Lavoie. She trusted Miss Finley as a friend, so you leveraged this friendship to get into Ms. Lavoie's room, where she had no idea her death was imminent," Anna went on.

Mr. Rossini was turning as red as pasta sauce now.

"Giles may be the worst of all," Anna went on. "Miss Finley had established a trusting relationship with the simple-minded man. She fostered a sense of care and friendship with him, which served you both well when she lured him to the attic where you finished him off."

"You have no idea what you are talking about," Mr. Rossini fumed.

"But perhaps the most brilliant move of all, Mr. Rossini, was your feigned sadness and worry for Miss Finley when she seemingly disappeared," Anna stated. "Miss Finley's disappearance provided you with the freedom to roam the estate and manor without anyone questioning your whereabouts. You were the concerned lover looking for his beloved when, in all actuality, Miss Finley was already dead, murdered by your hand to prevent her from ratting you out."

"What about Ms. Simmons? Or Merriweather? Whatever you want to call her?" Mr. Rossini asked.

"She likely made the connection the day she spent searching the grounds with you," Anna said. "Remember that Ms. Simmons confronted you directly, Mr. Rossini, suggesting that Miss Finley was not missing at all but, instead, had been the one to murder Giles. This accusation likely hit a bit too close to the truth for you. Worried she might reveal your misdeeds, you waited until the rest of us went to bed, snuck down to the foyer, grabbed the pendulum from the clock, and went out to find Ms. Merriweather."

"Ah, yes, this pendulum," Mr. Rossini said. "Why would I choose such an inconvenient weapon when there were knives in the kitchen? And what of this connection to the author you have claimed?"

"That was all Miss Finley," Anna suggested. "The books in her room gave her away. I doubt the woman initially had murderous intentions, but people do foolish things for love, particularly when it is built on such a fragile foundation in the first place."

I must say, in that moment I wanted to stand and give Ms. Winthrop a round of applause for her outstanding performance. Had I not suspected Mr. Rossini *before* Anna pleaded her case, I had no doubt after. Again, I felt a bit embarrassed that I had not made several of the connections that my assistant had made. Perhaps I was not as observant as I used to be. Still, I was the one responsible for hiring Ms.

Winthrop, so I felt entitled to take a bit of credit for her work.

"Mr. Rossini," said Mr. Richter, "Anna has levied quite a serious charge against you. Do you have anything to say in defence of yourself and Miss Finley?"

"Indeed, I do," Mr. Rossini said, glaring at Anna, "and it is less a defence for me and Mary Jane, as no defence is needed…"

Anna did not break her stare with Mr. Rossini.

"…it is, instead, more of an accusation," Mr. Rossini continued, "for Mary Jane and I did not kill anyone here at Raven's Point Manor."

"Then, who did?" I asked.

Mr. Rossini now sat back comfortably, even putting his shoes on the coffee table before lighting a cigar and responding…

"Anna Winthrop."

*     *     *

After the show-stopping spectacle from Anna, I will admit that the cards were stacked against Mr. Rossini. As far as I was concerned, the authorities would find him to be guilty of the murders per Anna's reasoning, and given that it was my job to summarize everything that had just happened, well, the future looked bleak for Mr. Marvin Rossini.

Mr. Richter and I were now sitting on the same sofa, Anna sat in a chair nearby, and Mr. Rossini was the one pacing the parlour as it had magically transformed into a courtroom after Anna's prosecutorial performance. I found myself wishing I had some more tea and biscuits to snack on in preparation of what was to come next.

"Who is Anna Winthrop?" Mr. Rossini began. "Her own employer admitted that even she did not know her new assistant's former occupation," Mr. Rossini said, gesturing my direction. "So, if her own employer did not know her very well, how could any of the rest of us?"

Anna seemed unamused and unaffected by Mr. Rossini's opening statement.

"I will tell you what kind of person Ms. Winthrop is," Mr. Rossini continued. "Forgettable. Unexciting. Reclusive. Envious. From the moment Anna arrived here at Raven's Point Manor, she has only succeeded at one thing: disappearing into the background."

I had to agree with Mr. Rossini there. I was constantly forgetting about the poor girl.

"And if a murderer could only succeed at one skill—besides murder itself, of course—what would that skill be? Disappearing into the background," Mr. Rossini reasoned. "Being so adept at being ignored that no one would ever consider her a key suspect in murder because no one would ever think of her in the first place."

Anna stared straight ahead appearing to bite the inside of her check. That last comment seemed to sting a bit.

"I noticed Ms. Winthrop's peculiar behaviour the very first evening we all gathered together after she arrived. Never one to mingle with the crowd and never one to share any personal, private information about her past, I quickly got the impression that Anna either had something to hide or wanted to remain hidden herself," Mr. Rossini said. "She attempted to explain her abnormal quiet behaviour as being a function of her work as a librarian, but this just added to the mystery and intrigue: what kind of learned librarian leaves such work to become a lowly assistant?"

Anna fidgeted in her chair a bit, visibly uncomfortable.

"I will tell you who: a criminal. Not necessarily a murderer, mind you," Mr. Rossini went on, "but someone with a past. Someone who was running from something or someone, maybe even the authorities. Someone who would be willing to take a demotion in life to obtain some peace of mind that eluded her."

"A lot of people change positions for no good reason, Mr. Rossini," Mr. Richter chimed in.

"Perhaps, Richter, but what else do we really know of Ms. Winthrop?" Mr. Rossini asked. "I would argue not very much. She has spoken of no family. No husband. No prior work save for her time as a librarian. No childhood or upbringing. No details of *any* kind."

"Some people are rather quiet by nature, though," I offered.

"Indeed, but Anna was not *always* quiet. She had a series of outbursts the past several days at significant times, like the moment she called Ms. Merriweather to task when her bogus story about visiting her parents with her brother did not ring true. It was Anna who suggested we make the arduous trek to the throughway, which resulted in the death of Mr. Powell. Yet when pressed to tell us why she left Birmingham in such a hurry, Ms. Winthrop was quite quick to shut down conversation."

Anna kept her head facing forward, but I saw her eyes watching Mr. Rossini's every move, like a predator waiting in the brush watching its prey.

"In fact, we never did find out why it was Ms. Winthrop left her comfortable life in Birmingham working as a librarian to take a job as a lowly housekeeper and then personal assistant in London, did we?" Mr. Rossini asked. "Would you care to tell us, Anna?"

Anna sat in silence and refused to answer the man's question.

"I thought so. But, when it comes to motive, the very thing that Ms. Winthrop, herself, suggested should drive our present logic, I can see a very clear motive that puts Ms. Winthrop at the heart of all the murders: jealousy. A poor, working class girl from Birmingham gets whisked away by a wealthy, successful author on a trip of a lifetime, across the ocean even! Why, I bet Ms. Winthrop never thought she would the see the day that she might sail across the ocean," Mr. Rossini said with a tone of such condescension.

Again, Anna refused to flinch and just let the man's criticisms hang in the air.

"I watched Ms. Winthrop as she observed our fellow guests. Claudette Lavoie, attractive, successful, and nearly the same age as Ms. Winthrop was like a Shakespearean foil, opposite in so many ways to Anna that she worried her own deficiencies were heightened with someone like Claudette in the room," Mr. Rossini argued. "She was used to this, of course, as Anna Winthrop was never the prettiest nor the most successful girl in any room."

I found Mr. Rossini's approach to be quite inconsiderate, but I dare not interrupt him at this juncture.

"Mr. and Mrs. Powell represented a kind of love Ms. Winthrop would never know, and seeing them together was another clear reminder of her own life's deficiencies," Mr. Rossini went on. "Giles was likely just an easy target, and Mrs. Flaherty just an annoyance who treated Ms. Winthrop less as a guest and more as a servant."

"What about Miss Finley? Ms. Merriweather?" Mr. Richter asked.

"Ever since Ms. Winthrop and I explored the grounds together the other day, I was worried she might try to use what I said against me," Mr. Rossini continued, "and so here we are. I told her the truth about my intentions toward Miss Finley regarding the end of our affair, so she has twisted my own words to frame me for the murder of Mary Jane."

Anna sat perfectly still, not indicating any hint of truth or falsehood in what Mr. Rossini was saying.

"Ms. Merriweather is a bit trickier, but my best guess is that her death was the result of a demented sociopath's need for recognition," Mr. Rossini said. "Anna Winthrop had concocted an elaborate scheme with particular theming and no one had picked up on her design. Why, who was it that pointed out the connection to *The Pit and the Pendulum* first?"

"It was Anna," I said aloud, a bit shocked.

"And who was it that then connected each murder to the stories of Edgar Allan Poe?" Mr. Rossini asked.

"Anna," I replied. "But the girl was a librarian! She *would* be familiar with his work."

"Do not be so naïve, Dame James," said Mr. Rossini. "It the old country we have a saying, '*Fidarsi è bene non fidarsi è meglio.*'"

"To trust is good, but not to trust is better," Mr. Richter translated.

"Precisely," Mr. Rossini nodded, "and I dare say that Ms. Anna Winthrop is not to be trusted."

There was a moment of silence as Mr. Rossini walked over to an open chair near the fireplace and sat down. Then, at that moment, Anna stood up from her chair, faced Mr. Rossini, and started clapping.

"Bravo, good man," Anna said dryly. "I imagine it took a great deal of imagination to come up with such a foolish, nonsensical story."

Anna walked over to the fireplace, directly up to Mr. Rossini. I was worried she might strike the man, but I also thought she had more grace and elegance than that of a common barfly.

"Do you want to know who I am, Mr. Rossini?" Anna asked. "I shall tell you. I was an orphaned child adopted by two abusive parents. I lived a miserable life in the Midlands until I met a kind gentleman and fell in love. We had plans to be married, and then he went off to war and never came home. I left Birmingham because I wanted to forget the pain that consumed me there, even if that meant taking whatever job was available in London. And *that* is how I came to Raven's Point Manor."

Anna walked away from the fireplace toward the door to the foyer. She turned around and faced the group.

"His name was Thomas Wright. There is a picture of him on my desk upstairs," she paused briefly before adding, "now you know the tragic story of Anna Winthrop."

Then she left the room.

\*     \*     \*

Having written extensively about the trials of characters

in my books, I knew very well that courtrooms were the setting of a great deal of drama. One day, I thought, people would likely entertain themselves by watching the goings-on of a legal proceeding, particularly those cases rooted in murder, crimes of the heart, and other stories that the human species just finds so fascinating.

Here, we had just witnessed Anna and Mr. Rossini putting each other on trial, presumably with Mr. Richter and I serving as both judge and jury. We did not ask for these roles, of course, but they were thrust upon us once Anna lobbed her accusation at Mr. Rossini. If I am being honest, I felt that Anna had done a far better job arguing the case against Marvin Rossini than Marvin did arguing a case against Anna. However, there were certain elements of Mr. Rossini's story that did strike me as interesting. Anna's extensive knowledge of Poe, for one. The fact that she left a decent job in Birmingham to take a job as a housekeeper being another. Sure, she managed to provide an explanation for these oddities in the end, but I had also learned from my writing that a pathological liar is capable of creating a compelling story on the spot. We had no way to know if what Anna was saying was true or false.

After Anna left the room, Mr. Rossini followed shortly thereafter, taking a sharp turn to the left to go smoke a cigar in the front yard of the manor. Mr. Richter and I were able to keep an eye on the man through the large window in the parlour that faced the massive front yard.

"So, what do you think?" Mr. Richter said, breaking the silence.

"About what?" I asked, pretending not to know.

"Who did it?" Mr. Richter replied, surprised at my apparent daftness. "Mr. Rossini? Anna? Were you not just paying attention to those accusations, Dame James?"

"No, I was," I replied, "but I also know that people often start grasping at straws when they are desperate. And if we, the lot of us, are anything, it *is* desperate."

"What do you mean, Dame James?" Mr. Richter asked.

"The four of us have witnessed unspeakable crimes here the past several days," I began, "from deaths we assumed were accidental to murders that we know were deliberate, calculated homicides."

"Go on," Mr. Richter said.

"As a man of science, Mr. Richter, you understand that the human species sets itself apart from its primate ancestry, like your friend Darwin upstairs, in part by its desire to solve problems," I continued, "to provide explanations in the absence of understanding, to provide reason in situations that seem unreasonable."

"Certainly, that is true," Mr. Richter nodded.

"When there are gaps in a story or when information is missing, the human brain is well adapted to fill in those holes with inventions of its own," I continued.

"Making stuff up?" Mr. Richter asked.

"Sometimes, yes," I replied. "It may be the case that the inventions of the brain are accurate and pull the pieces of a narrative together in a way that truly represents reality."

I stood and walked closer to the large fireplace. With my back to Mr. Richter, I continued, "And sometimes it is the case that the daydreams of the mind are pure fantasy, ideas we embrace because we long for the gaps in the story to be filled even if the result is not an accurate representation of reality."

"So, you are saying that Anna and Mr. Rossini are lying?" Mr. Richter asked.

"No," I replied, turning around, "I would not say *lying*. I believe that both Ms. Winthrop and Mr. Rossini genuinely believe the stories they have concocted in their minds. They are attempting to plug the holes with a narrative that makes sense and is, at least in part, supported by some of the tangible evidence available."

"But this speculation could have serious consequences," Mr. Richter argued. "If the authorities believe one story over another, it could mean that either Anna or Mr. Rossini are convicted of crimes, serious crimes."

I nodded, "That is true."

"This is why I am a scientist," Mr. Richter said in somewhat of an aside. "There is no speculation, no plugging in the holes with what feels interesting or good. There are facts. There is evidence. There is data. Your experiment either worked or it did not. You run a new study. You replicate your results. There is no room for loose interpretation."

"I know that about you, Mr. Richter," I replied.

"Is that so, Dame James?" Mr. Richter asked.

"Indeed, this is why *I* am an author. There is no hiding, no anonymity, no pretending to be someone else without revealing truths about who you *really* are in front of an author. Everyone is a character, and it is my job to identify a person's character, to notice the attributes and behaviours that reinforce that character, and to spot the feigned actions that would be out of character for a particular person. One's character may be complex and varied, of course, but an author always knows one's character in the end. *Always.*"

"Fascinating," Mr. Richter said. "And what would you say is my character? Researcher? Academic? Mad scientist?"

"No," I replied softly, "I could describe your character in just one word."

"And what word would that be?" Mr. Richter asked.

"Misunderstood."

\*　　　\*　　　\*

When Mr. Rossini and Anna returned to the parlour, the animosity the two had created for each other was readily apparent. Not wanting to appear biased given my professional relationship with Anna, I let Mr. Richter do the talking.

"Ms. Winthrop. Mr. Rossini," Mr. Richter began, "Dame James and I have deliberated over the accusations each of you has levied against the other. We found some merit in the points both of you have raised, yet several doubts still remain that make it difficult to pinpoint blame with a clear conscience."

In that moment, Mr. Rossini and Anna both seemed to have the same genuine expression of fear on their faces

"It is for this reason that we have proposed the following solution. Until the authorities are able to arrive, Ms. Winthrop will surrender the key to her room to Dame James and Mr. Rossini will surrender the key to his room to me. We are *all* to stay locked in our respective rooms until the access road is clear or the phone wires are fixed and the police can be alerted. We shall dine together at breakfast, lunch, and dinner as a group of four so that, should anyone in this room be dangerous, the others will be present for safety and protection."

Mr. Richter paused.

"Your acceptance of this plan is assumed, and any resistance or objection to this plan will be interpreted as an admission of your guilt of at least one of the crimes that have taken place here at Raven's Point Manor in the past several days. Are there any objections to the proposed plan?"

Mr. Rossini and Anna shared the same defeated expression.

"No," Anna replied.

"No objection," Mr. Rossini added.

The two accused guests each passed the key to their room to the assigned guardian. When Anna pressed her key into my palm, I did my best to communicate that I thought she *was* innocent, that Mr. Rossini's accusation was nowhere near as compelling as her indictment of him. Whether or not that was the message she received is anyone's guess.

Given that the hour had already grown late, the group decided it would grab dinner from the kitchen to eat in the dining room and then proceed up to the second floor for an early bedtime. We agreed that Mr. Richter and I would leave our rooms in the morning at 8 o'clock sharp, relying on our synced pocket watches given that the grandfather's clock was out of commission. We would then let out our temporary prisoners so they could come downstairs and grab breakfast in such a way that the four of us were never alone save for when we were locked away safely in our bedrooms. Raven's Point Manor now felt much more like a county jail and much less like a luxurious bed and breakfast.

Not surprisingly, no one said *one word* at dinner. The tension between Mr. Rossini and Ms. Winthrop was still simmering, fresh off the stove, and any attempt at carrying on normal conversation would just feel like one was making light of the very serious episode preceding dinner. When we finished eating, we took our used utensils to the kitchen, washed them, and then grabbed a few snacks from the pantry to take to our rooms. Surprising no one, I took several biscuits.

We took our temporary prisoners to their respective bedroom doors, let them enter their room and close their door, and then locked the doors simultaneously. I realized in that moment, that I was now alone with Mr. Richter in the hallway, granted a safe distance away.

"Goodnight, Mr. Richter," I offered, scurrying to my room in a way that I tried to make look as normal as possible.

"Goodnight, Dame James," he replied.

I entered my room, locked my door, and began my ritual of stacking furniture to create my barricade. I found that the excitement of the day's events had been quite exhausting, but I felt obligated to type up the details before they slipped my mind.

I sat at my desk and began typing. From the discovery of Ms. Merriweather's body to finding Miss Finley behind the brick wall in the cellar, from the diabolical connection to Edgar Allan Poe's works to the very serious accusations of murder lobbed by Mr. Rossini and Ms. Winthrop, the day had easily been the most unique and one of the worst of my storied life. Retyping the day's events just made the insanity of them all the more apparent. I knew it was my obligation to capture these details for the authorities, but I would be lying if I said my heart and my brain did not suffer reliving the details of the day.

I am not sure when it happened, what time it was or what my last thought had been, but despite my best effort to stay awake and finish capturing all the specific details of the tragic day, I fell asleep.

No dreams.

No nightmares.

Just darkness.

# 12 | THE REVEAL

I awoke to the sound of songbirds and beams of sunlight peeking through the heavy curtain hanging at my bedroom window. Upon pulling back the curtain, I was relieved to see that the weather outside finally seemed more characteristic of a warm June day. With any luck, the sun would dry up some of the saturated ground that had suffered so much flooding over the previous week.

I began to ready myself for the day, keeping a close eye on the time as I did. The last thing I wanted was to be late stepping into the hallway at 8 o'clock with Mr. Richter to set Mr. Rossini and Ms. Winthrop free. I also found myself strangely relieved that, for the first time in a while, my morning would not begin with a scream or the discovery of a deceased person. Small victories, I suppose.

I opened my door just as soon as the second hand landed on the twelve and my clock face read eight o'clock. I was surprised, then, when not only did I not see Mr. Richter emerge from his room, but his tardiness extended well past one minute, then past two minutes, and then past five minutes.

"He must be running late," I told myself. "No need to panic, Maggie."

As I was standing just outside Anna's door, I was a bit startled when there was a knock from the other side. Anna asked, "Dame James? Are you there?"

I should not have been surprised, I know, as I had planned on unlocking Ms. Winthrop's door at eight o'clock sharp and might as well have expected she was standing on the other side, anxiously awaiting her freedom. Still, I suppose my worry about Mr. Richter's tardiness made me temporarily forget that Anna was just beyond the door waiting to be released.

"Yes! Yes, I am here," I replied. "But, Anna, the strangest thing is happening."

"Strange? After this week?" she replied dryly. "Try me."

She had a point.

"Well, it would seem that Mr. Richter is either running extremely late or is, perhaps, indisposed," I replied. "He has not yet set foot out of his room, and it is almost ten full minutes after the time we agreed upon."

"Hmm, that *is* peculiar," Anna replied. "What about Mr. Rossini? Is he knocking to get out?"

"Not that I can hear," I replied, "but his room *is* at the opposite end of the hallway, and my ears are certainly not as sensitive as they used to be."

We stood in silence for a moment.

"Perhaps you should go knock on Mr. Richter's door then?" Anna suggested. "Maybe he has just overslept?"

"Ah, yes, that does seem to be the wisest course of action," I replied, "and forgive me, Anna, for not just letting you out. I am afraid both Mr. Richter and Mr. Rossini would be quite cross with me if I did given our agreement."

"I understand," Anna replied before adding, "but, to be fair, Mr. Richter is not holding up his end of the deal with his tardiness."

"Too true, my dear girl," I replied, "too true. Sit tight. I shall return."

I walked down the hallway slowly, keeping a careful eye on the foyer stairs, as well as the stairs leading up to the attic should anyone be hiding in the corners. When I got to Mr. Richter's door, I first listened to see if I could hear signs of life beyond the door. Then, hearing nothing, I gave the door a light tap.

"Mr. Richter? Good morning! It is Dame James," I said.

There was no response.

"Mr. Richter? Hello? It is me, Dame James!" I repeated. "We had agreed to meet in the hallway at eight o'clock to open the doors of Mr. Rossini and Ms. Winthrop."

Still nothing.

Figuring the young man might be in a deep sleep, I knocked on the door even louder and said, "Mr. Richter! Are you awake? Hello?"

This time, I heard something, but I was able to make out the source of the noise: Darwin. Apparently, my loud knocking had roused the monkey in the room, yet it failed to elicit a reaction from the human on the other side of the door.

I am not sure if it was instinct or just dumb luck, but I reached down to the door handle of Mr. Richter's room and gave it a turn. Much to my surprise, the door *opened*.

The room was an absolute mess. It appeared as if a small cyclone had scattered Mr. Richter's papers and belongings. Whatever sense of organized clutter his room had during the search of the manor gave way to complete and utter chaos. Even poor Darwin's cage was on its side, which I felt compelled to fix.

Curiously, Mr. Richter was nowhere to be found.

"Oh, dear," I said to myself, "this is not good."

My heart racing a bit and fearing for my safety, I hurried back to Anna's room and started fumbling with her room key in my hand as I tried to unlock her door.

"Anna," I said, "something is not right."

"What? What is it?" Anna asked from behind her door.

"Mr. Richter. He's...he's not in his room," I managed to get out while unlocking the door.

"Not in his room?" Anna asked as she opened her door. "Where is he?"

"I don't know," I replied. "I knocked several times, called his name, and then, hearing nothing, tried the door figuring it would be locked, but it opened right up!"

"Are his personal belongings still here? His luggage?" Anna asked.

"Yes," I nodded. "His room is a mess, but all of his personal items are still here."

"So, he probably did not flee the manor. And what about Mr. Rossini? Is he still in his room?" Anna asked.

In my panic upon discovering Mr. Richter's empty room I had completely forgotten about Mr. Rossini.

"I do not know," I replied. "I came running to you upon discovering Mr. Richter's empty room."

"Then let us go check for Mr. Rossini together," Anna suggested.

My assistant and I walked cautiously toward the other end of the hallway. As we passed Mr. Richter's room, I pushed the door open so Anna could see the mess I saw.

"Oh, dear!" Anna exclaimed. "Did he do this himself? *Would* he do this himself?"

I shrugged.

"Let's keep going," Anna suggested as we continued toward Mr. Rossini's room.

When we arrived at his door, Anna did the knocking.

"Mr. Rossini?" Anna called out. "Are you in there?"

No response.

"Marvin? If you are in there, can you please let us know?" I yelled.

We waited. Again, no reply. Something was off.

I looked at Anna and began, "Should we just…"

I couldn't even get the sentence out before Anna reached down, grabbed the door handle, and tried to open the door. Strangely, as had been the case with Mr. Richter's room, the door was unlocked and swung wide open.

Unfortunately, *unlike* Mr. Richter's room, Mr. Rossini's room was *not* empty. There, sprawled out in the middle of the bedroom floor was Mr. Marvin Rossini. The bright sunlight shining in from his window illuminated exactly the area where his body was. Although we could not tell from that distance whether or not Mr. Rossini was alive or dead, we had an established pattern of finding murder victims throughout Raven's Point Manor by now. We assumed the worst.

I let out a soft scream while Anna ran toward Mr. Rossini's body to check for a pulse.

"He is dead," Anna said, looking up at me with a worried expression.

"But how?" I asked.

Mr. Rossini was on his stomach, face down. A white powder was sprinkled all over the carpet and left some residue on Mr. Rossini's face and clothing. Also, about half a metre away from his head, a syringe was lying on the floor. Mr. Rossini had tied a small golden handkerchief tightly around his forearm, which likely was used to help make his veins more visible.

"Drugs?" Anna asked.

I nodded in agreement. "I am afraid so, Anna," I replied.

I realized at that moment that the powder I thought had been talcum powder a few days prior may not have been powder at all but, instead, cocaine. It was unclear what substance was in the syringe near his body, but the idea that Mr. Rossini had a drug problem was not altogether surprising. What we thought had been a runny nose or a slight cold could have very well been a side effect of the man's cocaine use. It also explained his manic energy at times.

"So, he died of an overdose then?" Anna reasoned.

"That's what it seems," I agreed, "but, if that is true, then why was his door unlocked?"

Anna had not thought about that.

"If Mr. Richter had the key, then he must have been in here," Anna suggested. "Perhaps he saw the scene and fled?"

"But *why* would Mr. Richter have come in here?" I asked. "We had agreed not to leave our rooms until eight o'clock. He would have been breaking the rules to come to Mr. Rossini's room at any point before our designated time."

"And why would he not have woken us up to tell us what he saw if he saw that Mr. Rossini had died?" Anna asked.

The writing was on the wall, clearly, but I think we were both too busy trying to avoid the truth to just come out and say it. Almost instinctively, Anna and I looked up toward the raven painting in Mr. Rossini's bedroom. Our intuition was confirmed: the lone, black raven in the painting had its eyes crossed out with two red Xs.

"Does this mean that…" Anna began to ask.

"It *wasn't* Mr. Rossini?" I finished. "It is certainly looking that way."

I walked over to the syringe lying next to Mr. Rossini and picked it up to examine it more closely.

"Careful, Dame James," Anna said. "You cannot be sure what is inside."

I carefully positioned the syringe in my hand to see what its label said.

"Heroin," I read aloud.

"Heroin?!" Anna responded, shocked. "What was he doing with heroin?"

I paused for a second and re-read the label just to make sure I was not mistaken.

"It was not *his*," I replied.

"Not his? Then whose was it?" Anna asked.

I lowered the syringe and looked at Anna with a face of shear panic, I am certain.

"Mr. Richter," I answered, "Dr. Ellard Fredrich Richter."

Anna's jaw dropped. She seemed to stop breathing as whatever little colour she had drained from the poor girl's already pale face.

"Ellard Richter? E.R.?," she said, "Elliott Radcliffe."

*       *       *

What happened next was a blur of emotion, quick thinking, and survival instinct. I opened the window and threw the syringe outside to prevent accidentally pricking ourselves with it. I should have known at once upon seeing the syringe and its contents that it came from Mr. Richter's mysterious bag of chemicals and substances we had uncovered during the search of the manor days before. We left Mr. Rossini's body in the room and shut the door behind us.

"Come with me," Anna said. "We need to check something."

She proceeded to lead me to Miss Finley's room where a quick survey of the raven painting in that room revealed what Anna feared we would discover: the eyes of the raven in that painting had been crossed out with red Xs just like the others.

She then pulled my arm and led me down the hallway to the rooms of Mabel Merriweather and Walter Ripley. Their paintings, too, had been defaced: red Xs on the eyes of the ravens.

"He has marked all his victims' rooms," Anna pointed out. "This is no murderer, Dame James. It is a deranged serial killer!"

We cautiously returned to Mr. Richter's room to see if there was any evidence that might have pointed to his plans; had he left with a suitcase, for example, then we might have reasoned that he had left the manor. The disorganization of the room did not lend itself to any useful clues except for one.

"Look, Dame James," Anna said as she pointed to the raven painting."

Unlike the other paintings throughout the rest of the manor, the eyes of the raven in Mr. Richter's room were untouched. Black, cold, staring eyes. It almost felt like Mr. Richter was staring right back at us as we gazed into the eyes of the raven.

"Anna, we need to get help," I suggested. "Perhaps the phone line is working again? We can go check in the library?"

"I agree," she replied, "but we must be careful. Mr. Richter could still be in the house."

We quietly snuck back down the hallway to our rooms where I grabbed my oversized umbrella and Anna grabbed a small knife from the kitchen she must have left in her room. To be truthful, neither of our little weapons would have done much to save us from a madman, but we did not want to venture down into the foyer empty handed.

We crept down the stairs cautiously, keeping one eye on the landing of the second floor, and another on the visible areas of the first floor. So far, there was no sign of Mr. Richter, and if he *were* wandering about the house, he was doing so without making one bit of sound.

As we reached the library, Anna stood in the doorway and instructed, "You go check the phone line, and I will stand here and keep watch. If I see anything, I will scream."

I did as I was told and walked my way to the far corner of the library, keeping an eye out just in case Mr. Richter was hiding behind any of the room's large furniture. Seeing no one, I hurried toward the phone. I picked up the handpiece and earpiece expecting the phone to still be dead.

But it wasn't.

"Operator?!" I yelled, then, worried I might attract attention to us, repeated in a whisper, "operator? Yes? Hello, my name is Dame Margaret James, and I need to be connected with the local police. I am at Raven's Point Manor on the grounds of the Radcliffe Estate. Yes. Yes, whatever is closest."

I looked over to Anna who, upon hearing my successful connection with the operator, seemed jubilant.

"Hello? Hello, yes. My name is Dame Margaret James, and I am a guest at Raven's Point Manor where a terrible crime has been committed. Several crimes, actually. There are two of us here who may be in grave danger. Yes. Yes, that's right: Raven's Point Manor. Radcliffe? Correct. Oh, thank you! Thank you so much!"

I hung up the phone and ran to Anna.

"The authorities have been notified and they are on their way!" I said joyfully.

"Oh, Dame James, that is terrific news! Just terrific!" Anna replied.

To be clear, I was ecstatic. How fortunate for us to have evaded the insane plot of Mr. Ellard Fredrich Richter–or Elliot Radcliffe–in whatever sick game of vengeance or retribution he was seeking. Still, this all seemed too good to be true. I had written enough murder mysteries to know that the story is not over until the story is over. It was with this in mind that I addressed Ms. Winthrop.

"Anna, my dear girl," I began, "we cannot count our blessings just yet. We still do not know if Mr. Richter is on the estate grounds. The authorities are on their way, yes, but it is unclear how long it will take for them to arrive. We should be extra cautious this close to the finish line."

"I agree," Anna replied. "One cannot be too careful in such a moment."

We paused for a second to look around and devise a plan.

"Let us go to the kitchen and get some food," I suggested, "definitely a pot of tea and some biscuits."

A lady knows what she likes.

"And then we can lock ourselves in my room or your room until the authorities arrive just to be certain that we are safe from harm," I added.

"That sounds like a marvellous plan to me, Dame James," Anna agreed.

With that we began our way to the kitchen, crossing the large foyer and making our way through the dining room. I was about to step foot in the kitchen when I felt Anna grab my arm from behind.

"Dame James," she said, "look at the painting on the wall."

The painting in the dining room, which consisted of three ravens perched on an old, wicked-looking tree, had been defaced. Two of the ravens sat on their perches, undisturbed. But the third raven, positioned on a branch just below the other two, had both of its eyes marked out with red Xs just like the raven paintings in the bedroom.

"That is odd," Anna said aloud.

"Indeed," I agreed. "What could it mean?"

We positioned ourselves at the head of the dining table so that we could see the painting straight on.

"I do not understand," Anna began. "Each of the other ravens corresponded with the rooms and deaths of the guests in those rooms, but no one lived *here* in the dining room."

I thought for a moment.

"Maybe it signified the death of good cooking with Mrs. Flaherty's dreadful meals," I offered. It seemed humour could lighten the otherwise rather dark moment.

Anna smiled.

"I supposed it could have signified the death of Mrs. Flaherty," she suggested before adding, "but you mentioned a raven statue in Kath's room with its eyes marked with Xs."

"That is correct," I agreed, "and I do think we would have noticed that this painting had been defaced long before now if Mr. Richter did it after killing Mrs. Flaherty."

We stood and stared at the painting a bit longer, completely perplexed by what it was supposed to signify, worried that we might never figure it out.

"Ah, well," I said, "probably best to leave well enough alone and get upstairs where we know we will be safe."

"I concur," Anna said and turned around toward the doorway of the dining room.

I took a step toward the kitchen when I felt Anna grab my arm *again*.

Surprised by this, I naturally looked toward Anna's face. She seemed distracted, staring off into the foyer as if she had seen a ghost.

I panicked. "What is it?! Is it Mr. Richter?" I asked.

I looked in the direction of Anna's gaze. No one was there. Not Mr. Richter. Not a ghost. Nothing. Just air. Still, the girl stared straight ahead. I looked beyond the foyer into the parlour where the fireplace was burning and the large painting of the Radcliffe family sat atop the mantle.

That is when it hit me.

I looked at the painting of the Radcliffe family, turned around to the far wall of the dining room, and looked at the painting of a conspiracy of ravens. I turned back to the parlour. Mr. Radcliffe, Mrs. Radcliffe, and young Elliott Radcliffe. The three members of the Radcliffe family. I turned once again to the dining room painting. Three ravens, with the eyes of the raven corresponding to Elliott Radcliffe crossed out with the red Xs.

Anna and I looked once more at the paintings, then at each other.

She began, "It would seem that Elliott Radcliffe is...dead?"

"It would seem that way," I agreed. "Or maybe Dr. Ellard Fredrich Richter *wants* it to seem that way."

A concerned look flashed across Anna's face.

"Anna, my dear girl, we best hurry and get upstairs."

And, with that, we grabbed whatever we could get our hands on in the pantry, and ran up to Anna's room to wait for the authorities.

\*　　　\*　　　\*

After locking ourselves inside Anna's room, my assistant and I began to think through the events of the previous days in a world where Mr. Fred Richter had committed the murders.

"We knew from the first evening that Mr. Richter was a socially odd sort," Anna began, "obsessed with science, the human brain, and—most importantly—the ability for the human brain to be controlled or manipulated with chemical substances."

"Correct," I agreed.

"If we operate under the assumption that Mr. Richter *was*, in fact, Elliott Radcliffe, then his motive to murder Kath is quite clear: the woman and her husband had taken the boy's inheritance and never bothered themselves with trying to locate him," Anna went on. "They may have even sent him away for all we know."

"Indeed," I added, "and the same logic works for Giles. As we discussed the other day, I am convinced Giles was most likely Mr. and Mrs. Flaherty's own son who, as a result of having developmental issues, was treated in the most inhumane fashion."

"I think you are definitely right with that connection," Anna responded. "What is less clear was Mr. Richter's motivation to murder the others—Ms. Lavoie, for example, or Miss Finley and Mr. Rossini."

"Well, the boy did seem emotionally disturbed," I offered. "That is often reason enough for some to murder."

"True," Anna continued, "I do think, however, there may have been a connection between Mr. Richter and Ms. Simmons, er, Merriweather, whatever we want to call her."

This intrigued me.

"We know that Ms. Merriweather was a patient at a nearby asylum," said Anna, "and we also know that Mr. Richter's research focus was biological chemistry. He went out of his way to discuss how chemicals affect the mind and the ability for the brain to think properly."

"Yes!" I exclaimed. "He even spoke about how one's emotions and mental health were a function of these chemical reactions!"

"Precisely," Anna said, "which leads me to believe that Mr. Richter and Ms. Merriweather had a prior relationship to her arrival to Raven's Point Manor. How else would she have known that there was a house hidden so far in these parts?"

"Indeed! Why would she wander through the rain if she did not have some indication that there was safe shelter ahead?" I added. "She *was* insane, but that always seemed so peculiar to me."

"So, if Ms. Merriweather and Mr. Richter had some pre-existing relationship, it could have been possible that he intended to pin the crimes on her, a poor, mentally unstable asylum escapee," Anna continued, "which would have allowed him to take vengeance on his missed fortune and childhood while also evading any of the suspicion or criminal charges that would have followed."

"And the Poe connection?" I asked. "What of that?"

"Well, I would not be surprised if Mr. Richter had been exposed to the work of Poe even as a child. A bit dark, yes, but I imagine the school his parents could afford likely taught the classics at a young age," Anna suggested. "Even if not, however, he would have most certainly been exposed to the great works during his university studies."

"That is my thinking exactly," I concurred. "There was never any doubt in my mind that Mr. Richter, a man who clearly spoke several languages, would not have crossed paths with the work of Chaucer, Shakespeare, Poe, and the sort."

"Precisely," Anna responded.

There was a brief pause.

"But what about the German bit?" I asked. "Why pretend to be German and then do it so incredibly poorly, I might add?"

"A cover, I suppose," Anna went on. "He clearly could not book a room under his birth name, and who even knows if he continued to use the name Elliott Radcliffe when he left Raven's Point Manor."

"Of course," I added, "his occasional use of a few German words was enough to throw the rest of us off. That is true."

"And he would have studied several of the classic languages given his pedigree," Anna added. "The way he translated Mr. Rossini's Italian, for example. Responding in French to Ms. Lavoie. Pretending to be German was not so much of a challenge for him, even if it was not perfectly executed."

"But then why run off?" I asked. "Assuming he is not still here in the manor with us, why murder all these innocent people and then leave if what you wanted was what was rightfully yours in the first place?"

"Dame James," Anna said softly, "you know how it is with these types. You, yourself, were once of a lower-class and, through hard work, are now of the same level as families like the Radcliffes."

"I would not say at the *exact* same level," I laughed.

"Back home in Birmingham, I recognized the difference between those of us who had to work, many who struggled to get by, and those who just 'got by' with little to no effort thanks to the fortunes their family had accumulated, the wealthy connections and opportunities their name, alone, was able to procure," Anna said. "Only one of those groups truly ever appreciated what they had, and we both know which group it was."

I understood exactly what the girl was saying.

"So, he did not truly care about the house or his assets," I offered. "He just wanted to make sure *no one else* could benefit from *his* family's resources."

"I'm afraid so," Anna said.

There was a moment that felt like a deep sigh or an exhale.

"I suppose I should apologize to you, Ms. Winthrop," I began.

Anna looked at me curiously.

"I never expected that when I hired you to be my assistant that I would be putting you in harm's way quite like this," I added. "You have proven to be an exceptionally good assistant and quite an incredible detective at that!"

Anna laughed. "Thank you, Dame James," she said. "It has been quite an adventure."

We sat in silence for some time, Anna enjoying her tea and I enjoying my biscuits, relieved that the madness of what was supposed to be an uneventful, peaceful writing retreat was now over.

*     *     *

An hour or so had passed and then several more before it struck us as odd that the authorities had not yet arrived.

"Do you think the access road is still flooded?" I asked. "It has not been sunny or warm for very long in comparison to how much rain we have had."

"That is possible," Anna replied.

I walked over to the window to see what we could observe from the safety of Anna's room.

"Oh, dear," Anna said. "Dame James, you do not think the authorities have already been here but found the front door locked and went away?"

Bloody hell. I had *not* thought of that. In our haste to get upstairs to safety, we had left the front door locked and secured.

"I suppose that *is* possible, Anna," I replied.

The dread that had been absent from our faces for a few hours quickly returned, as we both realized what this meant.

"We have to go open the door," Anna suggested.

I will admit that I gave half a thought to asking Anna if she would not mind going downstairs to unlock the door on her own. She was much younger and faster than me, and I thought it might be safer for both of us if I just stood in the doorway and kept watch. Realizing how unfair that was, I reluctantly agreed to join Anna on a quick trip downstairs to unlock the door for the authorities.

We took down the makeshift barricade we fashioned like the ones I had been setting up in my room. I grabbed my large umbrella, and Anna went to grab her small knife before realizing she had left it down in the kitchen when we grabbed food and hurried back upstairs.

Realizing that the knife was no longer in our possession, we exchanged a look of worry, although I tried to hide any disappointment in my face even if that was what I was feeling. We opened the door to the bedroom slowly and made our way to the stairs. The house was silent, not even the tick-tock of the grandfather's clock. This was both reassuring and alarming, as I half-expected Mr. Richter to jump out from one of the downstairs rooms at any moment.

We reached the bottom of the stairs and then hurried across the large foyer to the front door. I reached down to unlock it but found that it was *already unlocked.*

"It is already open!" I said to Anna. We both realized that this meant the authorities had not yet arrived, because if they had, they would have had no difficulty entering the manor.

We opened the door and stepped outside to the sunny, humid afternoon. Everything outside seemed...peaceful. A light breeze was blowing, birds were looking for worms in the front yard, and the trees were swaying in the light wind that was moving warm air across the estate.

"It feels so nice to be outside," I said.

Anna, however, seemed a bit preoccupied with something further down toward the far end of the house beyond the parlour.

"What is that there in the yard?" she asked as she advanced toward the side yard.

Looking out into the grass, I saw what she was talking about. Pieces of something, like shards of glass from a mirror, were reflecting the rays of the sun creating what looked like one hundred miniature lighthouses sending their beacons our direction. And, like ships, we followed their call.

As we approached the edge of the house, we saw that it was not, in fact, pieces of a broken mirror but, instead, pieces from a shattered window. And just a few metres in front of us, in the midst of all the broken glass and fragments of wood, was the very item that broke the attic window now scattered across the side yard: Mr. Fredrich Richter.

"Oh, my God!" I yelled.

"Suicide!" Anna said. "Of course he would!"

There, lying on the ground, in the most contorted shape I have ever seen was the mangled body of Ellard Fredrich

Richter—Elliot Radcliffe—bleeding from where the glass had cut him, bones breaking the skin in some places from the fall.

I could barely stomach to look at the sight much longer when I noticed that a rope had been tied around one of his ankles. The other end of the rope was tied around the most curious thing, an item that made complete sense once I stepped closer to get a look at what it was: the black raven statue from Mrs. Flaherty's room, the two eyes crossed out in red paint.

Anna, upon seeing the black marble raven statue I was looking at, spoke up, "An insurance policy, I gather; in case he chickened out at the moment of jumping. The coward."

Between the rope and the raven statue, a small, handwritten note was wedged. Anna grabbed the note and read it aloud:

*To Whom It May Concern:*

*By the time you find this letter, I will have taken my own life after taking the lives of strangers, people who infiltrated my home and enjoyed my family's personal belongings as if they were their own. This coveting is what led me to flee Raven's Point Manor as a child, and I vowed one day to return and seek my revenge. That day has now come and gone, and I can rest easily knowing that no undeserving filth is contaminating our manor, our estate, or the Radcliffe family name. Nevermore.*

*-E.F. Radcliffe*

"A suicide note?" Anna went on. "Such a peculiar man."

I nodded my head.

"It truly does not make any sense," she continued. "Why would he let *us* live if his goal were to rid the house of 'undeserving filth?'"

"That *is* puzzling, my dear girl," I replied. "He knew that we were…"

I stopped talking.

"Anna, do you hear that?" I asked.

"Hear what?" Anna replied.

"Shh," I quieted her so that I could hear the noise better. "It is faint, but there's a noise coming from the direction of the trees over there," I said, pointing toward the back of the house.

I began heading in the direction of the sound.

"Be careful, Dame James," Anna said following me. "You don't know who might be back there!"

I picked up my pace. The noise was getting louder, which meant we were getting closer.

Thump, thump. Thump, thump.

We walked past the first few trees of the green forest in the back of the manor. Up ahead in the distance was the dilapidated guesthouse Mr. Richter and Ms. Merriweather had located the other day during the search of the grounds.

"Of course!" I said, "Richter was the one who found the old guesthouse!"

We were practically sprinting to the source of the sound.

"I cannot hear the sound as well as you do, Dame James, but I am right behind you," Anna said.

"*How can she not hear this?*" I thought to myself. I began to worry that her inability to hear the drumming sound was a deliberate attempt to throw my attention.

Thump, thump. Thump, thump.

"Surely there isn't someone else being held captive or buried alive again?!" Anna asked.

"I am not sure, Anna," I replied. "I wouldn't put anything past Mr. Richter at this point."

Upon entering the crooked doorway of the guesthouse, the pulsing became almost unbearable.

Anna's eyes widened and looked at me with a curious, altogether creepy gaze. Her steel grey eyes cut through me with an icy coldness that made my skin crawl.

"I *do* hear it," Anna whispered with the wild look in her eyes now spreading across her entire face.

"I *told* you!" I barked back, a bit stunned that my aged ears could hear better than Anna's younger ones.

*"It's as if she pretended not to hear anything until she could pretend no longer,"* I thought to myself.

As we entered the rotting kitchen, the sound grew louder.

Thump, thump. Thump, thump.

"It's here! Under here!" Anna screamed, pointing to the floorboards near where the abandoned pantry was.

It may very well have been my own breathing, which was greatly exaggerated in all the excitement, but it seemed as though the floorboards, themselves, were pulsing to the beat of this invisible drum.

"Well, don't just stand there," I commanded. "Let's grab something to get these boards up!"

The pantry had a mix of old tools and supplies among its shelves of dry foods and canned goods. Anna, searching a dark corner of the pantry, returned with a metal crowbar that must have been used to open crates stacked nearby. I, instinctively, grabbed a shovel I saw among the brooms. Its placement did not seem particularly odd at the time, nor did my gravitation toward grabbing this particular tool upon seeing Anna approach with a crowbar.

I attempted to plunge the shovel into the floorboards, but my aged back was as creaky as the boards I was hoping to break. I struggled a bit trying to figure out the best position while also keeping a watchful eye on Anna and her crowbar.

"Stand back. I'll do it," Anna insisted, pushing me aside as she knelt down on the floor.

The next few minutes felt like mere seconds as Anna began prying up pieces of the hardwood floor. "I hear it," she screamed maniacally. "Can you hear it?! It's getting louder, Dame James. Louder!"

Thump, thump. Thump, thump.

Then, Anna pried away a final piece of the flooring, gazed deep into the hole she had created, and turned to face me with the most deranged expression I had ever seen. Her hand gripped the crowbar tightly, her cold eyes suddenly raging with fire.

I had just a brief moment to glance at the hole in the floor before returning my complete attention to Anna who was starting to stand from her kneeling position. That's when I saw it.

There, in a sliver of light bleeding into the darkness of the cellar, was a beating heart...

Thump, thump. Thump, thump.

...right where I left it.

# 13 | THE END

Poor Anna did not have enough time to stand up from her kneeling position before my shovel came down across her face. She must have had her suspicions all along, of course; she was not a daft girl. It is just unfortunate that she was just a tad bit too slow to figure it out. The look of realisation upon her face when she turned around was truly unforgettable: the whites of her eyes, the bewildered expression. It is possible that I imagined it, but I think I saw her mouth the words, "It's you!" right before the shovel smacked into her pale face.

Of course, getting Anna out to the guesthouse was no accident. I deliberately led her to the guesthouse just as I deliberately struggled to get myself in position to dig up the floorboards because I *needed* her to push me out of the way. I needed her to kneel on the floor. I needed her to think that I was not at all in charge of what was occurring in these final moments.

The use of the Victrola was truly a stroke of sudden genius. A few days before, when we had been listening to music in the parlour, I noticed the needle skipping at the end of the record sounded like the soft beating of a heart. I just had to get Anna close enough to hear it coming from under the floor of the guesthouse pantry. Had she been a bit more observant, she would have seen the trapdoor I used to place the device in the crawlspace in the first place. The old house was rotten, indeed, but the electricity worked just fine, which Mr. Richter made the mistake of mentioning.

What sounded like a beating heart was enough to trick

Anna's mind into thinking the liver I had placed under the floorboards was actually a heart. I mean, honestly, where was I going to get a real beating heart at that point? Everyone was already dead! Thankfully, my many trips to the kitchen made me keenly aware of the meat supply Kath had kept stored in the freezer. One, partially-thawed liver in a dimly lit crawlspace did exactly what I needed it to do. Elaborate, I know, but this was to be my grand finale.

To be honest, I was not surprised that Anna made it until the very end of the story. It wound up being quite poetic, actually: the smart, quiet type outwitting the others and *almost* figuring out the mystery only to succumb to the same fate as everyone else in the end. Well, *almost* everyone else, for I had different plans for Anna. You see, Anna was a sweet girl, but thankfully she had no family to miss her and no family to come looking for her. Indeed, if the police were to suspect anyone upon their discovery of the horrific scenes at Raven's Point Manor, it would most likely be the mysterious young woman with no connections, no established reputation, and no other reason to be there except something nefarious. I had removed the fake suicide note I wrote for Mr. Richter, so Anna would likely be the top suspect.

Perhaps most important, my name would never even be connected to Raven's Point Manor, its guests, or anything to do with the weekend's unfortunate events. You see, when I instructed Anna to book our rooms under a false name, I was not trying to throw off obsessed fans or the local townsfolk. No, I was deliberately removing myself from the scene of a crime. Clever, no?

But what about when I phoned the authorities? I spoke my name to the operator and to the police, didn't I? Did you hear the conversation? Did Anna? Did *anyone*? Of course not. The phone was still down; I took care of cutting the wire in the cellar during my self-guided tour of the manor. As far as anyone knew, Dame Margaret James never even stepped one foot in Raven's Point Manor. Even the driver booked for our arrival had a different name. As far as anyone knew, I spent a lovely holiday in New York City.

Planning a well-executed murder takes careful, advanced preparation. I should know, after all, as I have planned intricate murders on at least 39 different occasions from places as exotic as the French Riviera to as mundane as the English countryside. That this, my 40th foray into a murderous affair, actually came to fruition was a bit of a happy accident. But decades of planning all the fictitious murders that came before certainly made it easier to plan these murders.

Now, before I go into detail explaining *how* I did it, I should acknowledge that I understand if you, the reader of this novel, are quite cross with me for having led you down so many dead ends, so many possible murderers and motives that left you second-guessing yourself throughout the story (particularly near the end). However, if you are expecting an apology, well, let me just remind you of one, simple fact: I *told* you it was me at the very, very beginning.

Do you remember the first line of this book? If not, I shall retype it here: "As a writer of murder mysteries, I never expected to be at the *heart of such a crime*, and yet here we are." Perhaps you thought the heart of a crime would be its victim, but I am here writing this novel, aren't I? Thus, you should have properly deduced that if I were not the victim of said crime then I must certainly have been the perpetrator, the guilty party. Witnesses are mere bystanders and are not central to the story; more capillaries and arteries than the heart, itself. In fact, if you return to the first chapter of this book and read it once more, you may realize that the introduction of this book was, in fact, my confession, why I wanted to commit these murders in the first place.

More on that shortly, but first, let me shed some light on how I managed to murder ten strangers in cold blood, with an eleventh stranger killed for me (thank you very much, Mabel Merriweather). I truly hope you do not think of me as a crazy person, for I assure you that I am *not* insane.

Instead, perhaps you will try to appreciate, maybe even admire, the careful planning and sophistication of my plan.

We shall begin with the very first death: Mrs. Flaherty. Kathleen Flaherty was too much of a busybody to leave well enough alone. I recognized this early on and figured that her clockwork planning and stubborn regimen would be quite problematic if I were to be successful on my mission. Anything out of the ordinary at the manor would most certainly be noticed by Kath Flaherty. She had to go. Killing her was easy enough, of course, and I knew that using the grungy dinner bell she nagged Giles about would be enough to throw suspicion his way. If you recall, I awoke early that morning of Kath's death, proceeded downstairs, saw that Giles had already gone out for the day, and lured Mrs. Flaherty to the basement with a promise to polish that dirty bell. I knew the cleaning supplies were downstairs from my self-guided tour of the manor, a tour that Mrs. Flaherty herself encouraged. Silly woman. When she turned around to reach for the light, I shoved the bell right into eye socket, piercing the brain and causing a quick, not so bloody, death. I quickly checked my clothing for any blood, rearranged her body to make it seem like a falling accident, and then screamed as loudly as I could. I was pleased when Mr. Rossini and Mr. Powell concluded that Mrs. Flaherty's death was an accident, even as I realized I likely should have created some extra scratches and bruises to make the fall seem more convincing. Alas, one cannot think of *everything.*

At this point, the other guests were none the wiser that a cold, calculating murderer was among them. Mrs. Flaherty's death was but a mere accident, and I realised that there was value in leveraging this notion of a "naturally occurring" death theme as long as I could. Why raise suspicion if you do not have to? Thus, you can imagine my absolute delight when Mr. Powell revealed that his favourite cocktail was a little mix known as the "Corpse Reviver," which was part gin, Cointreau, a bit of Lillet Blonde, some fresh lemon juice, and, importantly, some Absinthe. The night before his death when we were all gathered in the library enjoying a post-dinner drink, Mr. Powell commented on how much he just *loved* this particularly cocktail, which led to several reactions of disgust from the rest of the guests. So, when Mr. Powell and the others left the next day to walk to the throughway for assistance in dealing with Mrs. Flaherty's body, I took it upon myself to "borrow" some of the sedatives Ms. Simmons brought for her brother and conveniently mixed them into the Absinthe. I knew no one *but* Mr. Powell would be drinking Absinthe, and the amount of sedative I put into the bottle should have killed him. Of course, you can imagine my surprise when we later learned that he had actually been buried alive. My mistake, I suppose, but after some additional reflection on the situation I was *delighted*: a drink called the Corpse Reviver led to a man being buried alive. That was almost too perfect to plan!

It was actually at this point that I thought of the Poe connection. You see, as a young girl, I used to *love* reading Poe's work while lying on the beach by the sea, so I was intimately familiar with all his macabre stories. In fact, I often think it was my early fascination with Poe that led me to take an interest in writing mysteries in the first place. One tale, *The Premature Burial*, told the story of a man who was terrified at the thought of being buried alive. He awakens at one point in pitch black darkness convinced his worst fear has come true. It turns out that it has not: he has just fallen asleep in the berth of a small boat. Unfortunately for Mr. Powell, he *had* been buried alive. Too bad, I suppose. If you can recall, Anna incorrectly thought Mr. Powell's death was based on *The Tell-Tale Heart*, but she was mistaken. If only she had gotten it right, well, she might have later guessed what was truly happening before that shovel came down on her face. The bell used to murder Mrs. Flaherty fit nicely with the Poe poem *The Bells*, and so I had found my motif. No great murder mystery should be without one.

Next came our French fashion designer, Mademoiselle

Claudette Lavoie. The day of her death, Ms. Simmons' odd outburst at the chess table was enough to distract the other guests in our company just long enough for me to grab the jade-handled dagger from its place on the shelf and slip it into my handbag. I figured if anyone turned to see me grabbing the knife, I would just pretend to be looking at it up-close; for all they knew it was my first time seeing the dagger. However, I had remembered the dagger from spending some time in the parlour the day I arrived. The fact that everyone retired earlier that night meant that everyone would also be falling asleep earlier; what *else* was there to do, after all? Once I heard Mr. Richter go into his room, I snuck down the hallway and slipped into Ms. Lavoie's room. How, you ask? It was surprising to me that no one ever thought about the skeleton key in Mrs. Flaherty's possession as the woman who cleaned the rooms and changed the linens each day. Killing her first gave me access to this key, and this key then gave me access to *any* room that I wanted. This would come in very handy later to throw off suspicion when *I* would be the one to suggest that we all lock ourselves in our rooms. What did I care if the others locked themselves away? *I* could still get to them.

Ms. Lavoie's room was already dark, lit only by a single lamp on the nightstand, and Ms. Lavoie was nowhere to be seen. I could hear her singing some pleasant little French tune from the washroom, so I hid behind the wardrobe figuring she would likely exit the washroom, climb into bed, turn off the light, and fall asleep in the dark. Too easy. Thus, you can imagine my surprise when she left the washroom and then sat at her vanity to brush her hair for what seemed like hours. I was growing so tired from just standing there that I was half tempted to crawl on my hands and knees to the door just to escape, a failed attempt. It was *then* that I saw it: a furry little creature, sitting on top of the canopy bed. I recognized it as a small monkey of some sort but wondered why in the world Ms. Lavoie had a small monkey in her room. A rooster? Sure. A poodle? Even better. But a monkey? And then it hit me: this was the lost "item" for which Mr. Richter had been searching. A marvellous idea then sprang into my mind per my new murderous motif. While Ms. Lavoie turned her head to the side to brush out her long hair, I took my opportunity, stabbing her right in the side of the neck. I don't believe the poor girl saw me coming, not in person or in the reflection of the vanity, which was a relief. I quite liked Ms. Lavoie, but she also had to go. I realized during our conversation earlier that evening, the one about Miss Finley and Mr. Rossini, as well as in some of our prior conversations, that Ms. Lavoie was supremely observant...*too* observant...and having her around would have made my job *that* much more difficult. As much as it pained me to do it, particularly given that she was such a splendid chef, the writing was on the proverbial wall.

I knew that the other guests would suspect murder following Ms. Lavoie's death, so to add some excitement to the game, I thought it would be fun to leave a "calling card" of sorts. I took the brightest red lipstick I could find from atop Ms. Lavoie's vanity and used it to cross out the eyes of the raven in the painting hanging on her bedroom wall. And, with that, my murderous plan became "a conspiracy of ravens," a fun play on words and the perfect title for what would be my final novel.

It was also after Ms. Lavoie's murder that Miss Finley and Mr. Rossini suggested that I, Dame Margaret James, take on the role of recordkeeper and investigator for no other reason than the fact that I had written a series of successful murder mysteries in my time. The secret to using this to my advantage was to protest the idea immediately, to shun the suggestion as if it made no sense at all. "I *write* murder mysteries," I said, "I do not *solve* them. And I certainly am no detective." Had I jumped at the opportunity when Mr. Rossini suggested I play such a significant role as detective, then the others might have been suspicious that I was *trying* to avoid being seen as a suspect. Playing it the opposite direction worked very much to my advantage. From the perspective of the other guests, I was no longer a suspect; I was the detective on the hunt of said suspect, quite a comfortable position in which to be.

Giles was next, and coordinating his murder was made much easier following the top-to-bottom search of the manor. You will notice that I never assigned myself to work with Anna. This was deliberate, of course, because I knew that, as my assistant, she and I would confer on matters pertaining to the searching, the guests, and other topics. By splitting up, I was able to get twice as much information as anyone else in the house, which allowed me to keep on top of everything and everyone. When Anna mentioned the attic and the odd area in which countless painted portraits of Giles were created, I knew then that I would likely be able to lure the young man up to the attic.

However, it was my discovery of the photos in Mrs. Flaherty's room that made something abundantly clear: there *was* a connection between Kathleen Flaherty and Giles, but it was *not* that he was her son. This idea seemed like quite a good one, if you can recall, and was the prevailing theory after it was presented, but do you recall whose idea it was? Remember, when Anna was speculating that Mr. and Mrs. Flaherty might have had a child, it was *I* who posed the question, "Do you mean to think that Giles was actually Mrs. Flaherty's son?" From that point, the investigation operated under the assumption that Giles was Mrs. Flaherty's son. The photos I found in Kath's room, however, included several of her with Elliott Radcliffe. There were photos from when the young Mr. Radcliffe was a toddler, several from when he was seven or eight (right around when his parents died), and, quite importantly, more photos of him as a young teenager and then as a young adult. This gradual evolution revealed one very important fact: Giles was *not* Mrs. Flaherty's son. Giles was Elliott Radcliffe.

The deterioration of the boy's physical appearance was

unmistakable. Mr. and Mrs. Flaherty certainly did *not* look after Elliott Radcliffe as if he were one of their own. I can only imagine the abuse the poor boy suffered at the hands of Kath and her husband if her treatment of "Giles" as an adult were any indication. The fact that the young master of the Radcliffe family was banished to the basement and had suffered mental limitations as a result of what I am *certain* was cruel and unusual treatment from the Flahertys was unacceptable. The young man never went to war; he just fought a constant battle with the unloving, abusive Flahertys. Their clear animosity toward each other made so much more sense in light of this discovery. Not that I ever had any regret after killing Kath, but the evidence of her abusive behaviour certainly justified her death. Good riddance.

I know, I know. That sounds rich coming from someone who murdered ten strangers, but I am no sociopath. I *do* have feelings; I have just grown numb to most of them.

Luring "Giles" upstairs was simple, the poor fellow. I told him it was time for a painting, and he just followed me. He did not understand what was happening when I tied the rope around the chair; I pretended like we were playing a game, which he actually enjoyed. That made it even worse, to be honest. I told him to close his eyes and count to ten, and that is when I stabbed him in the back, literally and figuratively, before marking his eyes. I did not *want* to do it, you see, but I *had* to.

The inspiration for this death came from a lesser known Poe story, *The Oval Portrait*, in which an artist has his wife sit for a portrait he is painting of her. The man paints and paints while the woman just sits there growing sicker, paler, and thinner until one day she just dies of negligence because of her husband's obsession with his craft. If ever there were a better story to capture Mrs. Flaherty's obsession about her own interest creating her "inn" and the negligence that led to Elliott Radcliffe's deterioration into "Giles," well, I have yet to discover it.

And then there was Miss Mary Jane Finley, schoolteacher, hopeful mistress, and, in the end, the most challenging kill. The partially constructed wall in the cellar was just too perfect to ignore given my Poe-themed killing spree. Think about it: it simply would not be compelling enough for a final book in a series of forty books to stick to just stabbings or poisonings. No, what would be needed was something remarkable, something memorable, something that would make the reader appreciate the cleverness the author put into her work. If I were truly going to pay homage to Mr. Poe, then I should seize the opportunity to recreate one of his best works: *The Cask of Amontillado.*

You might remember the day that the able-bodied guests went searching the grounds to see if another, as-yet-identified person was on the Radcliffe estate. I knew, of course, that there was no one else behind the murders, and I had been assigned to stay at the manor with Mrs. Powell. I was supposed to type up all the happenings of the previous days, including the previous night's searches, while Mrs. Powell could, I don't know, sleep or layer on her makeup or something. I made mention to Miss Finley that morning that Anna had found something suspicious in Giles' room. I suggested that Miss Finley, being a staunch defender of Giles, would likely be interested in seeing what it was Anna had found. I instructed her to find any excuse to hurry back to the house as soon as possible after leaving with her search partner to explore the grounds so that we could deal with it together without anyone else there to interrupt us.

Miss Finley did as I instructed, of course, having no reason to suspect malintent. With Mrs. Powell asleep (as usual), Miss Finley and I snuck down to the cellar where I had already started bricking in part of the doorway leading to the new storage room. I fumbled for the light switch and asked Miss Finley to "find a torch" while I quickly picked up one of the bricks on the pile and struck her head with it. It was easy enough, then, to lift her limp body over the small opening remaining in the brick wall and to continue stacking bricks undetected. Just before reaching the very top of the cellar ceiling, I doused some of the work rags in kerosene, lit a match, and tossed the items into the small room with Miss Finley's body, closing off the rest of the wall just thereafter. If Miss Finley were to wake in time, she would have found herself trapped in a brick-walled room with no windows, no exit, and—quite importantly—no ventilation for the smoke that was collecting in the small space. If panic did not do the poor girl in, then smoke inhalation certainly would have. A morbid way to go, indeed, but a stunning tribute to Edgar Allan Poe. I was quite pleased with my work.

The next two deaths were completely insane due largely in part to the fact that one of the two victims was legitimately *insane*. Ms. Betty Simmons and her "brother," Walter, were peculiar from the moment they arrived. As someone who has spent her lifetime introducing odd characters at opportune moments in stories, I imagine I was particularly sensitive to the improbable chance that two random strangers would somehow *accidentally* arrive at Raven's Point Manor (and in the middle of a torrential rain no less)! The lack of luggage, the inconsistent story, and, of course, the absence of any broken-down vehicle near the access road confirmed my suspicions.

Almost as if a sign of divine intervention, or perhaps divine *endorsement* even, the ultimate reveal that Ms. Simmons was, in fact, Ms. Mabel Merriweather, an escaped patient from an asylum, and Mr. Walter Simmons was truly Dr. Walter Ripley, unwitting hostage, reminded me of another famous Poe story. In his work *The System of Doctor Tarr and Professor Fether*, the narrator attends a dinner party hosted by the director of an insane asylum. The other dinner guests are dressed in odd outfits and are acting strangely, but the narrator thinks nothing of it. Before the dinner ends, it is revealed that the party guests are actually escaped patients who have, quite humorously, locked up the doctors in the patients' rooms. The doctors break free just in time, but the story still has such a haunting feel to it. When it was uncovered that nurse, Betty Simmons, was actually an insane person named Mabel Merriweather and her "patient," Walter Simmons, was actually Dr. Walter Ripley, well, it was as satisfying as wonderful poetry!

Ms. Merriweather's brutal killing of Dr. Ripley was impressive, even for someone who has dreamed up countless creative ways to murder someone for a living. I had no idea her dousing him in alcohol was part of a grander plan to push him into the fireplace, but brava, Ms. Merriweather. Brava, indeed! Unfortunately, I had to reward Ms. Merriweather's contribution to my killing spree with a wallop to the head. After Mr. Rossini, Mr. Richter, Anna, and I agreed to lock ourselves in our rooms for the evening, I realized that I could not carry out my plan very well with a mentally unstable person running around the house getting in the way. I was up half the night worrying about it, so when I awoke earlier than usual, I figured I could use this extra time to my benefit.

I crept out of my room, snuck down the foyer stairs, and searched for something to carry as a weapon. Of course, the ticking and tocking of the grandfather's clock was a familiar, early morning sound by now and a reminder that I was usually the only person awake for several hours each morning. I also realized that if I were to take the pendulum from the clock, then the clock would not chime to alert the others about our agreed upon meeting time. Perfect.

Now, looking for Ms. Merriweather *would* have been a challenge except the previous night's rain meant she left footprints in the mud that directed me right to her. The poor thing had *not* actually fallen into one of "Giles'" holes but was sleeping nearby. I snuck up slowly, positioned the pendulum, and then swung as if working on my golf game. Then I swung again. And again. And then once more. Once I realized Ms. Merriweather was dead, I slid her body over to one of the holes, a "pit" as it were, and dumped her lifeless body inside. I tossed the pendulum a few metres away and delighted in my homage to *The Pit and the Pendulum.* I hurried back upstairs and, when the grandfather's clock failed to chime at eight o'clock as expected, simply pretended to be shocked and confused by this curious phenomenon. The rest of the guests were none the wiser.

Mrs. Powell died next, but her death had actually been coordinated several days before. You may recall that it was I who assembled the teams that would search the Radcliffe estate for a mysterious person that may have been hiding on the property. I knew there was no such person, and I also made it a point to stay behind at the manor while sending everyone else away except for Mrs. Powell and "Mr. Simmons." Knowing that Walter would be kept sedated in his room, I took this opportunity to pay a visit to Mr. Richter's room so that I could access his bag of goodies. You know, the bag that contained spores from his walk, medicines, and other chemicals for his studies. It was then that I procured the spores that I would sprinkle into Ms. Powell's face powder on her vanity. I offered to get her tea not to be kind or polite—she never deserved that kind of treatment as she never provided that kind of treatment to anyone else—but, instead, to place the tray on her vanity with my body blocking her line of sight as I dispensed of the spores into her makeup. I knew two things about Mrs. Powell. First, she would not go one day without making up her face. And second, she was extremely allergic to most everything. While she thought she had caught a cold from someone or was simply having a reaction to the manor's dust and germs, she was actually coating her face with allergens that made her sicker and sicker until her poor immune system could take no more. The old woman died, likely from her body's ongoing, exhausting fight to rid itself of these contaminants. Too bad for Mrs. Powell.

Lest you think I would let this opportunity slip by without a connection to Poe's work, well, you would be mistaken. I had noticed Mrs. Powell's extreme aversion to dust, germs, and just about everything, in fact. It made her most unpleasant, just like how guests who complain all the time tend to be obnoxious and unwanted. The great lengths Mrs. Powell went to in order to avoid germs reminded me of *The Masque of the Red Death*, one of my favourite Poe stories. I was delighted to see that Mrs. Powell kept a red sleeping mask in her room, which I was all too happy to put over her eyes prior to "our" discovery of her dead body.

The final three deaths were a bit tricky. In murder mysteries, particularly those featuring multiple murders, it is often the case that the first death is relatively inconsequential. A "warm-up" if you will. The characters are not yet fully developed, their relationships are unknown, and guessing "whodunit" feels a bit premature. However, by the end of the book, all cards are face up on the table. Everyone knows everyone else. People's backstories are now front and centre. Strained relationships and animosities are well known. Thus, the reader is ever so much more likely to start settling on the *one* character he or she suspects the most.

Mr. Rossini, Mr. Richter, and Anna each had plenty of mysterious qualities that made them easy suspects. Mr. Rossini was trying to end his affair, ran a questionable business, and had his roots in Palermo, which often meant having relationships with some of New York's seedier types. Mr. Richter was a socially inept, curious sort, quick to judge in an intellectually stimulating way, but also a bit of a misunderstood recluse. Speaking of recluses, Anna Winthrop spent the better of her life blending into the background on purpose. Her brilliance and sneakiness made her an ideal candidate as a prospective murderer, but truth be told she was a much better detective than anything else…almost *too* good of a detective.

Once Anna and Mr. Rossini accused one another of committing some of the murders, I took time to talk to Mr. Richter separately, not only to deliberate about the accusations, but also for another important purpose. I omitted this part of the conversation earlier because I had a very clear plan in mind of how you needed to hear this story, dear reader. Please forgive me. It will all make sense shortly, I promise. During this conversation with Mr. Richter, I let him know that young scholars often do not run from their research institutions with specimens, chemicals, and even a live monkey. Clearly, he had done something that required he flee from his university, and given his talk of using chemicals to study the brain, I assumed it had something to do with that. Mr. Richter's inability to read social cues, or to temper his own social cues, gave him away: he was quite uneasy when I challenged him on this issue.

Another curious part of Mr. Richter was the way he was trying to disguise his German accent. Anna would later think that he was deliberately *trying* to sound German when, in reality, he was doing his best *not* to sound German. I noticed his accent tended to manifest when he was anxious, stressed, or nervous, which is typically when most humans default to their innate tendencies. I reminded him that, following the war, there was already a great deal of anti-German sentiment in the States, with pamphlets warning of German spies spread throughout the country. I told him that investigators would likely be quite suspicious of a young, German scientist traveling by himself with various medicines, specimens, and, of course, a monkey, particularly if it was determined that some of his materials were used in the crimes. The fact that Mr. Richter would be even peripherally involved in some diabolic plot that resulted in the murder of ten people would hardly play well for him. Even if he did manage to escape criminal prosecution, what university would be open to hiring a young scholar with such a scandalous mark on his record, worse yet, a young *German* scholar with a past?

By the end of our conversation, I could tell that poor Mr. Richter was as emotionally fragile as I thought he was. I told him about the raven statue in Mrs. Flaherty's room, the rope still lying on the floor of the attic where "Giles" was found, and the unlikeliness of surviving a leap out the attic window should one be looking for a "way out." I could not literally *push* Mr. Richter from the nest, so to speak, but I could nudge him in the right direction and hope that he would take care of the rest. Eventually, he would, with the heavy black marble raven statue holding his soul to the ground *just like* the famous bird from Poe's beloved poem *The Raven.*

The same night Mr. Richter jumped to his death, Mr. Rossini died of an "overdose" in his room. Poor Mr. Rossini's sniffling and manic energy was quite telling from the very first moment I met him in the library. Having lived in London for several decades I am no stranger to seeing individuals ravaged by drugs, and Marvin Rossini's behaviour was not too different from what I was used to seeing from the drug-addicted vagrants on the streets. When we conducted the top-to-bottom search of the manor, the talcum powder found in Mr. Rossini's washroom stuck in my mind. When I saw the powder on the man's clothing and face just a few days later, I had a hunch that Mr. Rossini's "talcum powder" might actually be cocaine. This, of course, could be put to an empirical test by contaminating Mr. Rossini's talcum powder with rat poison from the cellar storage. It was easy enough to sprinkle some of the poison inside the "talcum powder" so that if Mr. Rossini *were* snorting cocaine, then the rat poison would certainly lead to his death. As expected, when left alone, locked in his room for several hours, Mr. Rossini snorted some of the powder and died sometime thereafter.

However, as I mentioned, there is an extra challenge that one faces in a murder mystery when there are just a few suspects remaining. One must be hyper-aware of opportunities to throw suspicion in someone else's direction and then to do so. With Mr. Rossini dead, there would only be three of us remaining. If Anna suspected Mr. Richter, I would be safe. But if Anna suspected me, then my entire plan could have fallen apart.

So, once I was confident that Mr. Richter, far gone off

the deep end, had left his room, I hurried to mess it up a bit and then to procure one of the syringes from his bag. I set the syringe next to Mr. Rossini's dead body and tied one of his handkerchiefs tightly around his forearm. When Anna and I discovered his body, I made certain that *I* was the one who grabbed the syringe. When asked what the label said, I made it up. "Heroin," I told her. Why heroin? Well, it is widely assumed that the brother in *The Fall of the House of Usher* is an opium addict, so telling Anna the syringe was full of an opioid was one clever way to continue my theme and for whom better than a man representing a broken home.

But my second lie was even more ingenious. When I said the name that appeared on the label, I added the name Ellard to Mr. Richter's name: Ellard Fredrich Richter. The syringe label actually said nothing of the sort. However, I knew Anna had suspected that Mr. Richter was truly young Elliot Radcliffe under cover, having returned home to take back what was rightfully his. As such, this simple trick regarding the name was enough for Anna to believe that her theory was correct and to get her on my side, which I desperately needed if I were to finish my ruse successfully. Importantly, Anna never did get to see the syringe, as I was careful to keep it in my hand and then to dispose of it out the window so that she would not have the chance to observe it up-close.

And, of course, there was Anna. I had taken great care to make her think Elliott Radcliffe had returned for his revenge, even typing up that silly suicide note to tuck between the rope and Mr. Richter's ankle, and I actually believe I had her convinced all the way up to the very, very end, until just before she turned around and mouthed that soft, sweet, "It's you."

Eleven murders, ten of my own, inspired by the great works of Edgar Allan Poe, are the final crimes that conclude a long series of intriguing murder mysteries.

But why? Why murder innocent people? And why do so in such elaborate ways, with grotesque murders and a variety of dead-end suspects?

Simple: this is what you wanted, isn't it?

This is what you *all* wanted.

I left London to go to New England to write my fortieth and final murder mystery. One would think that thirty-nine novels should be enough, but it was *not* enough for readers, for the newspapers, or for the publisher. Everyone always wanted *more*, and no one was satisfied with just *enough*.

I suppose it was all the extra time alone, all the lonely days and nights since my beloved Harry passed, that led me to reflect on how my life had changed as a result of my work. I went from being a carefree soul spending most of my time with my one true love to a working woman spending barely any time with my love. It was a cruel coincidence that the day I finished my last book was the very day Harry's illness started. One cannot help but think how much more time we could have spent together, how many more memories we could have made, how many young children we could have had if I had not been so focused on my work and career.

After Harry had been gone for some time and the external pressure resumed for me to produce one final book, it struck me just how much I had sacrificed my happiness and quality of life in order to please others and to accommodate their requests. It was infuriating, actually, and unlike the pages of a book, the years of a life cannot be reread or relived.

I figured if people wanted me to give them one last book, then I should make it a truly memorable one. It is often suggested that as an author you should "write what you know," so I resolved in that moment that I would do precisely that: place myself in the centre of a real-life murder mystery and then write every detail of that experience to serve as my final book.

That, my dear reader, is the book you just read.

During my time at Raven's Point Manor, when I was supposed to be typing the events of the day for the authorities, I was writing *this* book. So, much of the book is truly a transcription of what *actually* took place, while other elements of the book are deliberately obscured, twisted, and manipulated to keep you, dear reader, entertained and guessing all the way from cover to cover. In the words of Poe himself, "Believe nothing you hear and only one half that you see." Had you followed this sage advice from the very beginning of this book, you might have been onto the game I was playing with you throughout: directing your attention and suspicion to everyone else *but* me, even though I was just as capable as committing the murders as the others.

As I finish this book, certainly my last, I cannot help but think of how it all played out in the end. When the authorities arrived, did they suspect Mr. Richter or Anna Winthrop the most? What did they make of the dead bodies placed in the crate coffins of the wine cellar? Did they imagine that it was one, single murderer or a team of accomplices?

I left a typed copy of this book sitting on the dining room table at Raven's Point Manor, under the watchful eyes of the conspiracy of ravens in the painting. By the time the authorities discover it and actually take the time to read the work, I will be long gone, en route back to London where I have a very specific plan to avoid having to deal with the notoriety the confession of this book is likely to generate.

You see, after I return back to London, I plan to take the train out to the lovely seaside town in which I was raised, Southend-on-Sea. I shall walk the beaches my parents used to take me to as a girl. I shall see the shop where my Harry and I first met. I will relive those happier days of my life, when I knew no worry and no stress, when I could walk the pier and remain anonymous, when I did not feel a constant pressure to satisfy the demands and needs of others. A lifetime before my fame, before my books, before my burdens. I will take a crate of my books—all 39 of them, one of each title, plus my copy of the current manuscript—and carry it all the way to the end of the pier. Past the amusement rides and carnival games, past the soda shops and families laughing and frolicking all about, past the parents and their beloved children. Then, once I reach the end of the pier, I will sit on the edge and look at the water, into the same beautiful blue waves that I adored as a child. I will remove one of the ropes keeping the crate of my books sealed tight. I will fashion a knot out of that rope, connecting it tightly to the crate of books. I will then take the other end of the rope and fasten it around my ankle in a knot that is exceptionally difficult to untie, especially for a panicked person who potentially could find herself regretting her decision. I will look around the pier to make sure no one is watching, taking one last look at the beach and sea that brought me so much joy at one point in my life, and then, lastly but most important, I will push the crate off the edge of the pier into the sea.

And with that, my final story will have come to an end.

# ABOUT THE AUTHOR

Dame Margaret James was born in Southend-on-Sea, a beach resort town due east of London. As a young girl she enjoyed reading novels on the beach and taking in the amusements of the Southend Pier with her parents. Upon moving to London with her husband Harold, Dame James began writing short stories for *The Evening News* and the London *Evening Standard*, which gained a loyal following. Upon signing a book deal with Stillings and Sons, Dame James went on to write 39 bestselling novels including *The Crimes of the Vicar*, *Death in the Hedge Maze*, and *Rhythm of the Riviera*. This book, *A Conspiracy of Ravens,* is Dame James' 40th and final novel.

Made in the USA
Columbia, SC
12 June 2020